# GODS OF DAWN

## Baen Books
## by Steve White

### The Jason Thanou Series:
*Blood of the Heroes*
*Sunset of the Gods*
*Pirates of the Timestream*
*Ghosts of Time*
*Soldiers Out of Time*
*Gods of Dawn*

*The Prometheus Project*
*Demon's Gate*
*Forge of the Titans*
*Eagle Against the Stars*
*Wolf Among the Stars*
*Prince of Sunset*
*The Disinherited*
*Legacy*
*Debt of Ages*
*St. Antony's Fire*

### The Starfire Series:
### by David Weber & Steve White
*Crusade*
*In Death Ground*
*The Stars at War*
*Insurrection*
*The Shiva Option*
*The Stars at War II*

### by Steve White & Shirley Meier
*Exodus*

### by Steve White & Charles E. Gannon
*Extremis*
*Imperative*
[[THIRD STARFIRE WHITE GANNON]]

# GODS OF DAWN

## STEVE WHITE

GODS OF DAWN

This is a work of fiction. All the characters and events portrayed in this book are fictional, and any resemblance to real people or incidents is purely coincidental.

A Baen Books Original

Baen Publishing Enterprises
P.O. Box 1403
Riverdale, NY  10471
www.baen.com

ISBN: 978-1-4814-8257-8

Cover art by Don Maitz

First Baen mass market printing, August 2017

Distributed by Simon & Schuster
1230 Avenue of the Americas
New York, NY  10020


Printed in the United States of America

10  9  8  7  6  5  4  3  2  1

# GODS OF
# DAWN

# Temporal Regulatory Authority Timeline

**100,000 B.C.**—Teloi of the *Oratioi'Zhonglu* arrive on Earth, genetically engineer *Homo sapiens* from *Homo erectus*

**4000 B.C.**—Nagommo warship crashes in Persian Gulf; survivors begin to teach arts of civilization to Sumerians

**2000 B.C.**—Nagommo civilization collapses, after destroying Teloi (except for *Tuova'Zhonglu* remnant)

**1628 B.C.**—Santorini explosion; first-generation *Oratioi'Zhonglu* Teloi (the "Old Gods" or "Titans") trapped in their pocket universe

**490 B.C.**—Battle of Marathon; failure of attempted alliance of Transhumanist underground and surviving *Oratioi'Zhonglu* Teloi

**1669**—*Oratioi'Zhonglu* Teloi all dead by now; *Tuova'Zhonglu* Teloi battlestation enters Solar system, allies with Transhumanist underground, but is destroyed

**1880**—Transhumanist underground founds colony of Drakar in HC+32 8213 system

**1897**—Colony of Frey founded by ex-slaves on planet formerly named Drakar

**2090**—First STL interstellar probes; origins of Transhuman Movement

3

**2130**—Transhumanist takeover of Earth (for three generations) begins; STL interstellar colonization begins as a result

**2180**—War of human colonists against autochthones on Mithras (Zeta Tucanae III)

**2230**—Discovery of negative mass drive on a colony world; overthrow of Transhuman Dispensation begins

**2270**—Transhumanists believed to be wiped out (but, in fact, go underground

**2271**—Human Integrity Act passed

**2310**—Weintraub discovers "temporal energy potential"; Transhumanist underground soon steals his work

**2330**—Fujiwara and Weintraub perfect temporal displacement

**2332**—Temporal Regulatory Authority soon founded

**2364**—Revised Temporal Precautionary Act passed

**2380**—Expedition led by Jason Thanou departs for 1628 B.C. to observe Santorini explosion and its aftermath, and discovers the Teloi role in human history; subsequently, he leads an expedition to 490 B.C. Athens, and learns of the existence of the time-traveling Transhumanist underground

# Prologue

The door closed softly behind the departing visitor. Once again the tiny, dimly lit monastic cell was empty save for its occupant, who lay dying on the narrow bed. Dying, and in distress of soul.

Father Pellegrino Ernetti, *Ordo Sancti Benedicti*, sighed. The young man who had just left was, by blood, only the son of a distant relative. But ever since his childhood he had called Father Ernetti "Uncle Pellegrino" and delighted in the lute that the Benedictine priest—one of the world's leading authorities on archaic music—had fashioned for him. Later he had poured forth his adolescent troubles into Father Ernetti's patient ear. Even as a young adult he had come for visits whenever he was here in Venice, although the visits had grown less frequent during the last ten years, since he had married and had children. But the special relationship had endured, and Father Ernetti had never lost his fondness for the onetime amateurish little lute player.

He also knew him to be a bit of a blabbermouth, congenitally unable to keep a secret.

Which was the real reason why, knowing he would not outlive this spring of *Anno Domini* 1994, he had telephoned the young man, imploring him to come to the Abbey of San Giorgio Maggiore without delay, one last time. And why, when the young man had arrived, he had made a confession to him, knowing that sooner or later the confession would become public property.

And now his meager bed was like a rack on which his soul was stretched by his conscience. Partly he was tormented for making such calculated, almost cynical use of one who felt nothing for him but trust and affection. And partly because the confession was a lie.

But it was a lie which had had to be told, and which must come before the world carrying the conviction of a deathbed declaration by a man of God. Only thus could he, Father Pellegrino Ernetti, O.S.B., complete his decades-long work of discrediting himself so thoroughly that no one would follow in his footsteps.

It had called for subtlety. For him to have simply blurted out a claim that everything he had been saying had been a fraud and a hoax would have seemed suspicious. Those who insisted in seeing a conspiracy in everything (understandable, in this sad century) would have instantly assumed that pressure had been brought to bear on him by the Church hierarchy, or by whatever vast, all-powerful and probably imaginary conspiratorial organization was the currently fashionable secular substitute for the Adversary. Therefore, more indirect means had been required. He had made claims that were easily discredited. (The patently fake "photograph of Christ" had, he thought sorrowfully, been his masterstroke . . . but ah, what he *could* have shown them!) He had given talks to crank organizations of paranormal faddists that no one took seriously, in order that he himself would not be taken seriously either. And now, in a final bit of indirection, he had not actually denied to his young relative that his experiments had taken place, but only made the false assertion that they had failed.

In short, he had taken infinite pains to make sure no one else would ever build another machine like the one he had built and later destroyed.

He had known in his soul that it must be destroyed as far back as the early 1970s, for he had come to see that it could be the instrument of a dictatorship beyond the dreams of the most godless tyrants of history. But even then he had been weak, and listened to the poisonous whisperings of the Adversary. In his weakness he had not been able to draw back from the pathway once travelled by Faustus, and it had led him to Hell-mouth, where he had stared into an abyss compared to which his earlier fears had been as nothing. And he had finally understood that he had, in fact, built an engine of universal damnation. What he had learned would destroy men's faith. He knew this, for he knew how closely it had come to destroying his own.

Indeed, in his darkest, most tortured moments, a stubborn honesty forced him to ask himself whether he was merely indulging in self-deception in believing he had any faith left.

If he did have any shred of it to cling to as he faced death, it was probably owing to the men from the future.

Not all of them, of course. Some, indeed, only demonstrated the lengths to which human evil (and, he was convinced, demonic possession) could be carried, for they were men who had sought to become more than men . . . and, of course had succeeded only in becoming less, because that was the way the Adversary always worked.

But then, there had been Jason . . .

# Chapter One

The oddly bifurcated constellation of Serpens spilled across the sky, at least to the eyes of one who knew how to pick it out.

His ancient Greek ancestors, thought Jason Thanou, must have had one hell of an imagination, to see a snake among that chaos of stars.

Indeed, it must have taken even more imagination than had been required to discern a charioteer in the region of sky they had named Auriga. Heretofore, Jason's interest in the descriptive astronomy of Earth's heavens had begun and ended with that constellation, for on a moment's whim he had once tried to pick out Psi 5 Aurigae, the sun under which he had been born on the colony planet Hesperia. But of course a mere G0v main-sequence star, though slightly brighter than Sol, was not a naked-eye object across forty-eight and a half light years, and after a single glimpse through a telescope he had lost interest.

Now, however, whenever he was in the right place in the right season for it to be visible, he found his eyes wandering to Serpens, and to one region in particular. He had used another telescope (a more powerful one, for the star listed as HC+31 8213 was somewhat less luminous than Psi 5 Aurigae and over fifteen light-years more remote) and picked out a tiny yellow-white gleam that had raised more gooseflesh than his home sun had. For he knew that there, well beyond the outermost periphery of human exploration and unknown to Earth until very recently, the descendants of people he had known and fought beside inhabited a planet named Frey. He also knew that their colony had been there for almost five centuries, since Earth's year 1897, for he had been present at its inception.

To most people throughout history, that combination of thoughts would have seemed paradoxical to the point of lunacy. But those of the late twenty-fourth century could take them in stride, for Jason was a time traveler. Specifically, he was head of the Special Operations Section of the Temporal Service, enforcement arm of the Temporal Regulatory Authority that held exclusive legal jurisdiction of all ventures into the past.

He had also been the one to discover just how important—and terrifying—a qualifier that word *legal* was.

Alexandre Mondrago, the number two man in Special Ops, emerged onto the rooftop observation deck and cleared his throat. "The meeting's about to start," he said. "You'd better not keep them waiting."

"Right," Jason sighed. Serpens would soon be setting below the horizon anyway, for it was a northern constellation and it was now late southern hemisphere winter. Before many more weeks it wouldn't be visible at all from this facility in Australia's Great Sandy Desert which housed the great Fujiwara-Weintraub Temporal Displacer the Authority employed to send expeditions back in time.

But at the moment it could still be seen in the desert-clear moonless light. And Jason saw Mondrago's profile, with its outsize nose, turn in the darkness to gaze in the direction of that constellation, which for him held memories of unbearable poignancy.

Jason sighed again, knowing he could never hope to fathom the full depth of the Corsican-descended ex-mercenary's loss.

"Well," he said briskly, before the silence could stretch, "I suppose I'd better get inside, as much as I dread it."

"What are you complaining about? If they were going full speed ahead *without* asking for your input, you'd be bitching about that too. As it is, they even came here instead of summoning you."

"I know, I know," Jason grumbled as he went inside. Mondrago followed him, pausing to catch a final glimpse of Serpens.

The elegant conference room, in the style known as Third Neoclassical, was intended for meetings of the Authority's governing council. But tonight only five people sat at the long, gleaming-topped table, for Kyle Rutherford had decided to use it for this meeting, given the importance of his visitors.

As host, and by virtue of his position as the Authority's operations director, Rutherford himself sat at the head of the table—a spare elderly man with a neatly trimmed gray Van dyke, dressed in the dark, expensively fusty style affected by Earth's bureaucratized intelligentsia. He and Jason were living proof that opposites do not always attract. Indeed, each possessed a positive genius for irritating the other. But Rutherford grudgingly acknowledged Jason's capabilities. And Jason knew that Rutherford, for all his affectations, did not really share the pedantic impracticality of the governing council, against whose compulsion to interfere with the Service he could usually (not always) count on Rutherford for backing, if only in defense of his own administrative prerogatives. So, to a greater extent than either cared to admit, they understood each other.

Seated to Rutherford's left was a massively built middle-aged man in the dark-blue service dress uniform of the Internal Defense and Response Force. General Viktor Kermak was the IDRF's chief of staff, which made him the top military man of the Confederal Republic of Earth. Of course, the Republic's stubbornly independent member states stoutly denied that the IDRF was a military force. But as a practical matter, the Republic's security arm required the capacity to bring a certain amount of armed force to bear promptly and under conditions of security, without the cumbersome political negotiations, divided command and duplication of effort that inevitably accompanied any attempt at coordinated action by the five largest member states that continued to keep control of the means of waging large-scale space warfare. Form follows function, and the IDRF and taken on more and more of the aspect of a military service, including the traditional rank structure. (Unlike the Temporal Service, which the Authority primly denied was anything so horrid as even quasi-military.)

Jason sat beside Kermak. He had met the general in the course of planning his last extratemporal expedition, which had been a joint operation with the IDRF. That had been the expedition that had seen the founding of the colony of Frey, in the depths of Serpens. And it was because of their involvement in it that Jason and Kermak now sat looking across the table at the two people on Rutherford's right.

Both of these individuals held seats on the Confederal Republic's General Convocation, where each member state had only one vote but could send as many representatives as it wished. Both also wore other hats. Sadananda Naidu of the Hindustani Union was a prominent member of the Council of State, which carried out the Convocation's executive functions. Irina Andreyevna Golodets of the Russian Federation served on another standing committee: the Deep Space Council, which administered the Deep Space Fleet. In fact, the Deep Space Fleet was a paper organizational abstraction, with the actual running of the fleets still in the hands of the admiralties of the member-states that owned them. But it could be called into actual being in an emergency, and it needed to be represented here.

There was none of the gaggle of staffers that would normally accompany such political bigwigs, and the room was as secure as the IDRF's experts could make it. Jason devoutly hoped that was enough. In his experience, most governmental secrecy had no higher purpose than shielding politicians from accountability for their own self-serving stupidity. But in this case, it mattered. They were here to discuss a possible expedition to Frey, of whose existence only the highest placed had been allowed to know, and any leak of which could have consequences better not thought about.

At least, he told himself, he had reason to think these two were reliable, by the standard of politicians. Not a terrible rigorous standard, he reflected uneasily, even though he had met some of history's better specimens of the breed. (He recalled Themistocles, arguably one of the best of the lot.)

After the initial introductions and formalities had been dispensed with, Rutherford proceeded briskly. "Inasmuch as Commander Thanou led the extratemporal expedition that eventuated in the founding of the colony of Frey, I will ask him to give us the benefit of his experience by summarizing what has happened to lead us to this discussion. Commander, you have the floor."

"At the risk of belaboring facts of which you're already aware," Jason began, "I'd like to start by reviewing the overall background, starting three years ago—in terms of the linear present, of course—when I led an expedition to the Aegean Bronze Age to observe the volcanic explosion of Santorini in 1628 B.C. and its aftermath. This was by far the most far-reaching temporal displacement ever performed, taking us back into previously unobserved stretches of time. It was in the course of this expedition that we discovered, to our amazement, the existence of the Teloi, and the role played by them and their Nagommo enemies in human origins."

None of this was news to Naidu and Golodets, but they were visibly uncomfortable. They had not yet adjusted to the knowledge that *Homo sapiens* was the result of genetic engineering performed on *Homo erectus* by aliens who had desired suitable slaves and worshipers to support their twisted pantomime of godhood. Nor to the realization that the beginnings of autonomous human civilization in lower Mesopotamia had been owed to a shipwrecked survey vessel's crew of the amphibious Nagommo, whose race had smashed the Teloi but died doing it. But they could fully understand why all of this was still being kept from the generality of humankind, on whom its effects would have been difficult to predict.

"Fortunately," Jason continued, "my colleagues and I were able to strand the first generation Teloi—the Titans, as they were later known—in their extradimensional 'pocket universe' by arranging for its interface device to be consumed in the volcanic cataclysm of Santorini. Subsequently, I led an expedition to Athens in 490 B.C. to observe the Battle of Marathon—and, incidentally, to try and ascertain whether any of the younger-generation Teloi were still alive and active, posing as the Olympian gods. We discovered that they were. We also discovered something else . . . something worse. Transhumanists."

Now Naidu and Golodets were almost squirming, for Jason had pronounced a word that carried the same freight of meaning and evoked the same kind of visceral reaction that "Nazi" once had.

"It was bad enough, discovering that back in the last century the leaders of the Transhuman Dispensation, foreseeing defeat, had laid the groundwork for an extremely well-organized and well-equipped underground, which is still very active today," Jason went on. "Much worse was the discovery that early in this century they had stolen Weintraub's original work on temporal energy potential, and then gone on to anticipate Fujiwara's application of it, but avoiding certain false trails Fujiwara followed, and producing a temporal displacer infinitely more compact and energy-efficient than hers. Worst of all, they were using it to change the past."

Naidu looked deeply unhappy. "I've never really understood that last part, Commander. I always thought the Observer Effect prevented anyone from changing history."

"History can't be changed, sir . . . but the past can." Seeing bewilderment, Jason explained. "Whatever you do in the past has *always* been part of the past, if you follow me. And if you *don't* follow me, don't be troubled; you're in good company, including the last two generations of philosophers. No observed event can be changed. You can't go back and shoot one of your own ancestors, or do anything else that's going to create paradoxes. If you try, something will cause the attempt to fail. We have a saying that reality protects itself." A bleakness entered into Jason's soul as a stunningly beautiful black woman in flamboyant seventeenth-century garb swaggered across his memory. "I can personally testify that if you try to prevent a recorded event from occurring, like a loved one's death, you're as likely as not to end up being the cause of that event."

"But . . . see here, I distinctly heard you say the past can be changed! Now you're saying it can't."

"Observed, recorded history can't. But consider how much of the human past is unrecorded. You can't go back and shoot Hitler, because history says he wasn't shot. But you can get involved in a battle of that period and shoot any number of nameless soldiers. If the Observer Effect lets you shoot them, it won't affect the outcome of the war; those soldiers will *always* have been killed. And you can be assured that none of them was one of your own as-yet-childless ancestors.

"The Transhumanists are operating in the shadows, keeping to the vast stretches of time and space where the Observer Effect doesn't apply. They're filling those stretches with a kind of secret history, setting a multitude of biological, nanotechnological, psychological and sociological 'time bombs' that are all set to activate at a point they call *The Day*, when it will turn out that recorded history has just been a façade behind which *real* history has been silently building toward a Transhumanist return to power."

Naidu's face, normally the color of medium-strong coffee, seemed to acquire more cream. "But we've been unable to learn when that is?"

"Unfortunately, that's true. But we have reason to believe that it lies not too far in our future. And we have managed to acquire a certain amount of intelligence about them—including the location of their principal temporal displacer, which the IDRF subsequently captured more or less intact, enabling us to reverse-engineer it."

"An operation in which Commander Thanou was instrumental," Rutherford interjected, unable to resist an opportunity to toot the Authority's horn. Kermak grunted in acknowledgment.

"It was fortunate that we obtained Transhumanist temporal displacement technology when we did," Jason resumed, "for we used it to follow up the discovery that the Transhumanists were engaged in time-travel outside the Solar System."

"So we've been told," said Naidu with a frown. "But I always thought it could only be done on Earth."

Jason carefully didn't let his exasperation show. "It can only be done within, and in relation to, a fairly substantial planetary gravity field, sir. But there's no reason why that planet has to be Earth. It had just never occurred to us to do it anywhere else. At any rate, a joint Temporal Service/IDRF expedition went back almost five hundred years and discovered the most stupendous of all the Transhumanists' 'time bombs': a colony planted on a world they dubbed 'Drakar' almost sixty-four light-years away."

"Yes," said Golodets, obviously still not fully recovered from the shock of the secret to which she had recently been made privy. "Stranded there in the past where it was meant to grow into an industrialized, militarized world of Transhumanist fanatics—an instant ally that would appear from space on The Day, without our ever having known it existed." She shook her head as though to clear it of the nightmare vision of ravening space fleets sweeping in from the blackness beyond explored space. "But I gather you foiled their plot, Commander."

Jason shook his head emphatically. "It wasn't just me by any means, ma'am. Several IDRF personnel gave their lives, and one was stranded irretrievably in the past."

"Major Elena Rojas," said Kermak grimly. "One of my finest officers. And now maybe distant descendants of hers are my contemporaries, out there."

"Equally indispensable were the slaves the Transhumanists had brought in for a labor force, some temporally displaced from our era but mostly contemporaneous, captured in remote areas of late nineteenth-century North America and India." Jason smiled inwardly at the memory of a trio of disreputable British sergeants and a certain Indian *bhisti* or water-carrier, who had died heroically. "But their uprising almost failed, despite our help, because of the arrival of a warship of the *Tuova'Zhonglu* Teloi."

"The . . . ? Oh, yes, the surviving Teloi we were told of, who have been wandering the spacelanes for thousands of years since their war of mutual extermination against the Nagommo." Naidu nodded. "Another secret that has been kept from the public."

"With good reason, sir," Jason assured him. "They are fanatical militarists, raving mad even by Teloi standards. But they were stopped at Drakar thanks to the self-sacrifice of Dr. Chantal Frey." *Alexandre Mondrago's lover*, he thought. *And a onetime defector to the Transhumanists—a sin she expiated with interest.* "Afterwards, the former slaves, under Major Rojas' leadership, renamed the planet 'Frey.'"

"Very appropriately, I'm sure," nodded Golodets. "But, Commander, one thing still puzzles me. This planet is only about fourteen light-years beyond our current periphery of settlement. Why did the Transhumanists plant their secret colony there, knowing we'd happen onto it before much longer in the normal course of our expansion?"

"That," said Jason drily, "is one of the reasons we believe we don't have much longer to wait before The Day."

For a moment, the implications hung heavy in the air of the silent room.

"Well," said Naidu, brusquely asserting control, "this colony of Frey is presumably still out there, after having had five hundred years to develop in isolation, and the point of this meeting is to discuss the advisability of sending an expedition there to make contact with it."

"The Authority and the IDRF have both advised against that," Rutherford reminded him.

"Yes, I know. This is why we're here: to hear your reasons."

"The same reasons we didn't destroy the Transhumanist temporal displacer in the SS+28 9357 system which they had been using to go back in time and set up the Drakar colony. As Commander Thanou learned, the slave-catching expedition that scooped up him and his companions was the Transhumanists' final trip to Drakar. Afterwards, they intended to leave it strictly alone, to avoid any possible Observer

Effect issues. So as far as they know, their colony is developing as planned . . . and we know nothing of it. We want them to continue to cherish that belief, so we've carefully given them no indication to the contrary."

"Now you understand the stringent security measures surrounding this meeting," Jason put in.

"Yes, yes, of course," Golodets assured him. "But our expedition would naturally be mounted in secrecy."

Kermak answered her. "We still don't know how far the Transhumanist underground's sources of intel extend. They might get wind of the plan, and ask themselves why we should want to go to that particular remote system—a question to which there'd be only one possible answer." The general might project the image of a blunt warrior, but like all top-level military officers in this day and age he was a politician as well, and Jason noted that he diplomatically left unspoken his opinion of the Deep Space Fleet's sievelike security. "No. The smart move on our part will be to wait for The Day and then see the look on their faces when the space armada they're counting on *doesn't* appear."

"And," Jason added, "then and only then we should contact Frey and bring in *our* allies. Because what's been growing there from small beginnings for nearly half a millennium is the mirror image of what the Transhumanists intended: a society whose foundation myth is built around hatred of those who enslaved them."

Golodets leaned forward, and her broad Slavic face held them with its intensity. "I understand what you are saying, gentlemen. Only . . . when The Day arrives, and all these 'time bombs' on Earth that you haven't ferreted out yet come to fruition, will we still be in a position to send to Frey for help? And will it be too late for that help to save us?"

Rutherford and Kermak exchanged an uneasy glance. Then they both looked at Jason as though they expected him to respond— perhaps, he thought, because of his unique record against the Transhumanist underground and its sometime Teloi associates.

"That is a legitimate concern, Ms. Golodets. It cannot be ignored. But the fact that the Transhumanists are relying on the arrival of an unanticipated military ally from beyond the frontiers on The Day suggests to me that they feel they cannot entirely rely on whatever they have prepared on Earth."

"Hmm . . ." Naidu laid his hands on the table in a meeting-closing gesture. "Quite possibly a valid point, Commander. These matters must be deeply pondered before we reach a decision."

And there they left it. Truth to tell, Jason was just as happy with the deferral of action, for he was deeply conflicted, with caution and curiosity waging their immemorial war. He had meant every word he had told Naidu and Golodets, but at the same time he held within him a quivering eagerness to attach himself to an expedition to Frey—as he would undoubtedly be able to do, given his role in the foundation of the colony—and see what the descendants of those he had known had wrought there.

And so matters stood a few days later, when Jason received a summons that would rearrange his priorities in a totally unforeseen way.

# Chapter Two

Jason knew something out of the ordinary was afoot the moment he entered the office, for he recognized Rutherford's black-clad visitor even before he saw the clerical collar.

"Have a seat, Jason," Rutherford invited. "I don't believe you know Father Casinde, do you?"

"Actually, we've met briefly. A pleasure to see you again, Father," said Jason as he shook hands with Father Julian Casinde, Clerk Regular of the Society of Jesus. "And I certainly know of you: the only clergyman who is also an officer of the Temporal Service. When I first heard of it, I must admit I found it a little . . . incongruous."

"Not as much as you might think," said the Jesuit. He was a slender youngish man of medium height, pale-olive-complexioned, with regular features and very dark hair and eyes. "I'm associated with the Assistancy of St. Eligius." Seeing Jason's blank look, he elaborated with a smile. "St. Eligius is the patron of clockmakers. Hence it's an appropriate name for the Assistancy."

"Er . . . 'Assistancy'?"

"There are a number of them within the Order, under Assistants who advise the Superior General on matters pertaining to geographical regions or specialized subject areas—in our case, the theological implications of the discoveries made through time travel."

"The Authority," Rutherford explained, "reached an agreement with the Holy See, as it seemed in the interest of both parties. Father Casinde has been extremely useful to us, leading expeditions touching on matters of religious significance—to the extent that we are, as a matter of practical politics, allowed to investigate such sensitive matters."

"Of course." Jason recalled some of the ideas the Authority had had to quietly drop—an expedition to Jerusalem around Passover in 30 A.D., for instance.

It was, he thought, not a surprising arrangement on today's Earth, with its culture of conscious archaism. The Transhuman Dispensation, with its more-than-Stalinist compulsion to obliterate the human past, had been particularly hostile to all religions, persecuting them with an intensity which seemed almost gratuitous given the fact that they had been steadily losing ground for centuries. This, of course, had given those religions—at least in their outward aspects—a new lease on life. After the wars of liberation, the human race had sought in every way possible to nurture what was left of its history and traditions, like plants that had been torn up by the roots and carefully replanted. *Literal* belief in religion was rare on twenty-fourth century Earth, but there was widespread observance of its forms and ceremonies, and painstaking restoration of its shrines.

Still, Jason couldn't avoid a certain surprise that the slightly built, scholarly-looking Casinde had qualified for the Temporal Service, especially considering some of the unsanctified things its officers were sometimes called upon to do. But, on further reflection, he decided it wasn't so strange after all, given the Jesuits' almost military ethos, including willingness to live in extreme conditions when required. These, he reminded himself, were men who in past ages had hacked missions out of South American jungles and spirited Jews away from the SS.

"Most recently," Rutherford was saying, "Father Casinde led an expedition to Rome in 1978, seeking to settle certain persistent questions surrounding the death of Pope John Paul I."

"Uh, I'm afraid I'm not familiar with . . ."

"He was found dead, sitting up in bed, only thirty-three days after his election," explained Casinde. "It was one of the shortest pontificates in history—the first 'Year of Three Popes' since 1605. The Vatican reported it as a heart attack . . . but no autopsy was performed. This, plus certain irregularities in the issuance of a death certificate, provided fertile ground for conspiracy theories. One was that he was assassinated by the Soviet KGB because he was planning to change the Church's policy of accommodation with Communist regimes. Another was that he was poisoned by Bishop Paul Marcinikus, the head of the *Instituto per le Opere Religiosi*, or Institute of Religious Works—better known as the Vatican Bank—because he was about to order a thorough housecleaning of the bank's notorious corruption, exposing its ties to the Italian Mafia and also to the Freemasons, a favorite suspect of conspiracy theorists in those days. It didn't help when, four years later, Bishop Marcinikus' business associate Roberto Calvi was found murdered in what was claimed to be Masonic ritual fashion. I believe the Bavarian Illuminati were also dragged in, as they so often were. And other motives for murdering the Holy Father were also proposed: either he was going to please feminists with certain changes in Church doctrine, or he was going to please traditionalists by restoring the Tridentine Mass, or whatever, depending on who you read."

Jason cocked his head. "I get the impression that you don't take any of this too seriously."

"The Church has always denied these claims," the Jesuit answered obliquely. "But the doubts and questions have never gone away, and recently the Holy See has changed its position to the extent of agreeing to cooperate with the Authority in an attempt to resolve the matter once and for all."

"The fact that Father Casinde was to be the mission leader helped to reconcile them to the project," Rutherford added.

"At any rate," Casinde resumed, "I took a party of researchers back to Rome in the relevant time period of September, 1978. While there, to my amazement, my implant detected nearby use of bionics."

For a fraction of a second, it didn't even register on Jason. Then he sat bolt upright, his entire consciousness in a state of quaveringly focused attention.

Direct neural computer interfacing was one of the things proscribed by the Human Integrity Act. But there were special exceptions, one of which was for the benefit of law enforcement officers and certain others, including Temporal Service officers who functioned as mission leaders. They had a brain implant that served various useful functions such as the recording of aural and visual sensory input, and the projection directly onto the optic nerve of a wealth of information, including a map of the user's environs. Almost incidentally, it incorporated a sensor which detected functioning bionics within a very limited range.

And bionics in twentieth-century Italy could mean only one thing . . .

"Transhumanist time travelers," Jason said softly.

"That was my own conclusion. Exercising my legal authority as mission leader, I declared a state of extraordinary emergency and made investigation of this new development our first priority. However, our TRDs of course activated at the set time—"

"Of course," Jason echoed. The implanted "temporal retrieval devices" which restored time travelers' temporal energy potential so that they reappeared on the displacer stage from which they had originally departed were normally timed to do so at a predetermined instant, thus facilitating "traffic control" on the displacer stage. The "controllable" variety, activated by the mission leader at his own discretion, was used only for Special Ops missions, which required more flexibility.

"—before we were able to make any headway. And at any rate, I was uncomfortable with exposing the academicians in my party to potential danger. So we learned essentially nothing." Casinde paused, and spoke with what seemed like great reluctance. "We did obtain certain clues as to the Transhumanists' activities that pointed in the direction of Venice."

"So," said Rutherford to Jason, "you can see that this is a job for the Special Operations Section."

"Right. We'll go back to a point slightly earlier than Father Casinde here spotted them, and determine what kind of 'time bomb' they've planted."

"Yes. And you'll have to exercise extreme caution to avoid running afoul of the Observer Effect, because Father Casinde certainly didn't encounter his own very slightly older self at any time."

"What? You mean you intend to send him back with us?"

"Yes. He has volunteered for it. And his knowledge of the milieu, together with his recent first-hand experience of it, should be invaluable. Indispensable, in fact."

Jason gave the slightly built Casinde a sidelong glance. "Father, I mean no reflection on you, but you're not a member of the Special Operations Section."

Casinde seemed only slightly miffed. "I am, however, an officer of the Temporal Service. So I have met the qualifications, and received the training, for surviving and functioning in lower-technology historical epochs."

"Of course you have. But in Special Ops we do things just a little differently than the rest of the Service." Jason pretended not to notice the faint choking noises from Rutherford's direction. "Sometimes our missions unavoidably entail violence, because we exist to combat extremely ruthless people—people who have no regard for the lives of 'Pugs,' as they call normal, unmodified humans. If it should become necessary, are you going to be able to . . . that is, are your vows going to allow you to—?"

"Commander, my unique dual status has frequently forced me to reconcile knotty questions of right and wrong—cases of conscience, as we call them. In fact, I've often had to resort to the kind of casuistry for which the Society of Jesus is renowned, if not notorious." Casinde's eyes took on a dark twinkle. "In this particular case, the fact that the Transhumanists were present to be detected at the time I did so, and evidently not exercising any special precautions, would seem to suggest that we had *not* come into violent contact with them before that point in time."

Jason chuckled. "No offense, Father, but I'm beginning to think there's something very appropriate about a Jesuit being a time traveler! All right: I'll want to put you through certain tests and expose you to a little . . . specialized training by my deputy, Superintendent Alexandre Mondrago. But, conditional on all that, you're in." He turned back to Rutherford. "The question is, where do we want to arrive? Rome would be the obvious place, but evidently there's some sort of Venetian connection. And there, at least, we'd avoid the Observer Effect issues you mentioned."

"True." The older man sighed. "It's a difficult choice, since we have nothing to go on. There's no event in that milieu with any obvious link to any Transhumanist machinations."

"No, there isn't." Jason was about to continue when he noticed, out of the corner of his eye, Casinde's troubled look. "What is it, Father?"

The Jesuit seemed to reach a decision. "Actually, there may just possibly be such a link."

"But what? The only major event in that temporal and geographical neighborhood was the death of the Pope, and they'd have no interest in that."

"No, it's not that. It's something else—something that occurred to me when Venice came into the picture. Something I've been unwilling to mention . . . even though it has a relation of sorts to the subject of time travel."

Jason recalled Casinde's odd hesitancy on the subject of Venice. "What was there in that time and place that could have anything to do with time travel? And why the reluctance to bring it to our attention?"

"Well . . . from the standpoint of the Church, it's slightly embarrassing. And it seems so far-fetched that I wasn't sure it was worth bothering you with."

"That's all right; any lead is better than the zero we have now. So what is it in Venice that year that might be of interest to the Transhumanists?"

Casinde took a deep breath. "Father Pellegrino Ernetti."

# Chapter Three

"Who?" asked Jason and Rutherford in unison.

"He was a Priest of the *Ordo Sancti Benedicti*—the Benedictine order—who lived from 1925 to 1994." Casinde had gotten past his unwillingness to speak, but he still seemed less than enthusiastic about doing so. "He was an eminent musicologist, specializing in archaic music. He was also renowned throughout Italy as an exorcist."

At first Jason wasn't sure he had heard correctly. "Did you say, 'exorcist'?"

"Indeed. Thousands of people made the journey to the Abbey of San Giorgio Maggiore in Venice where he resided, in order to be freed from demons."

"Uh . . . somehow I didn't think the Catholic Church was still doing that sort of thing in the second half of the twentieth century."

"Oh, but it was. So were certain other Christian denominations. The Anglicans, for example, codified exorcism rites as late as 1972. Admittedly, starting in the nineteenth century its scope had become more limited, with the emergence of psychophysical explanations for numerous cases of what had once been attributed to possession. And efforts were made to restrain the enthusiasm of ignorant country priests and restrict the practice of exorcism to qualified specialists trained in the *Rituale Romanum*, thus minimizing the risk of contagion."

"Contagion?" Jason echoed faintly. Casinde had spoken in tones of unmistakable seriousness and utmost earnestness.

"Oh, yes. Exorcism is not without risk to the exorcist and others. Demonic possession is unfortunately communicable. In fact there have been veritable epidemics of it, especially in nunneries. However," Casinde concluded firmly, "Father Ernetti was without question one of those qualified specialists, and practiced with great success. In fact, in the mid-1970s the Conference of Bishops in Rome commanded him to set down his techniques. The result was a book, *La Cateschi di Satana*, or *Satan's Catechism*."

"Well," said Rutherford briskly, after a moment, "this is all very interesting. But I fail to see how this Father Ernetti's distinguished career as an exorcist could have had any possible connection with time travel."

"No, it wasn't that. The connection grew out of his *other* field of expertise: musicology."

Jason's bewilderment was now complete.

"As I said earlier, he was a recognized authority on archaic music, which means the 'prepolyphonic' music—a succession of single sounds—prevailing in the Western world from the tenth century B.C. to the tenth century A.D., and therefore including the Gregorian Chant, which emerged in the sixth century A.D. In fact, he held what was probably the world's only endowed chair in the subject, at the Benedetto Marcello Conservatory of Music in Venice. He also taught the subject at the music institute of the Giorgio Cini foundation, on the same island as the abbey, and wrote a number of definitive books on it. He also had some writing credits on scientific subjects in related fields—an article on the electronic oscilloscope, for instance."

"Clearly a multitalented individual," Rutherford intoned. "But I'm still unclear on the relevance of any of this to time travel."

All at once, Casinde's palpable unease was back in full force. "So far, everything I've told you is biographical fact. And I'll continue to speak in straightforward narrative form, for the sake of clarity. But from now on I am going to be recounting what might most charitably be characterized as 'urban legend.'" He drew a deep breath, as though about to plunge into murky waters. "The story goes that in 1952 Father Ernetti was working with Father Agostino Gemelli, one of the founders of the Catholic University of Milan and president of the

Pontifical Scientific Academy in Rome, at the latter's electro-acoustical laboratory. They were using oscilloscopes and electronic filter systems in an attempt to remove stray harmonics from recordings of Gregorian chants, producing clearer singing voices. In the course of recording a chant on one of that era's very crude tape recorders, they picked up the voice of Father Gemelli's father."

For a moment, Jason and Rutherford looked blank.

"His long-deceased father," Casinde added.

Something began to dawn in his listeners' eyes.

"Afterwards," Casinde continued in the same matter-of-fact way, "the two went to Rome and reported the incident to Pope Pius XII. The Holy Father took it very calmly and told them that whatever they might have discovered was a scientific fact, without any disturbing theological implications, and might even lead to evidence that would strengthen the faithful's belief in the afterlife. Father Gemelli was totally reassured, and said no more about it. But Father Ernetti began to think intensely. His studies of music had led him to suspect that the classical notions of Pythagoras and Aristotle that sounds and other harmonics never really cease to exist were true . . . and that he had recorded a voice, not from the afterlife, but from the past.

"Over the next few years, he made contact with a very distinguished group of scientists—including Enrico Fermi, of whom you undoubtedly know, up until Fermi's death in 1954. With their help, and working in great secrecy, he developed a device he called a 'chronovisor' which could focus on any of these harmonics—not just of sound but also of light—from any time in the past, and make audio and video recordings. The device consisted of—"

"Wait a minute! Wait a minute! Stop right there!" Jason came surging up out of his chair. "Are you telling me that four hundred years ago some Italian priest invented a means of observing the past without having to be physically displaced in time?"

"And if so," added Rutherford, seeming like Jason to finally realize that he was actually hearing what he thought he was hearing, "then why have we never heard about it? The implications for the Authority's activities—!"

"As I explained," said Casinde with a touch of asperity, "I'm only telling you the 'consensus' version of this story. A great deal of it is based on a conversation the French theologian Father François Brune said he had with Father Ernetti in the early 1960s. According to him, Father Ernetti disclaimed individual credit for the invention, which he attributed to the help of his colleagues and to sheer luck. At any rate, if I may continue, they tested out the machine by viewing and hearing a speech by Benito Mussolini, who was—"

"—An early twentieth century Italian dictator," said Rutherford, an authority on history, rather testily. "Yes, yes, I know."

"He was so recent that they felt that they could check their recording against contemporary footage of him for confirmation of its authenticity. Having satisfied themselves that it was actually him they were viewing, they tried for the more remote but still fairly well documented figure of Napoleon, and were able to observe him proclaiming Italy a republic. Then, growing more ambitious, they leaped back to Roman times. After catching a glimpse of a vegetable market in Trajan's time, they narrowed their focus to the first of Cicero's speeches against Catiline in 63 B.C. The speech has been preserved, so it was possible to verify it. It also proved possible to record part of a performance, in 169 B.C., of a play subsequently lost save for fragments: *Thyestes,* by Quintus Ennius, the 'father of Latin poetry.' Father Ernetti was quite fascinated by the musical accompaniment, just as he had been by the divergences between Cicero's Latin pronunciation and what had always been taught in modern times. The 'ae' ending, for example, turned out to have been sounded in one syllable, as a long 'a' . . ." Seeing the looks on his listeners' faces, Casinde dropped the subject. "Subsequently, in 1956, Father Ernetti decided to try to focus on the crucifixion and resurrection of Christ."

Jason and Rutherford simply stared.

"And did he make a video recording of all this?" Rutherford finally asked in a hushed voice. "Including . . . the resurrection?"

"So he claimed to Father Brune, although the film was black-and-white and lacked much of the fine detail." The Jesuit took on a thoughtful look. "The funny thing is that his description of the events surrounding the crucifixion—in particular, his denial that certain legends like that of Veronica and the veil had any basis in fact—accords with subsequent scholarship."

After a moment, Jason found his voice. "Wouldn't the Church have, uh, taken an interest in this?"

"Undoubtedly. According to Father Ernetti, he showed the film to Pope Pius XII, the President of Italy and members of the Pontifical

Academy. Afterwards, he said he dismantled the chronovisor as too dangerous. But at this point the story starts to unravel. Over the next couple of decades, contradictory reports kept appearing in the tabloid press about his activities, and in 1972 a couple of them printed what purported to be a photograph of Christ's face, from the film. But after 1986, after talking about the chronovisor at a conference of people associated with ESP and astrology, he fell silent about it—until 1993, when he admitted to a Spanish reporter that the 'photograph of Christ' did not come from the chronovisor—it had been a photograph of a sculpture by a Spanish sculptor, based on a certain nun's description of visions she said she'd had. And yet, that same year—the year before he died—he told Father Brune that he went to the Vatican with the last two surviving members of his team and gave a presentation of the chronovisor to Pope John Paul II, with four cardinals and an international committee of scientists in attendance." Casinde shook his head. "All very perplexing. Just to muddy the waters still further, in the year 2000 someone describing himself as a distant relative came forward—anonymously—and claimed that in 1994 the dying Father Ernetti had confessed to him that in fact the chronovisor hadn't worked . . . almost, but not quite. According to this same source, he also admitted that he himself had composed the Quintus Ennius segment, from the surviving fragments of the play. In the course of this admission he rambled about 'past lives' of his, something so foreign to Catholic belief as to seem almost bizarre, coming from such a source."

Casinde fell silent. Rutherford cleared his throat.

"Curiouser and curiouser," he quoted. "But surely, Father, you don't believe there is anything to all this."

Casinde gave a tight, rather grim smile. "I'm ninety-nine percent sure there isn't."

Rutherford lifted one frosty eyebrow. "Only ninety-nine?"

"Well . . . it's just that the whole thing seems so utterly out of character. Why would a man like that—a distinguished expert in other fields—have come up with such an implausible fabrication? It's . . . perplexing."

Jason spoke slowly. "These Pythagorean and Aristotelian ideas of 'harmonics' . . ."

"Yes," Casinde nodded. "It's a concept related to the idea of 'akashic records'—a kind of steady etheric accumulation of all events that have ever happened, if only they could be accessed."

Jason turned to Rutherford. "Is there any possibility that these notions could have some kind of basis in quantum physics?"

"I'm sure I'm not qualified to say."

"I'm even less so. But if there *is* anything to it, it might very well explain the Transhumanists' interest. I'm beginning to think that, since we're going to 1978 Italy anyway, it wouldn't hurt to drop in on Father Ernetti."

# Chapter Four

"So," asked Jason, setting his empty glass down on the bar of displacer installation's lounge, "how is the good Father coming along?"

"Not bad," Alexandre Mondrago admitted. "Remember, as a Service officer, he's had some training. After all, it was his job to keep the members of expeditions he led alive. The expeditions he's led generally haven't been the kind that were likely to get involved in anything violent. But still, he's had to be prepared for all eventualities."

"Right." Jason nodded, and touched the glowing LED display on the surface of the bar to order another Scotch and soda. "It was part of the agreement by which he was allowed to join the Temporal Service. He had to pass some courses in purely defensive forms of martial arts."

The Corsican gave a rather cynical grin. "'Offensive' and 'defensive' aren't 'pure' concepts. They're relative terms when it comes to weapons; it all depends on how you use them—"

"True. I wouldn't want to get banged over the head with a sixteen-pound *hoplon* shield like the one I carried when we were in the fifth century B.C."

"—and I suspect the same goes for martial arts. Anyway, I've been teaching him some new tricks. He's physically fit—a Service officer has to be—and he's a quick learner. And if he has any qualms, he must have rationalized them away."

Jason smiled as he snagged his drink from a tray that floated over on grav repulsion. "Jesuits have always had a reputation for being able to justify all sorts of things, to themselves as well as to others. Casuisitic justification, it was called. Historically, their image has sometimes been almost a sinister one, at least among non-Catholics. Even within the Church, they had their ups and downs. In the eighteenth century, they were suppressed in various countries, and between 1773 and 1814 the Order was officially abolished."

"Still, he can't completely get around his vows about shedding of blood. So I've had to limit it to non-lethal stuff—although, there again, a sharp enough blow of the knuckles to somebody's temple . . . Well, anyway, he knows we're going to be looking for Transhumanists, and you can just imagine how he feels about *them*."

"Yes. He told me what a transcendent experience it had been for him to see the Vatican in the twentieth century, before the Transhuman Dispensation got hold of it." The Transhumanists had used nano-disassemblers. St. Peter's Basilica . . . the Sistine Chapel . . . the *Laocoön* . . . the *Apollo Belvedere* . . . Michelangelo's *Pieta* . . . not to mention the bones of St. Peter . . . all reduced to the same gray sludge as other such places in Jerusalem and Mecca and Benares. Jason was not religious, even by his era's lenient standards, but he was looking forward to the opportunity to see that vanished grandeur at first hand.

"So," he said, changing the subject, "has he gotten his controllable Special Ops TRD implanted yet?"

"Yes, last night. He also had his brain implant deactivated. He wasn't quite as happy about that."

"Nobody ever is." The exemption from the Human Integrity Act that allowed Temporal Service officers to use neurally interfaced brain implants was hedged about with restrictions. For one thing, it was strictly limited to current mission leaders—in this case, Jason. It was a bit of nitpicking he had often cursed, for there had been times when it would have been very useful to have more than one member of a team who knew the locations of all the other members, marked on an optically projected map by means of the microscopic tracking devices incorporated in their TRDs. But the taboo involved was too powerful to be fought.

"Anyway," Jason continued, "he doesn't require as much preparation as we do, having just gotten back from his last mission.

For one thing, he's already got the language from his last mission." It was another area in which the rules of the Human Integrity Act were slightly bent for the benefit of time travelers. The language of their target milieu was imprinted on the speech centers of their brains by direct neural induction, a process that required buffering with drugs and a period of rest thereafter, followed by intense practice in actually forming the sounds. Jason and Mondrago had only just emerged from all that after acquiring twentieth-century Italian, which had come relatively easily to them given their familiarity with Romance languages. Mondrago had also had to undergo an in-depth orientation (by more or less conventional teaching techniques; again, the taboos were violated only when absolutely necessary) concerning twentieth-century civilization. Jason, who was practically an old hand in that century, had at least been able to skip all of that except the specifically Italian portions, and of course Casinde hadn't needed it at all.

"Anyway," said Jason, "let's drink up. It's almost time for the informal mission briefing."

"The expedition will consist only of the three of us," Jason said to Mondrago and Casinde. "It's simpler that way. For one thing, we've all already had our biological 'cleansing.'" It was a necessity, to protect the people of earlier eras from centuries-evolved microbes against which they would have been as vulnerable as the Amerindians had been against smallpox. "Also, it happens that we will all be physically inconspicuous in the milieu, which isn't the case with any of the other Special Ops personnel who're available at the moment." It was a perennial problem, and not even Jason would have advocated using genetic nanoviruses to tailor time travelers' ethnic appearance to order for the purpose of blending. The horrors of the Transhuman Dispensation had placed such things so far beyond the pale of acceptability that the Human Integrity Act's prohibition was almost superfluous.

"Remember, Commander," said Casinde, "by the late twentieth-century, Western Europe was already becoming a fairly cosmopolitan place. An African or an Asian walking down an Italian street in 1978 wouldn't have raised nearly as many eyebrows as he would have just a generation earlier. And North American and northern European tourists were a common sight."

"Still, we always like to have as little explaining to do as possible—preferably, none. And in our case, we can even use our own names. You'll be, essentially, yourself: a Jesuit priest visiting Venice after a time among the small Catholic community in Greece, the people who observe the traditions of the Greek Orthodox Church while obeying the Pope of Rome. Alexandre and I will be acquaintances of yours from there—of French extraction, in Alexandre's case. That will help explain any oddities in our Italian pronunciation." It was another problem the Authority always had to deal with, even in eras when recorded sound had existed and really accurate simulation of the local language was possible. Direct neural induction was not magic. So wherever they were, time travelers always claimed to be from somewhere else.

"We'll arrive in Venice on September 26, 1978, two days before John Paul I's death. By dropping the name of that Father Brune you mentioned, we ought to be able to get in to see Father Ernetti—all the while remaining on the alert for Transhumanists." *With my implant as the only one we'll have for detecting functioning bionics*, Jason grumpily added to himself. It was yet another reason why he wished his two companions' implants hadn't had to be deactivated. But Rutherford, who had to answer to the Authority's hidebound governing council, had refused to budge.

"And if nothing comes of that?" Casinde inquired.

"Then we'll proceed to Rome, where you got your first indications of Transhumanist activity anyway."

"You realize, of course—"

"—That you and your expedition were there during that same time period," Jason finished for the Jesuit. It had given Rutherford a case of the cold sweats which, in Jason's opinion, served him right. "Fortunately, you know where you were at any given time, so if we're careful we ought to be able to avoid stubbing our toes on the Observer Effect. And hopefully the problem won't arise because we'll be able to wrap things up in Venice."

"Speaking of Venice," said Mondrago, "are we going to go there for a familiarization tour?" It was a frequent means of supplementing virtual tours in preparation for extratemporal expeditions, at least in cases where the locale hadn't changed so much over the centuries as to make it impossible to get any sense of what it had been like in the target time-frame.

"We can if you want to. Venice is still more or less recognizable today. But Julian is already familiar with it. And I've seen it in both the present time and the thirteenth century. 1978 ought to be sort of a compromise between the two."

"Never mind, then. I'll just soak up the computer simulation. I've heard that even now it's a very picturesque place."

"Oh, yes," said Casinde with a reminiscent smile. "Of course, nowadays the picturesqueness is somewhat artificial—carefully maintained for the tourists. To a certain extent, that was probably already starting in 1978."

"Well, we're not going there as tourists anyway," Jason said firmly. "And we need to get busy on the final stages of our orientation. Our schedule is as follows . . ."

Not so very long ago, the enormous domed structure at the center of the facility had housed the Authority's only temporal displacer, a massive installation powered by the only antimatter reactor permitted on the surface of Earth or any inhabited planet. All that, as everyone knew, had been necessary to cancel the temporal energy potential of significant objects like human bodies, with an energy surge so prodigious as to send them back three hundred years into the past before it became controllable. (*Only* into the past. The future—that is, what lay beyond the constantly advancing wave-front known as "the present" was, in an absolute sense, nonexistent until it happened.)

But now, thanks to Jason, the Authority had reverse-engineered the Transhumanist Underground's time-travel technology. The three-hundred-year limit still obtained—but it was now possible to construct temporal displacers orders of magnitude less massive and energy-gluttonous than the old one.

A ring of such displacers now circled the old displacer installation. This was a very good thing for the Special Operations Section, for in the past extratemporal expeditions had had to be tied to prearranged retrieval times at the one existing displacer stage, for simultaneous appearance of matter in the same volume was a risk that could not be taken. But now a Special Ops mission leader could be allowed to exercise his own discretion as to retrieval, for a displacer stage could be placed at his exclusive disposal. Jason was thankful for this flexibility in their present mission, given the vagueness of his hints as to the Transhumanist presence in 1978 Italy.

The new multiplicity of displacers did, however, complicate Rutherford's traditional ritual of a farewell handshake with departing time travelers. Still, he managed it.

"You will, of course, not remain any longer than necessary," he admonished Jason, not for the first time. "The impossibility of your communicating with us—"

"Yes, I know, Kyle." The only way of communicating across time was the "message drop" system of writing on some very durable material and leaving it in a prearranged place so remote that it would lie undisturbed until the twenty-fourth century. It was highly unsatisfactory at best, and out of the question in northern and central Italy, as Jason would hardly have the opportunity to scramble up to some Apennine mountaintop.

"And do take all precautions," Rutherford continued in the same jittery way. "This expedition is, I fear, somewhat undermanned, and—"

"Hey, Kyle, you know how cautious I am."

Rutherford was still spluttering when the indescribable sensation of temporal displacement took Jason, and the interior of the displacer installation faded like the memory of a dream, and they were standing in a Mediterranean garden just after daybreak.

# Chapter Five

Temporal displacement was subject to no limitations on where, within the planetary gravity field, it could flick time travelers in the process of sending them back in time. So Jason had been able to pick his target with care.

It was, of course, equally possible to choose the time of day for arrival—but, in practice, the choice was always just after daybreak. It represented a compromise between the dark of night (which exacerbated the psychological disorientation of displacement, sometimes to a dangerous degree) and broad daylight (which would be too conspicuous).

Thus it was that Jason and his two companions found themselves among the trees of Venice's Giardini Ex Reali, or Palace Gardens, just as the eastern sky was turning from gray to pale blue. As Jason had confidently hoped, there was no one present at this hour to be upset at the sight of figures springing into existence out of nowhere—just one snoring individual sitting propped against a tree trunk and clutching a wine bottle, whose slumbers Jason did not disturb.

All three of them were veterans, so they took little time to regain their mental equilibrium after the profoundly unnatural experience they had just undergone. Following the directions provided by Jason's optically spliced map, they departed the formal gardens and walked down to the Riva degli Schiavoni, the walkway that led along the

Grand Canal. There they turned left and walked toward the rising sun that was dispelling all but the most tenuous strings of cloud, whose undersides glowed in red and gold. On their right was the canal, its wharves lined with gondolas. To the southeast, a little over a fifth of a mile across the water, the island of San Giorgio Maggiore was clearly visible through a thin mist, the basilica with its tall brick bell tower and Andrea Palladio's classical façade illuminated by the golden early morning sun. Adjacent to that church was the Benedictine abbey where Father Pellegrino Ernetti resided.

Presently, the Piazzetta San Marco opened up to their left in all its glory. At its far end was the Byzantine splendor of the Basilica di San Marco, with the instantly recognizable Campanile, or bell tower, to its left. Jason sardonically wondered how many tourists knew that tower had once been a place of punishment for corrupt clerics, who were suspended from it in wooden cages for as long as a year, with—or occasionally without, in extreme cases—bread and water. On its right was a magnificent Gothic fantasia: the façade of the Palazzo Ducale, the palace of the Doges who had once ruled Venice.

The palace had only begun to assume its present form in the mid-fourteenth century. But the residence of the Doges had always been there, as Jason had reason to know. He had seen it in its earlier, altogether less impressive, fortresslike incarnation in 1204, when Doge Enrico Dandolo—blind and in his nineties—had negotiated the contracts with the leaders of the Fourth Crusade that had by tortuous paths led to the sacking of Constantinople and the creation of the vacuum Venice had filled, becoming the largest and wealthiest city in Europe and the arbiter of trade between the West and the Orient.

They proceeded past the two columns supporting statues of St. Theodore and the winged lion of St. Mark, and continued on as the sun's rays spread a golden sheen over what the twentieth-century writer Luigi Barzini had called "undoubtedly the most beautiful city built by man," making it seem even more dreamlike. The slight chill of daybreak was now yielding to the kind of warmth to be expected in Venice in September. As they walked, Jason felt a nagging sense that something was missing. Then he realized what it was: the distinctive aroma he remembered from his experience in twentieth-century cities, densely packed with hydrocarbon-burning motor vehicles. It was bad enough in America, and even worse in Europe where emission standards were lower. But Venice was the only significant city in the world with no automobiles—nor, indeed, any streets that could have accommodated them. Here there were hardly any of the usual urban fumes, and there would have been none at all save for the *vaporetti*, or water buses, which (unlike the romantic but not especially practical gondolas) were how people got around.

Continuing on along the Riva degli Schiavoni, they crossed the bridge over the narrow Rio San Zulian (only the largest canals were called "canali"; each of the myriad smaller ones was a "rio") between the palace and the Prigioni Nuove, or New Prison. Looking to their left, up the canal, they could see the enclosed marble bridge—the Ponte di Sospiri, a name coined by Lord Byron in the nineteenth century—that directly connected the palace and its torture chamber with the prison. (Jason suspected a certain irony in that name, which meant "Bridge of Sighs.") By this time, more people were up and about, and Jason recalled that Venetians who had business in this part of the city always tried to get it done early in the morning, before the crowds of tourists thickened. He noted with relief that no one was paying the three of them any special attention. Not that he had expected anyone to; the Authority's outfitters were past masters at producing authentic period clothing, and there was nothing especially out of the ordinary about the small overnight bags in which they carried very basic strictly in-period toiletries and a change of underwear.

They next crossed another bridge, over another narrow canal, the Rio del Vin. As with the rest of their walk, they did so slowly and carefully, in deference to the walking cane Jason was using. It would have seemed odd for more than one of them to have a cane, although Jason would have preferred more, given its special qualities.

Ordinary extratemporal research expeditions were flatly prohibited from carrying any out-of-period equipment, including weapons, into the past. But Jason had been able to argue successfully, against the horrified opposition of certain members of the Authority's governing council, that Special Ops personnel could hardly be held to the usual guidelines when going up against enemies who were subject to no such restrictions. So there was now a workshop that specialized in concealing and disguising weaponry of the sort that the Transhumanists did not scruple to carry into the past.

Thus Jason's cane incorporated a scaled-down version of a

Takashima laser carbine. He was familiar with it, having used it in fifth century B.C. Athens—and, in fact, having had some input into its design. This one was even more miniaturized, but had the same two selectable modes: "stun," with a low-powered laser ionizing the air along a path which carried an electrical charge; and "kill," with the laser powered up to weapon grade. Either way, the beam was invisible, although the ionization produced a trail of sparks, and the lethal version resulted in a *snap!* as air rushed in to fill the vacuum drilled through it—certainly nothing like the special effects the people of the late twentieth century had been led to expect of a laser weapon by Hollywood science fiction movies. There was also a harmless visible-light setting, in case a flashlight should come in handy. The superconductor-loop energy cells that powered it were disguised as ordinary AA lead-acid batteries of the period. And it had no metal parts—an important point, in case they found themselves having to pass through one of the metal detectors that had started to come into use for security purposes in the early 1970s.

There had been a certain amount of pouting on the part of Mondrago, who thought he should be the one playing the slightly-lame role and carrying their only weapon. But Jason had pulled rank. And in truth he was the logical choice to feign lameness, having had experience with the real thing. The limp he affected reminded him all too well of the time, in the wake of the devastating Santorini explosion, he had had to trudge across the mountainous landscape of Bronze Age Crete with a broken foot. He still winced at the memory, even though twenty-fourth century medical science had long since regenerated the foot.

They had now passed the point where the water to their right was no longer the Grand Canal but had widened to become the Canale di San Marco, better known as St. Mark's Basin, for it was actually a branch of the Lagoon of Venice. They stepped onto the pier that was the San Zaccaria terminal of the *vaporetti* network. There they bought tickets with authentically aged and rumpled *lire* and waited for the next *vaporetto* for San Giorgio Maggiore. San Zaccaria was a terminus of six routes, but less than twenty minutes passed before the right passenger motorboat arrived and they filed aboard, finding seats among a few passengers who had boarded at other stops. As the *vaporetto* chugged away from the pier, Jason permitted himself to look back and admire the incomparable view astern.

His reverie was interrupted by Casinde's elbow jabbing him in the ribs.

"Commander!" the Jesuit whispered urgently. "Look over there." He pointed at a fellow passenger, seated forward, who like Jason had turned his head astern to admire the view. Jason hadn't noticed him, and indeed he was the sort of man who was easy not to notice, so inconspicuous as to be nearly invisible. He was a small man in his fifties wearing a clerical collar, with a shock of unruly salt-and-pepper hair, eyeglasses that looked as though they had been made by the Coca-Cola bottling company, and nondescript features. After a moment, he turned away again, and Casinde resumed whispering excitedly.

"I've only seen one photograph of Father Ernetti. But I think that may very well be—"

But Jason had abruptly ceased to listen, for at the outer edge of his field of vision a tiny blue dot had begun to flash on and off. And a quick scan of the other features revealed one man, cheaply dressed, who exhibited certain subtle indicia that Jason knew all too well.

"Yes," he whispered back. "I've seen that photo too, and yes, I think that's Father Ernetti. But there's also an upper-level goon-caste Transhumanist aboard this boat."

# Chapter Six

The *vaporetti* landing was a small pier in front of the church of San Giorgio Maggiore, at the right end of the Palladian façade. To the right was the world's oldest continuously-operating Benedictine abbey, founded in 982, somewhat oppressive-looking in contrast to the splendid basilica. Even after the suppression of the monasteries in the early nineteenth century, a small number of monks had by sheer persistence won the right to remain in residence. They were still there, although the former monastery now housed the Cini Foundation.

The trip had been a short one, and Jason had had only a brief time to try and formulate a plan. He and his companions were seated at the stern of the boat, with a handful of early-rising tourists in front, along with Father Ernetti and the Transhumanist among them. He would simply have to wait until they were ashore and then play it by ear.

The boat docked, and the tourists began to disembark. Jason's party was unable to shove through the press, and by the time they were able to step onto the seawall and get past the tourists, Father Ernetti was walking briskly to the right . . . and the Transhumanist was hastening after him.

Jason thought frantically. The tourists were moving in a group to the left, toward the church. He motioned for Mondrago and Casinde to follow him. But by this time Father Ernetti was well ahead . . . and the Transhumanist had caught up with him. The two exchanged a few inaudible words, and then proceeded toward the heavy door in the abbey wall, continuing to talk.

The tourists were still outside the church, waiting for a tour to begin. Jason couldn't afford a scene. He continued to follow the two men ahead, trying to come up with an excuse to interrupt them. But then Father Ernetti reached the door, marked *Monaci Benedittine*, or "Benedictine monks," pushed a buzzer, and opened the door, admitting himself and the Transhumanist, who he evidently trusted. The door began to swing slowly shut behind them.

Jason shot a glance over his left shoulder. None of the waiting tourists seemed to be looking in their direction. He decided to take a chance. He sprinted forward and, without engaging in any attention-drawing acrobatics, managed to get his foot in the door before it closed. Mondrago and Casinde hurried up behind him and, carefully holding the door open, they slipped inside.

The interior corridors were no cheerier than the outside view. There was no one about. Father Ernetti and the goon—as the Temporal Service called Transhumanists of his caste, normally human to all outward appearances, but gengineered to be enforcers—had gone off in one direction or another, and Jason's implant was of no help in here. But he thought to hear a murmur of voices, and led the way in that direction.

After turning a couple of corners, they glimpsed a light ahead: a door opening onto a *cortile*, or cloistered courtyard. The monks' schedule must have had them occupied inside, for there was still no one in evidence—or so Jason thought at first. Then he looked to his left, down the colonnaded covered passage.

In the shadows, the Transhuanist had thrust Father Ernetti against the wall and was holding him there, his left forearm against the Benedictine's throat. He was muttering in low tones, as though trying to choke an answer out of him.

Jason let combat-trained reflexes think for him. He couldn't chance a shot with his laser weapon without risking hitting Father Ernetti—which, even on stun setting, would require some explanation. And he couldn't use his "cane" as a club without damaging the laser's delicate components. So, forgetting his pretended limp, he dropped the cane and launched himself forward, grabbing the goon by the wrist of his upraised right arm and bringing it down behind him and then sharply up, forcing him down on one knee so that he had to release Father Ernetti, who sagged back against the wall, gagging and clutching his bruised throat.

But only a heartbeat was required for the goon's genetically upgraded reflexes to snap his equally enhanced muscles into action. He sprang to his feet like a released steel spring, simultaneously jabbing his left elbow back into Jason's ribs. The two actions together caused Jason to lose his grip on the right wrist, and flung him back against a column with a force that momentarily winded him. With almost insectlike swiftness, the goon pivoted on him, poised for a killing blow.

At that moment Casinde dived forward, landed on his hands, and brought his legs around in a sweeping roundhouse kick that caught the goon's ankles and sent him sprawling, face forward. Before he could spring upright, Mondrago landed on his back, locked his right arm around his neck and, with his left hand, twisted the head around just so far but no farther, holding it at a precise angle.

The goon's caste was lacking in imagination and initiative, but was perfectly intelligent within its narrow scope; he realized at once that Mondrago could instantly break his neck. He stopped struggling and relaxed. Mondrago was not deceived into loosening his grip by so much as a dyne of force.

Jason took a deep breath. "Thanks," he said to the other two. He was particularly impressed by Casinde's performance. So, it seemed, was Father Ernetti, who was staring wide-eyed at the man in the clerical collar even as he continued to make faint choking noises while gasping for breath.

"See if you can help him," Jason told Casinde, who nodded and moved to Father Ernetti's side. Jason knelt, brought his face within a few inches of the goon's, and spoke in twenty-fourth century Standard International English. "All right. We know what you are. Why are you here, and what did you want with the good Father?"

Mondrago released his pressure on the goon's throat just enough to allow him to speak. "Why should I tell you anything?" he wheezed. "I'm as good as dead anyway."

Jason did not bother to deny this. "It can be quick . . . or my friend here can make it last."

The goon actually smiled. "No, he can't. And," he added mockingly, "you can't save the Pope, either!" And with that, he jerked spasmodically in Mondrago's grip and his eyes rolled up. There was the stench of death.

Jason sighed. He had hoped the Transhumanist wouldn't have one of their neurally activated suicide devices, or at least that if he did it would be one of the models activated by the mission leader. Evidently, this particular goon was operating alone and had been given one he himself could use to commit suicide in a manner undetectable by the medical science of the period. It also, Jason knew from past experience with captured Transhumanists, destroyed the brain beyond even the capacity of twenty-fourth century technology to retrieve information from it—not that he had any such technology available anyway—and caused all bionic implants to biodegrade tracelessly. He stood up, as did Mondrago after letting the corpse slump to the paving stones. Their eyes met. They had both heard what the goon has said about the Pope . . . and they both knew what it meant.

"Well," said Mondrago, "we've cleared up one mystery, anyway. Now we know how John Paul I died."

"And the Observer Effect won't let us do a damned thing about it," nodded Jason. He turned to Father Ernetti, whom Casinde now had sitting down, his back propped against the wall, and knelt beside him. "Are you all right, Father?" he asked in Italian.

"Yes . . . I think so," said the Benedictine, still speaking with difficulty. "Thank you, my son. God bless you. But . . . who are you? Where did you come from?" He sounded bewildered—understandably, Jason thought. "And what was that language you were speaking? It sounded rather like English, of which I can follow a little, but—"

"We came here hoping to see you," said Jason hastily, and launched into their cover story, including the connection with Father Brune, hoping it would distract the shaken Benedictine from pursuing the question of language, and from asking how they had gotten in without using the buzzer. "Then we saw this man attacking you."

This reminded Father Ernetti of his attacker, and he stared at the body. "Is he—?"

"Dead. Yes, Father. I'm afraid he must have had a heart attack or something." Actually, Jason was sure a 1978 autopsy would declare it a particularly severe cerebral hemorrhage.

Father Ernetti crossed himself. "But this is terrible! I must summon the brothers and—"

"Yes, of course, Father. But rest a moment longer, after the experience you've been through. Speaking of which . . . why did he assault you? What did he say he wanted? Did it by chance have anything to do with your chronovisor?"

The Benedictine's mild brown eyes grew round behind his thick glasses. "How did you know—?"

"Remember, Father," said Casinde, "we know Father Brune. He told us of his conversations with you."

"Yes, of course." Father Ernetti seemed to be recovering his composure. "To answer your question, this man approached me outside, and expressed interest in it. I was willing to discuss the theory with him. But then, once we were inside, I mentioned to him that I had destroyed the actual device. At that, he grew angry and accused me of lying, and began to use force and threaten me with death if I didn't give him the specifications for the machine . . . which was when you appeared."

The three time travelers' eyes met, and they exchanged a wordless *So the Transhumanists want the chronovisor.* Jason had already reached more or less this conclusion. The Observer Effect wouldn't have allowed them to kill Father Ernetti—history stated quite clearly that he was to die in his bed in 1994—but of course *he* couldn't have known that the threat was empty. And the Observer Effect wouldn't have prevented them from seizing the chronovisor, of whose existence there was no accepted proof. And besides, come to think of it, the Benedictine had said 'the *specifications* for the machine.' The plan must have been to copy it.

The thought of the Observer Effect reminded Jason of another matter. "Father," he said earnestly, "I have no time to explain why, but I have reason to believe that this man was involved with organized crime." That, he thought, should be easy enough for a twentieth-century Italian to swallow. "I must ask you a question, and it is urgent. Do you know of any reason why he and his criminal associates would have an interest in the Pope—even to the extent of posing a threat to his life?"

If Father Ernetti's eyes had widened before, they almost bugged out now. "Oh, God!" he moaned. "No! God forgive me!"

Jason and his companions exchanged puzzled looks. "But Father," said Jason, "you're not responsible for these evil men's actions."

"But I am—at least arguably." Father Ernetti drew a deep, unsteady breath. "You see, I spoke a falsehood earlier—first to this man, and then to you. I have not destroyed the chronovisor, although it is important that the world thinks I have. It is here, in a vault of the Cini Foundation. And a few weeks ago, shortly after his election, I obtained an audience with the Holy Father and told him of it. He was intensely interested, and commanded me to bring it to Rome. He even spoke of setting up a new Order within the Church, under my direction, charged with secretly investigating the past and seeking for confirmation of the faith. I am to go back to Rome in another week. And now you are saying that this may have something to do with a threat to . . ." He trailed off, staring into nothing, alone with his sense of guilt.

Jason stood up. "Father, you must make the arrangements for the proper disposal of this man's body. We have to go to Rome immediately."

"Yes!" Father Ernetti stood up too, and grasped Jason's lapels frantically. "You must warn the Holy See! You must protect the Holy Father's life!"

*How am I supposed to explain the Observer Effect to him?* thought Jason miserably. *How can I tell him that history says John Paul I is going to be found dead two days from now? The Transhumanists are going to kill him in some seemingly natural way that will be assumed to have been heart attack. That will be part of history, and will have always been part of history. And there's nothing anyone can do to prevent it.*

*But now I know the Transhumanists are in Rome. So I know where to look for them.*

"We'll try, Father," was all he said, trying to hold his dishonesty to a minimum. "Later, we'll return here to Venice and talk to you at greater length. But now we must go."

"Yes, go at once! And God go with you."

"Thank you, Father." Jason retrieved his cane and motioned to his followers. They departed hastily, with Jason not even bothering to simulate a limp.

As they left the abbey and hurried to the dock, Jason consulted his optically projected map. Yes: a couple of *vaporetto* connections would take them up the Grand Canal to the Venezia Santa Lucia railroad station.

In one of his previous twentieth-century sojourns he had been told that the one thing Mussolini had done right had been to make the trains run on time. Now he devoutly hoped that was true.

# Chapter Seven

*Bravo Mussolini!* thought Jason, offering up a wry mental salute to one of history's quintessential buffoons. He was now able to testify that, at least as late as the 1970s, you could set your watch by Italian trains.

The bad news was that they'd had to reach Bologna before they could make a connection with the high-speed line. But then the *rapido* had whisked them across the relatively low northern reaches of the Apennines (and under them, through tunnels), and then down through Tuscany toward Rome.

Jason had no eyes for the scenery. The enforced idleness of the trip gave him time to brood over the philosophical implications of what the Transhumanists were about to do, and to wonder how much more of recorded history was the result of their breathtakingly irresponsible god-playing. The three of them, with a compartment to themselves, talked about it in a desultory way.

"Well," said Mondrago, "Rutherford ought to be happy. We've cleared up one historical mystery. John Paul I did *not* die a natural death. And it wasn't the Mafia or the KGB."

"But why are they doing it?" asked Casinde, visibly anguished.

"As Father Ernetti told us—" Jason began.

"Oh, yes, I know their motivation. But why do they *need* to do it? They know that history says the Holy Father is going to die anyway,

49

without having had a chance to set up Father Ernetti's time-studying Order. Even urban legend is clear on the last part."

Mondrago, looking uncharacteristically thoughtful, turned to Jason. "Remember that business with you and Henry Morgan?"

"Vividly." A glimpse of his own very slightly older self had given Jason the solution to the problem posed by the knowledge the great pirate had obtained as they had gone into space and destroyed a Teloi battlestation. He, Jason, had had to return to the seventeenth century and wipe from Morgan's mind the memories that history had demanded he not possess, lest reality dissolve into a nightmare of paradox—and, while doing it, be glimpsed by himself. The incident had caused the Authority much soul-searching, for it had opened up the mind-destroying possibility that, by venturing into the timestream, humans might have unintentionally arrogated to themselves the role of guardians of inevitability, and that reality could no longer protect itself unaided.

"Well," Mondrago continued, "this must be something like that. They must have reason to think they have to *make* it happen."

They all looked at each other in silence. The notion of the *Transhumanists* as guardians of inevitability didn't bear talking about, or thinking about.

"Father," said Jason. (It had been some time since he had last called Casinde that.) "Is it possible that we mortals have dared too much?"

The Jesuit spread his hands. "God alone knows. But what's done is done. We can only make the most of what is given to us, with the aid of our conscience, which is also a gift."

The *rapido* finally pulled into Rome's huge but nonetheless congested Statzione Termini. Emerging into the vast parking lots, they found a taxi and explained that they wished to be taken to Vatican City. Using his map display, Jason confirmed that the driver, for all his somewhat disreputable appearance, was taking them by an honest route, not padding his fare by meandering through the urban labyrinth. (Casinde's clerical collar, and the fact that they obviously weren't American tourists, might have had something to do with it.) He drove past the remains of the Baths of Diocletian straight to the Via Nazionale, then past the bombastic Victor Emanuel Memorial and onto the Corso Vittorio Emanuel. Here, Jason noted, the twentieth-century gasoline miasma was present in full force amid Rome's often hair-raising traffic, in which their driver was an alarmingly enthusiastic participant. Then they crossed the Tiber under the shadow of the Castel Sant'Angelo and turned left onto the Via della Conciliazione. Ahead, visible at the far end of the canyon of buildings, the street opened out into the magnificent colonnade-fringed ellipse of Bernini's Piazza San Pietro, beyond which loomed the façade of St. Peter's Basilica, surmounted by Michelangelo's dome, the tallest in the world.

The driver let them out in the Square of Pope Pius XII. They alighted and, stepping across an invisible boundary line, left Italy and entered the Vatican city-state, the smallest sovereign state on Earth (no passports required) and one of its very few remaining absolute monarchies. They walked out onto the Piazza, joining the throngs of pilgrims and tourists. Jason couldn't help but glance around nervously, even though Casinde had assured him that he and his party of academics hadn't been at this location at this time and date.

"Now what?" Mondrago asked.

*A good question,* Jason admitted to himself. His eyes strayed to the right, where the Apostolic Palace soared up behind the colonnades, and focused on the last window to the right on the top floor—the Pope's bedroom. "John Paul I is going to be found dead, sitting up in his bed, shortly before dawn the day after tomorrow. No matter how high-tech the means by which the Transhumanists are arranging his death, laying the groundwork for it must have taken a certain amount of time, and a lot of infiltration. But now, with their work about to come to fruition, they must surely be around here. We just need to cover as much territory in Vatican City as possible, to give my short-range sensor function the maximum opportunity. The problem is, access to most of it is very limited. Isn't that right, Julian?"

Casinde blinked the rapture out of his eyes, which had been gazing on these surroundings, and swiftly turned businesslike. "True. Anyone who is decorously dressed can walk into the Basilica. The same is true of the museums and the Sistine Chapel, if you don't mind waiting in line and buying a ticket. But there seems no particular reason for the Transhumanists to be in those places. And as for the Apostolic Palace, where the Holy Father lives, there's normally no way to get into it unless you're . . ." He trailed off as his attention was caught by a group of people clustered at the center of the piazza, beside the obelisk that had once stood nearby in the Circus of Nero where Christians, including St. Peter, had been martyred. A priest was speaking to them, and began shepherding them toward the right.

"Wait here," Casinde said to Jason. He hurried over and greeted the priest. For a few moments the two of them conversed, with characteristically Mediterranean hand-accompaniment and occasional gestures by Casinde in the direction of Jason and Mondrago. The priest nodded, and Casinde, with an audible "*Grazie*," returned to his companions.

"It's as I thought," he told Jason. "You see, the Holy Father gives 'general audiences' for pilgrimages organized by people's home dioceses. This is one such group. I talked the priest into letting us join it."

"Good work."

"It's the same way I got my research party in. In this case it was easier; I told him about you two, and suggested that it would be a gracious gesture to our beleaguered fellow Catholics in Greece."

"Your research party? Uh, that wasn't by any chance—?"

"No, no," Casinde hastened to assure Jason. "That was yesterday. And with all the people that come through here, I doubt if anyone we encounter will remember me and notice that I'm here two days in a row."

They fell in behind the priest's flock as it moved to the colonnade to the right of the piazza. At the end of the colonnade was a gate, the Portone di Bronzo, guarded by Pontifical Swiss Guards in their Renaissance style uniforms of blue, red, orange and yellow, with black berets for headgear rather than the plumed slivery morions reserved for ceremonial occasions and particularly holy locations. They were armed with halberds, but Jason knew from his orientation that these men were also equipped with, and trained to use, a variety of up-to-date small arms. Even more emphasis would be placed on that training three years hence after the attempted assassination of John Paul II. But even now it was inadvisable to let oneself be fooled by the gorgeously anachronistic getups.

Passing through the Portone di Bronzo, they filed into the Portico of Constantine, with Bernini's equestrian statue of the first Christian emperor. Ahead was another work of Bernini: the Scala Regia, or

"Royal Staircase," so called because its two flights led up to the Sala Regia, the "Royal Hall" where Popes had received kings and emperors. The pilgrims moved through the barrel-vaulted hall in silent awe, and even Jason was not immune to the effect it created, with its walls covered in magnificent Mannerist frescoes depicting the earthly triumphs of various Medieval and Renaissance Popes.

The hall had four doors besides the one through which they had entered. The pilgrims' priest led them toward the one that led to the Sala Ducale, or "Ducal Hall" where dukes had once assembled to await meetings of the Consistory. Now it was the place for general audiences. Their group of pilgrims began to file reverently in . . . and as they did, a pair of blue dots began to flicker at the edge of Jason's vision.

He looked around intently, seeking to orient the direction of the bionics. They were nowhere near anyone in the group in front of them . . . and, in any event, any Transhumanist among that group would have already triggered the sensor. And besides, the flickering quality meant they were at the edge of the sensor's range, and behind these centuries-old walls—walls that suddenly seemed very confining.

Jason grasped Casinde by the arm and held him back while the pilgrims proceeded into the Sala Ducale. "Julian," he whispered, indicating the other doors. "Do you know where these lead?"

"I think so. That one leads to the Aula Della Benedizioni, or 'Hall of the Benedictions.' That one there goes to the Cappella Paolina, which is closed to the public. And that other one connects to the Sistine Chapel—but it's just an exit from it for private groups, and usually locked"

Jason completed his orientation just before the dots guttered out. There was no doubt as to where the Transhumanist pair were, or rather had been. He waited a moment until the door to the Sala Ducale closed behind the last pilgrim and the three of them were alone in the Sala Regia. Then he rushed to the door leading to the Sistine Chapel. It was locked, as he had more than half expected from what Casinde had told him.

"Let's go," he hissed. "And Julian, show me how you *do* get to the Sistine Chapel."

# Chapter Eight

"It's very roundabout," Casinde murmured to Jason as they hastened out through the Porto di Bronzo, past the Swiss guards who were there to control ingress, not egress. "The Sistine Chapel is only a stone's throw from here, but the only way the public can get to it is by going through the whole length of the Vatican Museums, the 'Long March,' as it's been aptly called—it's sort of a grand climax of the museum tour. So we'll have to go to the Museums entrance, which is—"

"I see it," said Jason, consulting his map display. "And yes, it *is* roundabout—but simple. Let's go!"

They emerged into Bernini's colonnade, followed it about halfway around that side of the ellipse, turned left, and followed the outside of the Renaissance defensive walls that defined the boundary of the Vatican city-state. They walked as rapidly as possible without attracting attention, with Jason simulating a limp only when there was obviously someone watching. First they took the Via di Porta Angelica, past St. Anne's Gate where Swiss Guards were on watch over the entrance used by Vatican employees. Then, at the Piazza del Risorgimento, they took another left turn, then right on the Via Leone IV. Ahead was a final left turn, on the Viale Vaticano. Another hundred yards or so beyond that, Jason knew, would bring them to where the wall was pierced by the monumental entrance to the Vatican Museums.

It wasn't a very long walk, but it gave Jason time to wonder what a pair of Transhumanists were doing in the Sistine Chapel. The answer, he decided, must be that they had been in the adjacent Vatican Palace, which they had somehow infiltrated, and were now trying to leave. But they had run into the same problem he himself had—the fact that the direct exit through the Sala Regia was closed. So now they were having to go the long way, along with the tourists. They and he were converging on the same destination, the main entryway, from opposite directions.

Jason's map display suggested that the Transhumanists had only about half as much ground to cover. But they wouldn't have any reason to be in a hurry, and indeed they wouldn't be able to hurry through the crowds without drawing attention. And besides . . . Jason wondered if even Transhumanists would be capable of hurrying through the Raphael Rooms, the galleries of maps and tapestries, and on past the Apollo Belvedere and the Laocoön, without pausing only briefly to gaze on what their twisted ideology would one day consign to molecular dissolution to sate that loathing of the human past that was, as always, an unconscious manifestation of self-loathing.

They had turned the corner onto the Viale Vaticano and were approaching the thirty-foot-plus-high entrance, surmounted with statues by Michelangelo and Raphael representing "Sculpture" and "Painting," when the flashing blue dots reappeared.

Jason halted his companions with a gesture and studied the gaggle of dazed-looking tourists emerging from the entrance. Two inconspicuously dressed men carrying small overnight bags not unlike their own, who seemed somehow out of place in that crowd, were hurrying purposefully toward one of the taxis parked in the small square. Their movements conformed to those of the blue dots in Jason's field of vision.

Jason rushed to one of the other taxis, not caring if any bystanders thought such speed incongruous in a man carrying a cane. He shook the shoulder of the drowsy driver and pointed to the taxi the Transhumanists had entered, which was now pulling away from the curb. "Follow that cab!"

The driver, who had probably never dreamed of hearing that phrase outside of American movies, stared round-eyed with mouth agape.

"*Basta!*" snapped Jason, pulling out a thick wad of high-denomination *lire* notes and waving them in the driver's face.

The driver needed no further urging. The three of them piled in, and the driver took them back the way they had come, past St. Peter's Square and down the Via Della Conciliazione toward the Tiber. Casinde gazed back at the receding Dome of St. Peter's with an unmistakable look of regret.

"Julian," said Jason softly, speaking in the Standard International English he was sure the driver wouldn't be able to follow even in the unlikely event that he knew the twentieth-century version of the language. "We couldn't have saved the Holy Father. We couldn't even have tried. You know that."

"Oh, yes, I know. I understand the Observer Effect as well as you do. It's just . . ." Casinde gave a smile that mingled sadness with embarrassment. "I hate to tell you the reason I'm sorry to be leaving so soon, since it seems frivolous, and I know we're not here to sight-see. But . . . have you ever been inside St. Peter's Basilica?"

"No."

Casinde paused a moment, then spoke with seeming irrelevance. "Have you ever seen the Grand Canyon, in North America?"

"Yes, I have. It was on a side trip I once treated myself to in our own time."

"Could you describe it—I mean, really convey the impact of it—to someone who had never seen it?"

"No. There's no point in trying. And photographs are meaningless."

"Well, the interior of St. Peter's is like that. Only, unlike the Grand Canyon, it was created not by God but by men inspired by God."

Jason could think of nothing to say, but he was beginning to share Casinde's regret. To take his mind off it, he concentrated on the route they and their quarry were taking. It soon became clear that it was the reverse of their earlier taxi ride. The Transhumanists had completed whatever they had done to give the Pope a seemingly natural death and were headed for the Termini station.

Mondrago deduced as much without the aid of a map display like Jason's, from his recollection of the streets. "Why don't they just activate their TRDs and get out of here?" he wondered aloud. "Assuming, that is, that they've got 'controllable' ones like ours."

"Maybe they're waiting to see if their assassination plot succeeds,"

Casinde speculated, then gave his forehead a Latin slap of annoyance. "But no—they *know* it's going to succeed, don't they?"

"We'll find out soon enough," muttered Jason, preoccupied with a question that always occurred to him whenever he encountered Transhumanist time travelers in the past: when were they from? He had never, as far as he knew, met one from further in the future than his own point of departure, which could mean any of a number of things, some good and some bad. It certainly tended to confirm something the Authority had already deduced from certain other indications: that *The Day* lay not very far in his own future.

They pulled into Termini station, with the Transhumanists' taxi still in sight ahead of them but too far for Jason's sensor to pick up their bionics. Jason gave the driver the tip of his life, then hurried after the two Transhumanists as they entered the building and proceeded through the milling crowds toward the ticket windows and got in a line. Jason and his companions managed to get into the same line, but several places behind.

The pair showed no sign of realizing they were being followed, indicating that whatever implants they had did not include a sensor function like Jason's—for which, still under the psychic influence of his recent surroundings, he offered up a quick, out-of-character prayer of thanks. On a more practical level, he activated his brain implant's recorder function, which preserved all that he saw and heard for later study by the Authority's experts. Of more immediate value was the fact that the audio pickup could be adjusted for amplification. Jason did so, and strained to hear what the leading Transhumanist was saying to the ticket clerk, over the general hubbub of the station. He couldn't make it all out, but *"Venezia"* came through.

"They're going to Venice," he told Mondrago and Casinde in a low voice.

"Hell!" muttered the Corsican. "We're going around in circles."

"But why?" Casinde wondered.

"I can make a pretty good guess," said Mondrago grimly. "They've got implant communicators, and their late friend in Venice hasn't reported in."

"And," Jason added, "they've concluded that he failed in his mission to force Father Ernetti to lead him to the chronovisor. So they're going there to do the job themselves."

Then they found themselves at the head of the line. To Jason's inexpressible relief, there were still three tickets available all the way through to Venice.

The train trip was an overnight one. It was also far too crowded for them to even think of trying to take any action against the Transhumanists enroute. All they could do was maintain contact with their quarry, even through the changeover at Bologna. Jason permitted himself a little sleep, on the theory that the Transhumanists wouldn't try to get off the moving train. But worry—his sensor function did not include any kind of alarm to awaken him if it detected movement—made his sleep fitful.

In the morning, as they finally pulled into Venice's Santa Lucia station, it occurred to him that John Paul I had less than twenty-four hours to live.

They followed the Transhumanists to the Ferrovia pier and boarded the same *vaporetto*, taking scattered seats so as not to appear to be a group. As they worked their way down the S-shaped course of the Grand Canal, Jason had no eyes for such iconic tourist sights as the Ca' d'Oro and the Ponte Rialto. And he studied the Transhumanists as closely as he dared. He now saw that one was an obvious goon, but the other had the indicia of a higher caste, genetically programmed for initiative and high—if somewhat narrow—intelligence. Both had features genetically sculpted into perfect forgetability.

Jason had expected the Transhumanists to take the *vaporetto* all the way to the San Zaccaria pier and make the connection to San Giorgio Maggiore. But they surprised him by getting off well short of that, at the pier beside the Ca' Rezzonico, in the *sestiere*, or district, of Dorsoduro, on the opposite side of the Grand Canal. He led Mondrago and Casinde after them, gesturing caution as they followed the Transhumanists into Dorsoduro, past prestigious tourist hotels like the Palazzo Stern and plunging into the Venetian maze for which "picturesque" was too weak a word, along little walkways and alleys and across humped bridges over minor canals. Finally, the pair they were following came to a tiny hostelry that, Jason somehow suspected, wasn't listed in Fodor's.

He had no idea how the Transhumanists knew about the place, or why they were confident they would be able to get a room in it in

September, not the height of Venice's tourist season but still busy. But they entered the inconspicuous door and didn't come back out. Jason waited a couple of minutes, then followed them in. They were nowhere in evidence, having evidently gone to their room. A short inquiry with a clerk at a desk that was more like a Dutch door confirmed Jason's expectation that no more rooms were available. However—also as per expectation—a flash of Jason's well-filled wallet overcame the clerk's momentary lapse of memory. The three of them filed into a tiny room, most charitably described as "authentic," *sans* view but complete with bidet and, Jason was certain before even testing it out, typically unusable European toilet paper.

He consulted his map display. The Transhumanists seemed to be on the floor above them. "We'll wait for a while and see if they move," he told the other two.

But the day dragged on, with no activity by the Transhumanists. After a while, Jason took the chance of sending Mondrago out to find a *trattoria* and bring back food. As day turned to night, they set up a schedule of napping, with one of their number on watch. Whenever that one wasn't Jason, he had to loiter near the stairwell.

"What is this shit?" demanded Mondrago irritably as he came off watch. "Do you think they're just playing some kind of mind games with us?"

"Well," yawned Jason, "even if they are, they can't stay here in this dump forever. We can wait as long as they can."

But his watch passed uneventfully. He turned the watch over to Casinde and tried to get back to sleep. He was just drifting off when the Jesuit rushed into the room and started shaking him.

"Commander! They're moving."

# Chapter Nine

It was the small hours of the morning, and the deserted alleys and walkways of Venice's Dorsoduro *sestiere* were lit only by a few lamps shining dimly through a thin fog. The air carried a chill, and dank odors rose from the canals. There was an indefinable sinister quality to the closely encroaching walls and shuttered windows, as though there lurked behind them a dark mysterious Venice the tourists were never allowed to see.

From the way the two Transhumanists were moving, Jason assumed their eyes must be bionic replacements with a light-gathering setting. They themselves had to proceed more cautiously, but Jason's map display showed him that they were working their way southward. Soon they came to the Fondamente Bonini, a walkway running alongside the Rio del Ognissanti canal. They turned left, came to the Campo San, then turned right and crossed a small bridge across the canal. Another minute's winding walk brought them to a more substantial walkway, the Fondamente Zattere Ponte Lungo, running along the north side of the wide (for Venice) Canale della Giudecca. At once a bridge took them across the mouth of the Rio de San Trovaso. To their right was the *vaporetto* terminal of Zattere, where boats were tied up for the night. There were actually several small piers, some of which accommodated *motoscafi*, or water taxis, smaller than the *vaporetti*. It was to one of these that the Transhumanists now purposefully went.

Lurking in the shadows of a recessed doorway, Jason could see what they were up to.

He turned back to Mondrago, who with Casinde was concealed behind him. They exchanged glances in the misty lamplight. Mondrago nodded. Jason set his cane on "flashlight" mode and handed it to Mondrago. The Corsican took it without turning it on and, like a swiftly flitting shadow blending with the general shadow-patterns, slipped away toward the nearest pier, where the Transhumanists' backs were to him.

There was no light from the *motoscafo* where the Transhumanists were hunched over the engine housing. There wouldn't be, thought Jason; they would be using their built-in starlight scopes to see as they employed some kind of twenty-fourth-century device to activate the boat's motor. For perhaps the millionth time, he mentally cursed the Authority's overcautious, hidebound attitude that denied Service personnel practically all high-tech tools, however artfully concealed, with only the occasional grudging, graceless concession to the need for things like his cane. At the same time, being inescapably a product of his culture, he felt horror at the Transhumanists' irresponsibility in allowing their own time-travelers such goodies, and in reflective moments he admitted to himself that he couldn't honestly deny the contradiction between the two feelings. Still, being constantly at a disadvantage got a bit tedious at times.

Fortunately, Mondrago had certain skills that sometimes helped even the odds.

Still silent, the Corsican slid into a *motoscafo* without being noticed by the Transhumanists at the other pier. With his back toward them to conceal the light, he held the cane in his mouth, activated the flashlight feature, and set to work on a job of low-tech hot-wiring.

He was still at it when the Transhumanists got their *motoscafo* going and, very slowly, eased away from the pier and putted down the Canale della Giudecca. They were still in sight when Mondrago signaled to Jason and Casinde, who slipped from the shadows and boarded the boat. With a caution equal to that of their quarry, they followed the Transhumanists just closely enough to keep them from vanishing into the darkness and the fog.

Not that Jason was in any doubt as to where they were headed.

The Transhumanists continued on their slow, inconspicuous way to the confluence of the Canale della Giudecca and the Canale di San Marco. There they entered the Laguna Veneta and turned a few degrees to starboard, toward the darkened mass of San Giorgio Maggiore.

"Drop back a little further," Jason whispered to Mondrago, who was doing the steering. In this somewhat more open water, he was worried that they might be more noticeable. But the Transhumanists clearly weren't concerned about being followed. Their attention seemed riveted on their destination, the *vaporetto* pier in front of the church.

Mondrago stepped their motor down to almost nothing and they hung back as the Transhumanists, almost invisible in the distance, moored their *motoscafo*, went ashore and walked to the right, toward the door to the abbey. Jason recalled that a buzzer had to be pressed to gain admittance, and he was sure there was no admittance at all at this hour. He was equally sure the Transhumanists were equipped to disable the door's security. He could only hope that it would stay disabled.

He gestured to Mondrago, and their motor began, very softly, to push them forward. As they neared the landing, they cut off the motor altogether and glided on by momentum and some judicious hand-paddling, in complete silence. By the time they drifted up to the pier, the Transhumanists were nowhere in sight.

They hastily tied up the *motoscafo* and hurried to the heavy wooden door. Jason heaved a sigh of relief when it opened. With their characteristic lack of subtlety, the Transhumanists hadn't tried to cover their tracks by reactivating the electronic lock behind them.

They entered into a darkness against which Jason's map display showed in colors brighter than its usual ghostliness. This time Jason's brain implant was helpful, having been in these corridors once before and built up a schematic of what his eyes had observed. With that help, and that of the flashlight, they swiftly negotiated the route they had previously followed and emerged into the cloistered courtyard.

Jason had hoped that by now the Transhumanists, bionics and all, would be within the very limited range of his sensor. But no little blue dots appeared before his eyes.

"Where are they?" whispered Mondrago.

"Unknown. But they can't be very far away. Let's cover as much ground as possible, running a search pattern to bring them within the pickup. Here, give me the flashlight."

The three of them started out, keeping close together. There was no point in spreading out when only Jason had the ability to detect their quarry, and at any rate they only had one flashlight. Turning to the right, they proceeded along the covered colonnaded passageway, past several doors, Jason tensely alert for the flashing little blue lights.

With startling suddenness, they appeared, blinking fitfully as they always did when the bionics being detected were at extreme range.

Jason took a bearing on them and shone the flashlight in the indicated direction. It revealed a door slightly ajar, with light showing through the crack.

"Come on!" Jason hissed. He retrieved the cane from Mondrago and released the safety catch with his thumb, with the one click that activated the "stun" setting rather than the two for "kill." Simultaneously, he plunged ahead and kicked the door open.

He found himself looking into a small, austere monastic cell, only about twelve feet square. To one side was a meager bed. Most of the center of the room was taken up by a large and obviously ancient desk, piled high with books, files and papers, including much sheet music. More books filled hanging shelves. In the center of the desk, as though benignly presiding over all the clutter, was a brass cross symbolizing the Benedictine Order.

But it was only afterwards that all that registered on Jason. In the first instant, all he had eye for was the two Transhumanists and Father Ernetti, whom the goon was forcing down over one end of the desk in an unbreakable grip while the leader bent over him, speaking in a low voice.

The tableau lasted only a tiny fraction of a second. The goon flung Father Ernetti aside and, as the Benedictine toppled over the bed, hurled himself at Jason. Such was his almost insectlike quickness that only about three feet separated them when Jason pressed the barely visible firing stud on the cane.

Even a low-powered weapon-grade laser like the Takashima produced instant unconsciousness. But without the knock-back effect of energy exchange produced when a lethal laser beam speared a predominantly-water human body and caused a small steam explosion, the goon continued forward on momentum, crashing into

Jason and toppling him over. As he fell under the goon's dead weight, he glimpsed the leader bringing an in-period pistol—a .25 caliber Beretta automatic, Jason guessed, with a silencer—into line but hesitating for fear of hitting the goon.

But then Mondrago lunged through the door past Jason and the goon, seized the wrist of the leader's gun-hand, and forced that arm down and back around at a painful angle, while grasping the leader around the neck from behind. The Beretta fired once with the muffled report of a silenced small-caliber pistol, putting a bullet into the floor of the cell, before Mondrago twisted it out of the Transhumanist's hand.

Jason extricated himself from under the goon with Casinde's help, and scooped up the Beretta. The whole business, he thought, had been practically noiseless; none of the half-dozen monks who were currently permitted to reside in the abbey would have been awakened. He turned to Father Ernetti, who was rising unsteadily from the bed and straightening his thick glasses, which had come askew. "Are you all right, Father?"

"Yes . . . yes. Thank you, my son. But who—?" At that moment the Benedictine got his glasses straightened, blinked several times, and saw Jason clearly. "*You?* Again? But . . . but I thought you had gone to Rome to warn the Holy Father!"

"We did go to Rome. It's a long story, Father. But right now, excuse me a moment." Jason turned purposefully to the Transhumanist leader, prudently motionless in Mondrago's potentially arm-dislocating grip.

"All right," he began, "what are you—?"

The Transhumanist smiled an irritating smile . . . and all at once Mondrago was holding nothing. Rather ludicrously, the Corsican's arms came together, with only air between them, and he lost his balance, looking sheepish. The unconscious goon likewise vanished. There was a double *pop* as air rushed in to fill the holes left by the two Transhumanists who were no longer in this century.

*So,* Jason thought bleakly, *they had TRDs like our Special Ops versions, that could be activated by thought control. And this one was the controller. So they didn't even need to kill themselves. Now they're safely back in the twenty-fourth century.*

*Well, at least there are no bodies to get rid of.*

He turned back to Father Ernetti, from whom there had been

absolutely no sound. The Benedictine had sagged down onto a stool. His mouth was working, in a futile attempt to form words, as he stared at the spaces from which two men had just disappeared into thin air.

Words finally came. "Who in God's name *are* you people?"

# Chapter Ten

Jason sat down wearily and faced Father Ernetti. "Let me start with the easy part of the answer to your question: our names. I'm Jason Thanou. This is Alexandre Mondrago. And this is Father Julian Casinde . . . who, by the way, really *is* a Clerk Regular of the Society of Jesus. That much is true. In everything else, I'm afraid we've been less than candid with you." He drew a deep breath, knowing that Rutherford would have a stroke at what he was about to do. "Before I go any further, I must ask for your promise to hold what I tell you in strictest confidence."

"Think of it as a confession of sorts, Father," Casinde suggested.

Father Ernetti's eyes flicked from one of them to the other nervously, as though fearful of what he might be about to hear. But his voice was steady. "I promise."

"Very well," said Jason, knowing it would be superfluous to ask the Benedictine to swear an oath. "This is going to be very hard for you to accept—although probably not as hard for you as it would be for almost anyone else of this century. The fact of the matter is, we are from your future—four centuries in the future, to be exact."

"Are you telling me," breathed Father Ernetti after a moment's stunned silence, "that you can actually travel, in your corporeal bodies, into the past, and not just observe it? But how?"

"I assure you that there's nothing supernatural about it—although,"

Jason added, remembering Clarke's Law, "it might well seem so to people of this time." He decided against attempting to explain the "temporal energy potential" that Aaron Weintraub would discover and Mariko Fujiwara would learn how to controllably cancel in the early twenty-fourth century. "By means of science that has advanced beyond this era's as far as its own has advanced beyond that of the Renaissance, it is possible to . . . cast a human being or an inanimate object loose from its temporal mooring, setting it adrift in the timestream—but adrift to a precisely designated destination in space and time."

"In the past . . . or the future?" Father Ernetti's shaky whisper was almost inaudible.

"No, only the past." Jason could almost feel the Benedictine's relief, for the concept of mortals being able to foretell their own future must have been a truly chilling one for him. "And this 'temporal displacement,' as we call it, is not easy to do—in fact the effort required is so great that it sends a time traveler a minimum of three hundred years into his own past. And it is such a deeply unnatural state of affairs that it can be reversed easily, so that one returns instantly to one's own time, to which one is inseparably linked."

Father Ernetti pointed unsteadily at the place from which the goon had vanished. "Is that how . . . ?"

"Yes. These two were also from the future. They have returned to their own time." Jason smiled. "If you turned the body of the one who died yesterday over to the police, they're going to be very surprised in the morning when they find that it's disappeared from their morgue." He abruptly turned serious again. "Perhaps you're thinking that I'm either a madman or a liar. But I ask you: how else do you explain what you've just seen here?"

Father Ernetti shook his head slowly. "I don't think you're mad. And a priest hears a great many lies. I usually know when I'm hearing one—and when I'm not. I'm prepared to grant that you're being truthful and even accurate when you tell me *how* you can travel in time. But . . . *why* have you chosen to come to this particular time and place?" A slight smile. "Not that I'm ungrateful, mind you! You've come to my rescue twice. But I can't believe that was your purpose in crossing the gulf of four centuries."

"Not exactly. You see, we are . . . law enforcement officers. And when I told you that the men who've attacked you belonged to a criminal organization, it wasn't a complete falsehood. They were *Transhumanists*—members of an underground movement of our time. It is our duty to combat them wherever and *when*ever we find them."

"But why do you fight them? What is their crime?"

"Actually, they are worse than mere criminals—far worse. Their organization seeks to reimpose a tyranny that ruled—or, I should say, will rule—the world but will be overthrown a century in our past. It will be a tyranny exceeding even the atrocities of the Fascists and Communists of your century. Its origins lie a little more than a hundred years in your future . . ."

A post-World War II writer named Gore Vidal had once said of his era's Western intelligentsia that "dealing so much in ink, they yearn for blood." It was certainly true that, like so many fads of that intelligentsia (such as its bizarrely self-contradictory infatuation with fundamentalist Islamic terrorism), the Transhuman movement of the late twenty-first century had been rooted in sick self-loathing. Self-mutilation is a common expression of self-loathing. But developments such as genetic engineering, nanotechnology and direct neural computer interfacing had opened up the possibility of self-mutilation taken to an entirely new level: the human race transformed into something no longer human. For some, this prospect—a race divided into specialized castes, with a genetically enhanced elite ruling over twisted abominations whose flesh blended into machinery and circuitry with no clear dividing line—had become the basis of a new ideology, calling for the human race to take conscious control of its evolution and transcend itself. That ideology had been like a new disease organism in a body with no immunity, for Western society had long since sacrificed its philosophical defenses against totalitarian fanaticism on the altar of political correctness. Under the charismatic leadership of Armin Drakar, the movement had swept its hopelessly conflicted opposition aside, and by 2130 Earth was entering into three generations of hell.

But by that time slower-than-light interstellar colonization had become possible, and Earth's irreconcilable elements had used it to flee the new order, which had been well pleased to have such a safety valve. It would have felt differently had it known that one of the libertarian colonies would eventually discover the negative-mass drive. Those exiles had returned to the Solar system on faster-than-light wings, bringing the message that there was something better and sparking a forty-year series of wars of liberation that had swept the Transhuman Dispensation away in a torrent of blood by 2270. The true humans, rising from the ashes, had enacted the Human Integrity Act that was the cornerstone of subsequent civilization, with its thundering commandment that man must remain man. The Transhumanist aberration had been forever consigned to the dustbin of humanity's grandiose mistakes.

Or so everyone had thought . . .

"Instead, they went underground," Jason concluded his account, having reverted to the past tense with which he was more comfortable. "Their leadership had foreseen the possibility of defeat, and laid the groundwork for an extremely well financed and well equipped secret organization."

Father Ernetti's eyes had glazed over with horror as Jason had told his tale. "You are right, my son: not even the Bolsheviks or the Nazis ever committed such an outrage against God Himself. They too attempted to eradicate religion. But they never sought to distort and pervert God's creation of man in His own image!"

"It gets worse. The Transhumanist Underground stole the secret of time travel, and improved on it. Only recently have we learned that they've been working to change the past and create a 'secret history,' thus setting up the preconditions for a return to power."

"Dear God!" gasped Father Ernetti. "This is beyond evil. It is a sin against the right order of Creation itself!"

"So now you understand why we must travel in time to forestall them."

"Yes, yes, of course . . ." Suddenly Father Ernetti's eyes, already magnified by his thick glasses, grew even larger as a new thought dawned. "Wait! Now I understand! These Transhumanists came back in time to kill the Holy Father. And you were sent to save him!" He leaned forward and grasped Jason's right forearm like a drowning man desperately grasping a life preserver. "Please, my son, tell me you succeeded!"

Jason sighed. This was a moment he had been dreading. "I'm sorry, Father, but in a few hours the morning news will announce that Pope John Paul has been found dead in his bed, of an apparent heart attack. And there was nothing we could do to prevent that."

"Why not?" asked Father Ernetti in a tiny, stricken voice.

"Because our history says that is how he died." Seeing bewilderment, Jason tried to explain. "A moment ago, you spoke of 'the right order of Creation.' That order—causality itself—would dissolve into chaos if we could go back in time and do things that would create paradoxes. A time traveler killing his own youthful grandfather, for instance. Or doing something that would contradict observed and recorded history. Such acts simply *can't happen.* Something will always prevent them. We call this the 'Observer Effect,' and it cannot be fought. If you try to fight it, the results can be tragic. In fact, if you try to avert a past tragedy, your own efforts may turn out to have been the cause of it." For a moment, a familiar cloud passed over Jason's soul. "Believe me, I know."

"In our era," Casinde put in, "the Church has taken the position that God does not permit time-travel paradoxes, which would violate His most fundamental laws."

"As good an explanation of the Observer Effect as any I've heard," Mondrago muttered.

Father Ernetti sank back onto his stool, a shapeless lump of misery. "I can't pretend to understand. But I believe you. And now I must live with the knowledge that my dealings with the Holy Father brought his doom upon him." Then he straightened, as a new thought seemed to occur to him. "But if you knew that you could not prevent his murder, then what *is* your purpose here?"

"We knew we couldn't stop the Transhumanists from killing the Pope, if indeed that was their intention. But the Observer Effect would still allow us to thwart any of the more surreptitious offenses they perform in our past—things that aren't part of recorded history." Jason didn't try to explain gengineered retroviruses, retroactive plagues, nanotechnological time bombs, deeply buried secret societies, and the rest of the Transhumanists' delayed-action repertoire. "Father Casinde thought there might be a connection with you, which is why we came here to Venice. And now we know their aims. First, to prevent the formation of a secret time-investigating Order by killing the Pope." *Which,* Jason reflected, *involved no Observer Effect complications, since the Order was to have been secret.* "And secondly, to obtain your chronovisor."

"But why? Surely people who possess this marvelous science of time travel have far better devices."

"It may surprise you to learn that we have never developed a means of observing the past without going into it physically. Such a capability would be a tremendous advantage to either side in our war with the Transhumanists."

"Actually, I'm not surprised. As I told Father Brune, it is wildly unlikely that the chronovisor would ever be independently reinvented, as it was only by a stroke of luck that I stumbled upon it."

Casinde spoke. "You also told Father Brune that you had dismantled the machine, because you felt that it was too dangerous—that it could lead to a frightening dictatorship in which there would be no secrets and no privacy."

"Yes—and when I said that to Father Brune in the early 1960s, it was true. But then, a couple of years later, I grew too ambitious. I managed to gather some of the original team that had worked with me in the mid-1950s, although many, such as Enrico Fermi, were no longer living. We reassembled the machine. Subsequently, I became almost addicted to it, using it to gratify my curiosity about many things. But then . . ." The Benedictine suddenly shuddered, and buried his face in his hands. When he could speak again, his voice was haunted. "Then I discovered that which made me realize that my earlier fears had been as nothing. I have not used the machine since."

"But more recently," Casinde prompted, "you've been doling out things like the photograph of Christ that appeared in 1972."

"Yes. I've made any number of claims that can easily be disproved, and associated my name with various crank organizations. I shall continue to do so. I and the chronovisor *must* be discredited!"

"Why?" asked Casinde, perplexed. "After all, your recent audience with the Holy Father—"

"I requested that audience because I was in distress of soul. I needed guidance. And that is why I haven't destroyed the chronovisor. The Holy Father commanded me not to do so, pending further investigation, however much I may wish to."

"Why do you wish to?" Casinde repeated.

"Because I now believe the machine is a fraud of Satan. No . . . I don't, really. But I *want* to believe it is. It *must* be! Because I have seen things which, if they become generally known, will destroy the faith."

# Chapter Eleven

Silence reigned as they waited for Father Ernetti to elaborate. When he finally spoke, he approached the subject obliquely.

"What is the earliest date to which your people have traveled?"

"1628 B.C. was the earliest by far; the second earliest was 490 B.C.," said Jason, recalling both occasions vividly. "You see, the amount of energy required for temporal displacement is a function of the mass being displaced and the stretch of time involved. This is true even of the Transhumanists' displacement technology—which we've recently obtained, by the way. With the energy-intensive equipment our organization has always used, the energy requirement for really long displacements is colossal, and can only be met by using extremely expensive . . . fuel."

"You mean atomic power?"

"Something like that." Jason didn't go into an explanation of antimatter.

Father Ernetti gave a sad little smile. "You should count yourselves fortunate. My own road to damnation was made all too easy. The chronovisor's power requirement is inconsequential, and does not seem to be affected by how far back one observes. So no limits were imposed on my curiosity—my hubris. I developed an interest in the Genesis Creation story—I wanted to track it down to its origins. So I focused the chronovisor on the year 4004 B.C."

Casinde gave him a sharp look. "Would that by any chance have been Sunday, October 23, 4004 B.C.?"

Father Ernetti looked up at him, and his eyes held a slight twinkle. "You've found me out. I see you are familiar with the Ussher chronology."

"The what?" Mondrago wanted to know.

"James Ussher," Casinde explained, "was a bishop in the seventeenth century—an Anglican bishop," he added parenthetically, in a *nobody's perfect* tone. "Specifically, his title was Archbishop of Armagh and Primate of All Ireland. By various methods, including the combined lifespans of all the male lineage from Adam to Solomon as given in the Bible, and cross-referencing later Biblical events and kings' reigns with datable events in other cultures, he concluded that the Creation as described in Genesis took place in 4004 B.C. He further concluded that it must have begun on a Sunday, since God rested on the seventh day, and the Jewish day of rest is Saturday. And, as it happens, the autumnal equinox—the start of the Jewish year—was Sunday, October 23, that year."

"Strictly speaking," Father Ernetti put in rather pedantically, "he calculated that the work of Creation began six hours before midnight—6:00 PM, that is—on the preceding day, October 22. He was able to build further calculations on this. For example, that Noah's Ark touched down on Mt. Ararat on Wednesday, May 5, 2348 B.C."

Jason, slightly dazed, looked from one priest to the other. "And all this was, uh, taken seriously?"

"Oh, yes," Father Ernetti nodded. "Starting in 1701, annotated editions of the King James Bible cited Ussher's chronology as authoritative."

"But . . . but . . . the fossil record . . ."

"Such things were easily explained away," Casinde assured Jason. "It was declared that Earth without a fossil record would be imperfect. God makes only perfect creations. Therefore, Earth was created complete with a fossil record."

"Now I truly believe that you are in fact a Jesuit," said Father Ernetti drily.

Jason stared at him. "Father, am I to understand that you thought you could actually observe the—"

"No, no! Of *course* not!" The Benedictine sounded more than a little defensive. "No modern theologian believes *literally* in the Genesis story. As I explained to you before, I was only interested in investigating its origins, which we know lie in Mesopotamia, probably as far back as the early Sumerian Uruk culture, or perhaps even its Ubaid predecessor. And we believe that the latter was yielding to the former right around the end of the fifth millennium B.C. or the beginning of the fourth. So you see, the time frame I chose made perfect sense." His bristling defensiveness began to shade over into embarrassment. "Admittedly, my choice of that precise date was, I suppose you could say, a bit of facetiousness on my part. But it *was* a reasonable choice. And," he repeated a little too firmly, "I was *only* interested in getting to the historical roots of Genesis."

"Of course, Father, of course," Jason soothed. *And yet, for all your protestations, I can't help suspecting that at the very back of your mind, against your will, you were wondering if maybe . . . just possibly . . .*

*And you just had to find out for sure.*

"At any rate," Father Ernetti resumed, "I chose the site of what was later to be the city-state of Uruk, on the lower Euphrates. Of course, it wasn't really a city-state then—that hadn't developed as yet. The Ubaid people had laid the groundwork for a proto-urban culture by using the annual flood of the Tigris and Euphrates to irrigate crops on a larger scale than anyone else had ever attempted, enabling them to build up an unprecedentedly dense network of settlements, some of them with populations of up to a thousand. The rise of the Uruk culture marked the transition from towns to actual cities, with features such as public buildings and occupational specialization that we associate with urban life."

"Right around the period you chose," Jason nodded.

"I observed them. I listened to them. By listening for certain sounds, I was able to settle one historical controversy: the people of the Ubaid and Uruk cultures were already speaking Sumerian, the language that was being spoken in the region half a millennium later, when writing was invented and history dawned. I recorded the sounds, hoping to solicit the aid of a specialist to translate them." Father Ernetti paused . . . and the pause continued, as he hunched over and seemed to withdraw into himself. It was, Jason thought, as though he had gone as far as he could before reaching the edge of an abyss of horror.

"Yes, Father?" he prompted. But the Benedictine appeared not to hear him, or even to be aware of anything except his private nightmare. "Tell us about what you saw."

A strong shudder ran through Father Ernetti. He drew a deep breath and sat up straight. "Yes. I must tell someone. I kept observing those incredibly long-ago people, unable to stop, even though after a while I began to feel like a voyeur—the fascination was like a drug. I was determined to penetrate to the core of their religion, so I followed them as they went about their rituals. And . . . and . . ." All at once he wailed and buried his face in his hands.

"What did you see, Father," said Jason gently.

Father Ernetti looked up, and his face was set with tears. "The Annunaki! The primal gods of the Sumerians! *They were real! They were alive!*" He looked from one of his stunned listeners to another. "Don't you see? The chronovisor must have somehow been lying. It *must!*" He sank back onto his stool in misery.

"Father," said Jason slowly, as a suspicion began to dawn, "tell me about these gods—these Annunaki."

"They were supposedly the offspring of the deities Anu and Ki—"

"Although," Casinde cut in tonelessly, "There is an alternative theory that the name means *those who from the heavens came to Earth.* And . . . they cohabited with the daughters of men and produced hybrids."

The three time travelers stared at each other in silence, for what was in all of their minds could not be said in the presence of the tormented priest, lest it destroy what was left of his faith.

Furthermore, they needed confirmation—not just of what Father Ernetti seemed to be saying, but of the fact that this "chronovisor" actually existed and worked, something Jason was still having difficulty accepting.

"Father Ernetti," said Jason, "may we be allowed to see these Annunaki?"

There was another *cortile* behind the first one. It surrounded the facilities of the Cini Foundation. Using Jason's flashlight to light the way without awakening anyone, they made their way through the cloisters and down several flights of steps into levels not known to the general public.

"I am uncomfortable with this," jittered Father Ernetti. "Remember,

I would already have destroyed the chronovisor had it not been for the Holy Father's command." But then they were at the lowest level, before a door that would have done credit to a bank vault. Father Ernetti keyed in a combination, and the massive door swung open. He flipped a switch and lights came on, to reveal . . . something Jason's mind had difficulty grasping at first. It did not look like a product of high technology, by the standards of Jason's world; but at the same time it somehow did not seem to belong in this one, even though as far as he could tell it was made from components that were commercially available in 1978 . . . with one possible exception. But those components were put together in what seemed a purposeless way, in three distinct blocs, connected by cables.

"How does it work, Father?" asked Casinde in a hushed voice.

"What you must understand is that memory has very little to do with the brain or nervous system," said Father Ernetti distractedly as he fiddled with instrumentation. "All matter has memory. In fact, it may be all-pervasive. The difficulty is one of accessing it. It appears to be stored in infinitesimally small 'memory traces' involving an electrical charge perhaps a millionth of that of an electron. The signal generator picks them up." He indicated the bloc of seemingly miscellaneous hardware to the left, at one end of a heavy table. "But to reactivate the memories thus stored in inanimate objects, they must be enhanced to a certain threshold. This is the function of the enhancer." He pointed at the largest and most featureless bloc, which filled the space under the table. "Finally, the analyzer, here on the right-hand end of the table, reactivates the memory traces and causes sensory impressions to appear in visible, audible and recordable form."

It was this last component that included the one item that seemed out of place. For in addition to ordinary audio ports, it supported a largish circular screen, nothing like the cathode-ray television screens of this era.

"And you can zero in on any time and place in the past?" asked Jason.

"Yes." The Benedictine, still busy, seemed not to notice the skepticism Jason had been unable to keep entirely out of his voice. "And since I always kept a careful log of all my usage of the machine, I know exactly where to focus. Ah . . . here!"

A low humming filled the room. The circular screen came to life.

There was something peculiar about that screen. Very peculiar. It was two-dimensional, but it drew the eyes in until the viewer seemed lost in it, immersed in a three-dimensional reality. And that reality was of a flat, marshy, canal-crisscrossed landscape under a sky whose blue was whitened by heat as though baked, even though it was October. Across the mudflats huts could be glimpsed, with reed as the basic building material, including roofs of bundles of reeds tied near the top to yield a graceful curve, with reed roofs. But the immediate surroundings were those of a town of sun-dried brick, thronged with a stocky, olive-skinned, aquiline-nosed people. The men's heads were mostly shaven, and they wore flounced tunics long enough to be describable as skirts. The women wore wraparound shawls over long dresses. The language in which they spoke meant nothing to Jason, but he had no difficulty making out the tone. It was one of hushed, reverent expectation. All attention was focused on what was by far the town's largest building.

That building was, of course, not one of the towering ziggurats that would, much later, dominate Mesopotamian cities. It was only a rather featureless rectangular structure of the usual mud brick. But it had been built atop an artificial mound of earth, a platform designed to raise it above its surroundings. And the reverence with which the crowd regarded it left no doubt that it functioned as a temple.

All of a sudden the dull clang of a crude gong sounded. A low moan arose from the crowd. And from the temple emerged that which laid Jason's last doubts to rest.

The proto-Sumerians were a short people, but this being—dressed in a colorful robe that must have fit current notions of what a god would wear—would have towered over even the humans of Jason's day, for he was at least seven and a half feet tall, and his miter-like headgear made him seem even taller. His form had roughly the proportions of an extremely slender, long-legged human. Straight, shimmering hair like an alloy of silver and gold framed a long, almost dead-white face whose sharp features included high cheekbones which, like the eyebrow ridges, slanted upward. Their slant paralleled that of the huge eyes, whose opaque blue irises seemed to have no clear line of demarcation from the pale-blue "whites." The overall effect was an exoticism that hovered uncertainly between the eerily beautiful and the flesh-crawlingly abnormal.

The crowd, moaning even louder, sank into a collective genuflection.

Another being like the first—this one female, although the distinction was not as obvious as it was in *Homo sapiens*—emerged behind the first one The two of them were flanked by human attendants, presumably priests or acolytes, dressed in a more elaborate version of the usual male attire and wearing a simpler version of the "gods'" headgear.

"You see?" came Father Ernetti's quavering voice. "It's a lie. It must be a lie of Satan! Mustn't it? These are the Annunaki as generally described—tall, golden-haired, awesome in a disturbingly strange way. Some believe their aspect may, much later, have contributed to the common visualization of angels."

*Believe me, Father, they're not angels,* thought Jason grimly.

"Commander," said Mondrago in the uncharacteristically flat voice that never failed to get Jason's full attention. "Look at those two priests."

Jason did. They were noticeably taller than the worshipers. That might have resulted from belonging to a well-nourished hereditary elite . . . but this seemed too rudimentary a society for that. They had a look of unsuccessfully concealed arrogance, again possibly a byproduct of social stratification, but with the same objection to that explanation. Then Jason looked beyond all that, and as certain subtle indicia began to emerge a chill ran through him.

*They have the typical local ethnic features,* he thought, forcing calmness on himself. *But nanomachines can resequence the genetic code to order, giving anyone dark-olive skin and a big hooked nose.*

*And yet . . . if you know what to look for . . .*

*And I know a Transhumanist middle-management level type, and a goon-caste one, when I see them.*

Abruptly, Father Ernetti turned off a switch—struck it, actually, as though he could bear to watch no more. The image vanished, leaving them all blinking in the dimness of the vault as the Mesopotamian sun vanished.

"Now do you see?" said Father Ernetti. "If this becomes general knowledge, imagine the consequences."

"Father," said Jason, speaking to himself as much as to the Benedictine, "you have *no* idea." He shook himself. "I must ask one more favor of you. You mentioned that the sights and sounds you pick up can be recorded. Did you make a recording of this?"

"Yes, among many others."

"It is urgent that we now return to our own time. Would you lend me this recording? I swear I will return it."

"He is known to be a man of his word, Father," said Casinde as the Benedictine hesitated. "And this is vitally important."

"Very well. The tapes are here." Father Ernetti walked over to a cabinet and withdrew a plastic case.

*Tapes!* thought Jason. The Authority's specialists should have fun cobbling together something that could project such archaic media.

"I implore you, my son," Father Ernetti told Jason as he handed over the case, "do not reveal this to the faithful of your era, lest you undermine their faith."

"Father," said Casinde with great seriousness, "I pledge by all that is holy that we will reveal nothing to suggest the possibility of supernatural pagan gods having had actual existence."

*A Jesuit indeed!* thought Jason with an inner smile. He prepared his mind to give a neural command. Then something occurred to him.

"Father Ernetti, remember what I told you before about the 'Observer Effect'? For reasons connected with it, I must ask you to not use the chronovisor to observe this same location during the period immediately following what you have just shown us."

"You need have no fear on that score! I could not bear to so torture myself."

"Good. Farewell for now, Father."

"Farewell. Go with God."

Jason saw Father Ernetti make the sign of the cross just before the reality of 1978 A.D. faded out.

# Chapter Twelve

Kyle Rutherford stopped the crude video recording that was projected onto a wall of his dimmed office, backed it up, and after a few seconds stopped it again. He had already done so several times, but seemed unable to stop. Finally he turned away, shaking his head slowly.

"Someday, Jason, you're going to shock me by going on an expedition and *not* coming back with something to give me nightmares." His glance once again went to the frozen frame, and he started to back it up again before looking away in obvious self-annoyance at what smacked of compulsive behavior. "Is there any possibility that this could have been faked?"

"Oh, absolutely, Kyle! Father Ernetti hired some eight-foot-tall actors and a really good makeup artist, and—"

"This is no time for sarcasm, Jason."

"This is a perfect time for sarcasm!" Jason waved his hand at the frozen image flickering on the wall in its charmingly retro-tech way. "Those are *Teloi*, damn it! You know that as well as I do. How could a twentieth-century person have known of their existence, much less what they looked like? And it's stretching coincidence too far to believe that fakery on his part would have just happened to resemble them this exactly—even assuming he had wanted to fake any such images."

"And he wouldn't have wanted to," said Casinde, his mild tone a counterpoint to Jason's vehemence. "Far from it. Trust me, Director: I was there. Father Ernetti would have sold the soul he absolutely believed he possessed for these images *not* to be true. In fact, he was trying desperately to convince himself that they were not—that the chronovisor was deceiving him, that it had somehow become a conduit for lies of the Adversary. But I could tell that he didn't really believe it."

"Very well," said Rutherford heavily. "I concede the lack of motive. We must accept Father Ernetti's good faith. And I suppose that the appearance of palpable Teloi in this recording means we must also accept the chronovisor's efficacy. But . . . *how*?" He was almost wringing his hands. "How could this device you've described to me, assembled out of bits and pieces of mid-twentieth-century technology, possibly have worked?"

Jason had turned thoughtful. "Remember what we were saying when Julian first told us about Father Ernetti?"

"I do. I must say it sounded like a lot of pseudoscientific tosh to me. 'Akashic records' indeed!"

"Maybe. But I've been doing some more reading. It's true that a lot of pseudoscience and outright mysticism got mixed up with the concept of the 'ether' that people used to think must fill the universe in order for energies and forces—light and gravity and whatever—to be transmitted. Then, in 1897, the Michaelson-Morley Experiment seemed to disprove the ether's existence; they measured the velocity of light, and it turned out to be the same whether the beam was aligned with or against the Earth's orbital motion, or perpendicular to it. And in 1905 Einstein's theory of relativity made it clear that light waves didn't need a propagating medium.

"But then, by the end of the twentieth century, many physicists began to admit that the concept of intangible quantum fields filling the universe—every particle having its own field that extends universally, and when excited with energy creates the associated particle—"

"The 'implicate order,' a physicist named David Bohm called it," interjected Casinde, who evidently had also been doing some reading.

"—is an awful lot like the 'ether' under a new name. Anyway, whatever you call it, maybe it accumulates thoughts, and sensory impressions." Jason gave a spread-hands gesture of helplessness. "I don't know. Not even Father Ernetti knew—he admitted he blundered onto this by accident, against transfinite odds. But *something* must explain it. Those Teloi images aren't going to go away."

"I know," said Rutherford bleakly. "So we must simply accept that the chronovisor is being truthful, as I gather Father Ernetti knew in his heart of hearts. But of course he didn't suspect that the reality he was seeing was even worse than what he *thought* he was seeing." A sudden suspicion awakened in his eyes. He turned a stern regard on Jason. "You are, of course, aware that you told him a great many things quite improperly."

"What was I supposed to do, Kyle? He had just seen two Transhumanists vanish into thin air. And don't think he was stupid . . . or that he was primitive. Remember, this was 1978—thirty-six years after the first atomic chain reaction, thirty-one years after the invention of the transistor, nine years after men had landed on the Moon. And he had personally known Enrico Fermi! He wouldn't have bought some mumbo-jumbo explanation."

"Perhaps. But as regards the real import of this recording . . . please tell me you didn't reveal *that* to him . . . did you?"

"Of course not, Kyle!" Jason firmly reined in his exasperation. "I'm not *quite* the lout you think I am. This was a Catholic clergyman, born and raised in the early twentieth century, who was trying to come to terms with what seemed to be unambiguous proof that pagan gods were real. I wasn't about to compound his torment by telling him that they were actually extraterrestrials who had created the human race by genetic manipulation of *Homo erectus* around 100,000 B.C."

"No, no. Of course not." But Rutherford still looked unhappy.

"Anyway, we shouldn't just be looking at the Teloi. We should be looking at those 'priests'. We know what *they* imply."

"Yes." Rutherford stared at the flickering image. "Believe it or not, Jason, I *do* have the utmost respect for your professional judgment. And you have more experience dealing with Transhumanist time-travelers than anyone else. If you say those were specialized medium-caste types in 4004 B.C., I accept that."

"Then you must also accept the fact that the Transhumanists have gone back two and a third millennia further back than we've ever gone—and even further back than that from the earliest period we know they've visited, which was the thirteenth century B.C."

"Not out of the question, given their temporal displacement technology," Rutherford mused.

Mondrago addressed Jason, looking very thoughtful. "Do you remember Franco, the leader of the Transhumanists we met in Athens in 490 B.C.?"

"I remember him very well."

"Then maybe you remember what he said about how they had linked up with the few surviving Teloi of that era, who were still posing as the Olympian gods."

"Right. He said he had encountered the Teloi in the course of an earlier visit to the late Greek Bronze Age when he'd gone back to lay the groundwork for the cult of the god Pan. That's how we know they've gone back that far. In fact, he told us that the Teloi had helped them gengineer the being they passed off to Pan's worshipers as the god himself. And . . . Hey! Wait a minute! I think I see what you're driving at."

"So do I," said Rutherford. "Franco said nothing about knowing of the existence of the Teloi at any period earlier than the thirteenth century B.C. So these Transhumanists in Father Ernetti's recording must have come from a period later than Franco's expedition."

"Which means they could quite possibly be from our own future," said Jason grimly. "Remember, Franco's expedition to fifth century B.C. Athens had departed from the twenty-fourth century at a time only slightly earlier than ours had—shortly after our earlier expedition to 1628 B.C., in fact."

"But surely not very far in our future," said Rutherford, as though appealing for reassurance. "After all, we have reason to believe that we haven't very long to wait before *The Day*. And . . ." He did not continue, for he was skirting a subject that always entered everyone's mind in connection with that of Transhumanist extratemporal expeditions from their own future: the possibility that *The Day* was going to succeed, and that the Transhumanist time travelers came from a nightmare future world in which their obscene tyranny had been reimposed. It was a thought which no one ever wanted to voice.

But after that first horrifying reaction, everyone always took refuge in the reassuring rationale that a victorious, reestablished Transhuman dispensation would have no reason to continue subverting the past. In other words, after *The Day* and regardless of its outcome, there should be no further Transhumanist time traveling. Therefore, no Transhumanist time travelers that one might ever encounter could be from further in the future than that.

Hence, nobody completed Rutherford's sentence or responded to it. By unspoken common consent, the subject was dropped into a well of silence.

"There's something else we should consider," said Casinde after a moment. "Jason, you were the first to learn the truth about the Teloi. As I understand it, the ones on Earth belonged to something called the *Oratioi'Zhonglu*—"

"That's right. *Zhonglu* is an apparently untranslatable Teloi word meaning . . . some kind of organization or group or society for a certain purpose. After the Teloi gengineered themselves into virtual immortality, they started coming up with more and more bizarre ways to fill their endless, meaningless lives. The *Oratioi'Zhonglu* essentially marooned themselves on Earth because it was a place where they could play at being gods—at least after they had created a race of slaves and worshipers."

"But from what I read in your report, the human slaves began to turn rebellious, running away from the Teloi core area of northeast Africa and southwest Asia to populate the rest of the Earth. And eventually the Teloi, exasperated, withdrew from their original river-valley areas and established themselves to the north and west as the Indo-European pantheon, known by various names from Ireland to northern India. Would they still have been active in lower Mesopotamia in 4004 B.C.?"

"Why, they *must* have," said Jason, indicating the still-frozen frame projected on the wall, with its image of "Annunaki."

"Perhaps. But," Casinde persisted, "your report of your later expedition to the seventeenth-century Caribbean spoke of a different *zhonglu*."

"Right—the *Tuova'Zhonglu*. As I said, the Teloi organize themselves around specific purposes. And for the purpose of fighting a war against their enemies the Nagommo they formed a military *zhonglu*. By the time I encountered them, the war was long over and the Teloi had been wiped out—except for the *Tuova'Zhonglu*, the hard-core remnant of the military, who were still roaming the galaxy, mad even by Teloi standards, dreaming of galactic conquest and obsessing about how they would have won the war if only they hadn't been betrayed by the decadent, effete remainder of their race, which had failed to give them its full support."

"But," Casinde persisted, "correct me if I'm wrong, but wasn't the Teloi-Nagommo war in still going on in 4004 B.C.?"

"Oh, yes. In fact, that would have been about the time Oannes, the Nagom we encountered, told me his ship had crash-landed in the Persian Gulf and . . ." Jason trailed off as the full implications of what Casinde was saying dawned on him. "Are you suggesting that these Teloi in the recording might have belonged to the *Tuova'Zhonglu*?"

Mondrago frowned. "And if so, they might have come to Earth in search of Oannes' ship. *That* could lead to a sticky situation."

"But," Jason protested, "Oannes told me nothing about having been pursued to Earth." He recalled the amphibious alien he had known, and who had saved his life—the alien who would leave a memory of a "fish-man" who had brought the arts of civilization to mankind. "He only said that his scout ship was crippled by the automated orbital defenses the *Oratioi'Zhouglu* had emplaced, before it destroyed those defenses, and that afterwards the survivors helped the early Sumerians create an independent civilization, starting with teaching them writing."

"A great many mysteries," Rutherford intoned.

"Altogether too damned many for my taste," said Jason. "I think it's become important that we pay a visit to Sumeria in 4004 B.C."

# Chapter Thirteen

"But . . . but . . . it's *unprecedented!*" Alcide Martiletto's voice almost broke as he pronounced the governing council's ultimate obscenity.

He—Jason decided the masculine pronoun was permissible—currently held the rotating chairmanship of the governing council, which Rutherford had convened at the Authority's Australian headquarters. There, the members had been shown Father Ernetti's recording, which after a certain number of arguments and objections had overcome even these people's capacity for self-deception and wishful thinking. Now they, along with Rutherford and Jason, sat around the long conference table in their elegantly appointed meeting room and listened to Jason's proposal.

"That, Mr. Chairman," Rutherford told Martiletto, "is precisely why I requested this meeting. Ordinarily, approval of extratemporal expeditions is within my discretion as Operations Director. But since this will involve incomparably the longest temporal displacement in the history of the Authority, I thought it well to involve the full council in the approval and planning process."

Several members started to speak, but unfortunately Serena Razmani got in first. She was the newest member of the council, and relatively young by its gerontocratic standards. She should, thought Jason, have been a breath of fresh air in these stuffy confines. Alas, her chief talent was for wasting time with irrelevancies occasioned by her inability to grasp things obvious even to the likes of Martilleto. She did not disappoint now, and as she spoke her face wore its habitual expression of vague puzzlement.

"But Commander Thanou, I *still* don't understand this Father Ernetti's connection with the Transhumanist underground. Or the connection of the Transhumanists you encountered to those in the recording from 4004 B.C."

"Perhaps, Madame Councilor, I can clarify what I explained in the earlier briefing." It was the closest Jason dared come to *Haven't you been listening?* "The Transhumanists had, by means as yet unknown to us, learned of Pope John Paul I's plan to create a secret Order, headed by Father Ernetti, to use the chronovisor to search the past for matters of theological significance. They evidently recognized it as a threat, for such an Order might very well have accidentally uncovered their activities in the nooks and crannies of history. Therefore, the Pope had to die."

"But didn't history say he was going to die anyway?"

Jason gave Razmani a sharp look. *Can it be that she's actually taken the trouble to inform herself about the Observer Effect? Maybe there's hope for her yet.* "That's a very valid point, Madame Councilor. But evidently they had reason to think they had to *make* it happen. We don't know what that reason was, and we may never know, but as you may recall we once found ourselves in such a situation."

"Yes," Alastair Kung interjected heavily, glaring at Jason with narrowed eyes, almost causing them to disappear into their nests of fat. "The Henry Morgan business."

"At any rate," said Jason, continuing to address Razmani, "since they were in 1978 Italy anyway, they decided to try and steal the chronovisor, which as you can imagine might be very useful to them. They had no reason to think the Observer Effect would have prevented it—although, come to think of it, maybe the fact that *we* prevented it was simply a case of the Observer Effect in action." The unease around the table was unvoiced but palpable. "And to answer your second question: we have no reason to think there is any connection between *that* Transhumanist operation and whatever it was they were doing in Sumer in 4004 B.C."

"But," Razmani persisted, "what *were* they doing there? How could they know the Teloi were going to be present?"

Jason forced himself to speak without any condescending display of long-suffering patience. "We have no reason to suppose that contacting the Teloi was their original reason for going back to that time and place. It could have been to plant any one of their various 'time bombs' ticking away toward *The Day*, all of which require different lengths of time to germinate, if I may mix my metaphors. Gengineered retroviruses and plagues, for example. And secret societies and cults, nurtured over the centuries by accurate 'prophecies' and periodic visitations by an apparently ageless 'prophet' performing displays of techno-magic. We've been able to abort or root out some of those, but there are bound to be others, unaware of each other's existence, waiting for the word. Creating one of those—the cult of Pan—was what they were doing in fifth century B.C. Athens. And I have a hunch that something of the sort is what they're up to in proto-historical Sumer. Probably they encountered the Teloi—of whose existence they already knew in general—by sheer coincidence. And it was another coincidence that Father Ernetti observed them there."

"A fortunate coincidence," Rutherford put in. "Now we know that they were active in that time period—and that they made contact with the Teloi, something we have previously thought they first did on their expedition to fifth century B.C. Athens." He paused, frowned in annoyance at the usual confusion of tenses, and continued. "The leader of that latter expedition thought the same thing, which is why we conclude that the expedition to Sumer departed at a later date than did his—possibly from our own future."

For a moment everyone was silent, uncomfortable with that line of thought as people always were. Rutherford took advantage of the pause. "So, thanks to this fortuitous set of happenstances, we now have the kind of precise date and location we need to target a Special Operations mission."

"But," rumbled Jadoukh Kubischev in the ponderous way that went with his massive frame, "as the chairman has pointed out, it's unprecedented. 4004 B.C. is almost twenty-four centuries further back than any temporal displacement we have ever attempted."

"And the *expense!*" squeaked Martilleto. A sympathetic twittering ran around the table.

"I suggest, Mr. Chairman," said Rutherford smoothly, "that our ideas concerning expense are still conditioned by our past assumptions. Under those assumptions, I grant that a displacement of almost sixty-four centuries would be ruinous. But using the Transhumanist technology that we now possess, our calculations suggest that is it perfectly feasible, as long as we limit ourselves to a small party."

Jason braced himself for a characteristically uninformed question from Razmani at this point, but none was forthcoming. Evidently even she understood that the energy requirement for temporal displacement was a function of two factors: the stretch of time involved and the mass to be displaced.

"If the Transhumanists did it, we can do it," he put in helpfully.

"You speak of a 'small party', Director," said Helene de Tredville. She was a tiny woman, old even by the council's standards, with white hair pulled tightly back into a severe bun. "How small?"

"We are thinking in terms of four: Commander Thanou, Superintendent Mondrago, and two other members of the Special Operations Section chosen for demonstrated competence and ability to blend physically in the target milieu."

"We would, of course, ideally like to send more," Jason added. He decided that the old military axiom *"The more you use the less you lose"* would be considered in questionable taste in this company. "But four should suffice, given the proper equipment."

Kung began to inflate, toadlike, as though disapproval was filling him like air. The Special Operations Section's limited exemption from the Authority's traditional ban on twenty-fourth-century weapons and other devices had never sat well with him—or, for that matter, with the council in general, even though the argument in favor of it was irrefutable. Permission to carry such things, ingeniously disguised, into the past was granted routinely, but never with any good grace.

"Also," Jason continued, before Kung could start huffing and puffing, "we should have the element of surprise. The Transhumanists—depending on when they displaced or will displace from—may very well know of Father Ernetti's chronovisor in general. But they should have no reason to think he observed them in 4004 B.C., or that he shared the knowledge with us. And they certainly won't be expecting *us* that much further back than any of our previous expeditions." *After all, they know how hidebound the Authority's leadership is,* he did not add.

Rutherford picked up the thread. "We're fortunate in the matter of language, since Father Ernetti recorded the local speech. Our linguists have confirmed that his supposition was correct: the language was an early form of Sumerian. This enables us to provide the expedition members with it by direct neural induction." There were no prim manifestations of disapproval at this exception to the Human Integrity Act; it was a long-established practice, and not even Kung and his ilk could deny the pointlessness of sending time travelers back without the ability to communicate.

"As usual, we won't be able to speak the language like natives," Jason cautioned, largely for Razmani's benefit; the others were aware of the technique's limitations. "Nor will we really look much like the locals, although as Director Rutherford indicated we'll do our best in the selection process. So we'll claim to be from the Zagros Mountains, further north, where we're pretty sure the people spoke languages ancestral to the Caucasian group."

"Unrelated to Sumerian, which was *sui generis*," Rutherford amplified.

De Tredville looked worried. "You'll have to get your biological 'cleansing' upgraded. Six and a third millennia for microorganisms to evolve . . . !"

"Including the forced-draft evolution of super-strains caused by the unintelligent overuse of antibiotics in the late twentieth century," Kubischev nodded grimly.

"We're well aware of the problem," Rutherford assured them, "and it will be attended to." He left unsaid the disturbing question that always entered people's minds when this subject was discussed: did the Transhumanists have sufficient sanity to take the same precautions with *their* time travelers? And if they did not, were some of history's great plagues their doing?

After only minimal ritualistic nitpicking, the basic plan as initially presented by Rutherford was approved and the meeting broke up. As Jason and Rutherford left and walked down the corridor side by side, the latter spoke in elaborately casual tones.

"I couldn't help but notice, Jason, that you did not bring up the possibility we discussed earlier: that the Teloi presence might be a result of the *Tuova'Zhonglu* having pursued the Nagommo to Earth during their war. Which, if true, means that the Nagommo warship will have already crash-landed in the Persian Gulf."

"Well, I saw no compelling reason to bother them with side issues."

"'Side issues'? Like the fact that the Nagom named Oannes might be present? And the fact that when you encountered him in 1628 B.C. he had never encountered *you*, and had no notion that time travel was possible." In a startlingly out-of-character gesture, he halted and grasped Jason's arm. "Have you considered the Observer Effect tangles this could enmesh you in?"

"Why, Kyle! Ending a sentence with a preposition! That's something up with which we will not put." Jason's attempt to crib a witticism from Winston Churchill—who he had once met, in 1897 India—fell flat. He turned serious. "Well, I'll just have to play it by ear, won't I?"

"With your customary success, I can only hope."

Jason cocked his head. "Kyle, am I imagining things or is it possible that you're actually concerned about my safety?"

"Let's say that finding a replacement for you would be a minor but nonetheless real inconvenience."

"I'm deeply touched."

# Chapter Fourteen

Jason ran his eyes over the biographical information on the holographically projected display screen, and thought hard. He scrolled up and down a few times, decided further temporizing would serve no purpose, and punched a few keys. Most of the information vanished, leaving two names and their accompanying data.

Mondrago looked over his shoulder. "So those are the ones?"

"Yes. You know the unique staffing problems this mission presents."

"That's an understatement. Normally, when we take a research expedition back, it includes at least one historian specializing in the target milieu, who—even if he's an obnoxious know-it-all—can give us tips about the local culture and even, sometimes, tell us what's going to happen next. And Special Ops missions which *don't* take academic types along generally go to a time and place that's already been scouted by a research expedition. But this time—"

"This time we've got the worst of both worlds," Jason glumly completed the thought. "We've never been to protohistorical Mesopotamia, or anywhere even remotely close to it. And when we're limited to four people, going up against Teloi and Transhumanists, they *have* to all be Special Ops personnel; we can't afford to have one of them be a noncombatant that the other three are responsible for keeping alive."

"Look on the bright side," Mondrago urged him. "That same

consideration persuaded even fatheads like Kung and his allies on the council that it wasn't practical to send a political watchdog along."

"I suppose so," Jason grudgingly conceded. "Anyway, the best I've been able to do is pick *him*." He indicated one of the two names with a cursor.

"Constable Ahmad Allawi," Mondrago read. "I've only met him a couple of times. Newbie, isn't he?"

"One of our newest. This will be his first extratemporal expedition. I would have preferred somebody with more experience, but he has certain special qualifications."

"From that part of the world, is he?"

"Actually, he's from Mithras, in the Zeta Tucanae system. Served with the militia there, which was why we accepted him for Special Ops."

Mondrago nodded, understanding. Three centuries earlier, the colonists of Zeta Tucanae III, who had arrived during the slower-than-light colonization surge from an Earth in the Transhumanist grip and were therefore strictly on their own, had found themselves locked in a desperate war of extermination against a previously unsuspected and insensately hostile autochthonous species. Even now the culture of Mithras had not altogether lost a certain militant flavor, and the colony's militia was better regarded than most such organizations.

"However," Jason continued, "while his ancestry is a good old Mithran mix on his mother's side, his father's family are relatively recent immigrants from Earth—specifically, from Iraq, and he more or less looks it. But the real point is this: from an early age he's had an interest in his paternal heritage. Sort of a Near Eastern history buff, in fact. Which is at least part of the reason why he came to Earth and signed up for the Temporal Service."

"Well, on this mission he ought to be like a pig in shit." Mondrago indicated the other name. "At least you picked an old sweat for the other slot."

"Right. We both know Sergeant Irma Shartava. In addition to being a combat veteran, she looks as Georgian as her name." Jason grinned. "So, unlike the rest of us, she actually comes close to the ethnic origin we're going to be claiming to belong to. Not that it will do her any good where we're going; I imagine what they were speaking in the Zagros

Mountains in 4004 B.C. resembled modern Caucasian languages like Georgian about as closely as the Proto-Indo-European of the same period resembled Standard International English."

"Still, you might as well let her use her own name. I don't imagine the Sumerians far to the south will know the difference. And at least it's one Georgian name that's less than five syllables! They're almost as bad as Greeks that way."

"You'll pay for that!" Jason punched more keys. The immaterial display screen vanished. "All right, they're locked in. I'll cut their orders. As soon as they arrive, we'll meet with them for a preliminary briefing."

"Do you know, Commander," said Ahmad Allawi brightly, "that the Arabic name 'Iraq' was derived from Uruk—or Erech, as it was later called in Aramaic?"

"No, I didn't know that," said Jason, smiling politely at the constable, who had been exuding enthusiasm ever since learning of their target location. Allawi was a dark, rather handsome young man, predominantly Near Eastern in appearance despite a few discordant notes like light hazel-green eyes with a very slight epicanthic fold. He was also an inch or two taller than Jason, which would stand out where they were going, but it couldn't be helped.

Sergeant Irma Shartava, on the other hand, was short by twenty-fourth century standards, and stocky. Her face was hard and nondescript, and her short hair was turning iron-gray even though she was only in her late thirties. She was as taciturn as Allawi was ebullient, and had taken the news of their destination with no apparent reaction.

"I didn't know it," Jason repeated, "although I've learned a little bit about the place in the course of studying up for this mission. We're here today for your initial orientation briefing. Let's get started."

The two new arrivals, along with Mondrago, sat down in the small briefing room. Jason activated the wall screen, and a map appeared. Allawi studied it and frowned.

"Er . . . Commander, there's something wrong with the courses of the Tigris and Euphrates rivers, and the coast of the Persian Gulf."

"No, there isn't. This map represents our best guess as to the geographic features as of the year we're going to. So far, all I've told you is that our geographical destination is Uruk; I haven't told you the target year. It is, in fact, 4004 B.C."

Even Shartava's eyes widened. Allawi's almost bugged out, and his jaw dropped.

"A little background information is in order—and I remind you that this briefing is classified 'Most Secret.' Superintendent Mondrago and I recently returned from an expedition to twentieth-century Italy . . ." As concisely as possible, Jason told them of Father Ernetti and his chronovisor, and of what the chronovisor had revealed. By the time he was finished, they had almost recovered from their initial stunned incredulity.

"Father Ernetti chose Uruk as the place to view simply because of its importance in that era. In fact, it was what the archaeologists call the 'type site' of the Uruk period, starting right about our target date, during which urban civilization arose in Sumeria. We'll observe our usual precautions, arriving outside it just after daybreak, October 24."

"How did you decide on that precise target date, Commander?" Shartava asked.

"More 'usual precautions.' Father Ernetti focused on October 23, and none of us appear in his imagery. We want to avoid any possibility of Observer Effect complications. He promised me he wouldn't look in on Uruk after that, and I believe him. So we'll arrive on the following day.

"This mission will be governed by Special Operations protocols. We'll have 'controllable' TRDs, and a dedicated displacer stage using Transhumanist technology will be kept open for us to return at my discretion. And we are permitted the Section's standard modified Takashima laser carbines, in this case disguised as walking sticks. Naturally, these weapons will have only a single energy cell's worth of shots, in an era when there are no replacement cells available and nothing which can really serve as a disguise for them. But this mission should be one of limited duration, so the problem isn't expected to be a serious one. My brain implant's sensor function will give us some warning of the presence of Transhumanist bionics. Superintendent Mondrago's implant will, of course, be deactivated." Jason pronounced the words *of course* in an expressionless tone of voice, while gritting his teeth mentally as he contemplated the Authority's inflexible rules-worship. "Over the next few days we will undergo microbiological cleansing and acquisition of the local language—the latter process facilitated by Father Ernetti's audio recording, although as always we won't be expected to pass as natives of the locality. We will then proceed with orientation for as many days as I deem necessary. During that time, all of us—except Sergeant Shartava, of course—will cultivate beards. For now, that's all. Any questions?"

Allawi spoke up with a hesitancy that seemed foreign to him. "Ah . . . Commander, since joining the Temporal Service I have of course had access to the information on the Teloi you gleaned on your earlier expeditions—the stuff that's been kept from the general public. From my reading of it, I gather that at some point in time those Teloi that created *Homo sapiens* and formed the basis for the later pantheons of gods—the, uh . . ."

"The *Oratioi'Zhonglu*," Jason supplied.

"Yes, sir. Anyway, your reports indicated that sometime around our target date they moved their activities further north."

"Correct. We don't know exactly when that occurred."

"But you also learned that they gengineered an enhanced 'Hero' subspecies of humans to serve them as proxy rulers over the masses—"

"That's right," Jason nodded, remembering Perseus. "Didn't exactly work out the way they planned."

"—and that one of the first of these was Gilgamesh. He ruled at Uruk. But as far as we can determine, he lived in the 27$^{th}$ century B.C."

"That does seem to involve a contradiction, doesn't it?" Jason acknowledged.

"Maybe they moved out and then later tried a comeback using their new approach of ruling through *übermenschen* 'herdsmen,'" suggested Shartava.

"Maybe. But another possibility, which we've already considered, is that *these* Teloi belong to a different group: the *Tuova'Zhonglu*, the military subculture that was, at that time, doing the actual fighting in the war against the Teloi's Nagommo enemies."

"You'd better hope not," Mondrago interjected grimly. "Believe me, they make the *Oratioi'Zhonglu* look like a bunch of pussycats."

"Too true," Jason affirmed. "You'll also know about them from the classified information you're privy to. For one thing you'll know that they were still at large in galaxy—the last survivors of their race—at least as recently as 1897 A.D., still obsessing about their war against the Nagommo thousands of years earlier. But in 4004 B.C., that war was in full swing. And . . . what is it, Ahmad?"

Allawi blinked away the haunted look Jason had noticed. "I've also read about the Nagommo in your reports, Commander. Including the facts that they were amphibious beings, and that at some point in time around the beginning of the fourth millennium B.C. one of their survey ships crashed in the Persian Gulf. And that its crew tried to get the local humans started on the road to civilization."

"Correct. And we've considered the possibility that the *Tuova'Zhonglu* might have followed it to Earth. But we don't know if that had already happened in 4004 B.C."

"There's something that might shed light on that, Commander. Look on the map a little to the southwest of Uruk, close to Ur."

Jason moved the cursor in the indicated direction, toward what was then the northwest end of the Persian Gulf. It rested over a locale labelled "Eridu" and marked with an ambiguous icon.

"Eridu has a claim to being the oldest town on Earth," Allawi explained. "It certainly dates back even before the Ubaid period, maybe to the mid-sixth millennium B.C. The reason it doesn't get the same icon as the other Sumerian towns is that it's not clear what its status was at the end of that period and the beginning of the Uruk period. One theory is that it was practically abandoned after that. And yet it was a major site in what's called the Early Dynastic period later in the fourth millennium B.C., although power shifted north to places like Uruk."

"Yes," said Jason with a touch of impatience. "But—?"

"Eridu," Allawi continued in a level voice, "was associated with the god Enki—a water-god. He was pictured as a half-human creature from the sea. And an early culture hero, Adapa, who brought civilization to the city, was associated with him. In fact, later stories told how Enki's daughter Inanna, the goddess of Uruk, had to go to Eridu to receive the gifts of civilization. And, by the way, 'Eridu' has been translated as meaning 'Guidance Place.'"

Jason and Mondrago looked at each other.

"Food for thought," the Corsican commented.

# Chapter Fifteen

Having a new language imprinted on the speech centers of one's brain by direct neural induction was one thing. After that, it was necessary to become accustomed to actually thinking in it. Fortunately for Jason, almost all the languages he had ever been required to wrap his mind around had been Indo-European ones, so the basic structural assumptions were already there, to be filled by new vocabulary like new wine in old bottles. The only exception had been the utterly alien Teloi language, and that experience still gave him nightmares.

The unique Sumerian tongue—a "language isolate," to use the jargon of linguists—proved almost as bad. The fact that Allawi's familiarity with Arabic didn't help him in the slightest was no great comfort to Jason. He wondered if perhaps Sumerian was a surviving remnant of the primordial speech of *Homo sapiens* before they had begun expanding from northeast Africa and southwest Asia, escaping the vast Teloi slave-pens and differentiating into the ethno-linguistic groupings of historical times. Rutherford was inclined to agree with the theory. But that didn't help either.

At least, Jason consoled himself, this time the imprinting process was cushioned by rest under antidepressant drugs—not like the way his Teloi captors had brutally rammed their language into his brain.

He considered requesting that Shartava and Allawi be provided with the Teloi language as well as the Sumerian one, but decided against it. In certain situations, it might well be advantageous if the Teloi they were seeking could be kept in ignorance of the fact that their private conversation was being understood. If Jason and Mondrago were the only ones who could do so, the chances of revealing that secret were minimized.

In addition to language practice, they went through the standard orientation on the local culture, fairly intense but conducted by conventional educational techniques with only minimal neuro-electronic stimulation of the relevant brain centers while asleep or otherwise unconscious. And in this case, the curriculum was more limited than usual. The plain fact was that, even with the glimpse afforded by Father Ernetti's chronovisor, the proto-Sumerian world was pretty much historical *terra incognita*. This was not one of the relatively well-documented eras to which Jason was accustomed. In fact, no time travelers—not even Jason, on his expedition to the Aegean Bronze Age—had ever ventured into a milieu about which so frustratingly little was known. They would have to play a lot more things by ear than usual—altogether too many for Jason's taste, in fact.

"We generally pose as foreigners or at least outsiders of some kind," he told the others, "just so it won't seem strange that we talk funny. But in this case, we're going to have to come across as especially ignorant."

"I've been wondering about that, Commander," said Shartava with a worried expression that seemed to come naturally to her. "Just how cosmopolitan *was* this early Uruk period? Not very, I wouldn't think. Are foreigners going to encounter a lot of hostility?"

"Maybe not," said Allawi before Jason could answer. "Remember, we're claiming to be from the Zagros range, to the north. And the proto-Sumerians must have had a long history of contact with that area, because it was from there that they originally learned agriculture."

"But," protested Mondrago with a frown, "wouldn't the original humans have already known about agriculture, from their time as Teloi slaves?"

Rutherford, who was sitting in on the conference, answered that one. "From what we have gathered, it seems they regressed to hunter-gatherers after they escaped and spread across the globe. Agriculture was reinvented in the rain-watered highlands to the north and east of Mesopotamia, probably in the ninth millennium B.C., and spread into the lowlands from there. The Sumerian contribution was to invent large-scale irrigation, which in turn required organization and social specialization." He smiled. "Prehistorians used to assume a little too readily that any new cultural innovation must have been accompanied by a wholesale migration of a new population and the displacement of a previous one. So the conventional wisdom was that the Sumerians must have migrated into southern Mesopotamia from the mountains. Now, of course, we know they were there all along, and Father Ernetti's findings confirm it."

"Anyway," said Jason, getting the conference back on track, "it seems likely that foreigners are not unknown, but not so familiar that much is known about them. The second part is good from our standpoint—we ought to be able to get away with simply making up details about the region we're supposed to be from. The hard part is going to be explaining what we're doing so far away from home."

"Itinerant merchants, maybe?" suggested Shartava.

"I doubt if any such thing existed at the level of social development we're talking about. Oh, yes, we'll be taking along some in-period trade goods to pay our way with—remember, this was over three thousand years before anybody thought of the idea of currency."

"What kind of trade goods?" Allawi wanted to know.

"Copper tools and trinkets. The Near Eastern farming communities had learned to smelt the stuff at least fifteen hundred years before our target date. At first, it was used mainly for beads and such. But by our target date they—and peoples as far afield as Austria and Yemen and Central Asia—were using it for implements, alongside the good old stone ones."

"The term for such a culture is 'chalcolithic,'" Rutherford put in primly.

"Anyway," Jason resumed, "we'll claim we were on the losing side of a blood feud between two clans, and the mountains were too hot to hold us—but that we got away with some of the goods. We'll also be carrying some in-period copper weapons in addition to our 'walking sticks.' Copper's no good for a sword—actually, it's too soft to be especially good for any weapon, and in 4004 B.C. nobody had learned how to alloy it with arsenic or tin to produced bronze. But we're pretty sure they used daggers and hatchets. And Alexandre is very good with a sling."

"Do we really know what copper weapons of that milieu looked like?" Shartava sounded skeptical.

"As with so much else, the answer is no," Jason admitted forthrightly. "Most of our knowledge of copper weapons comes from Egypt, at later periods. Our experts have tried to 'reverse-engineer' later bronze ones. Once again, we're hoping that people will take for granted that a bunch of foreign mountaineers will have their own style of arms.

"By the way, Irma, I was going to let you use your own name. On reflection, I think all of us may just as well do the same; to people in southern Mesopotamia, they'll all sound like undifferentiated foreign gibberish.

"And now I believe Director Rutherford has a few words."

Rutherford cleared his throat. "Traditionally, we often precede a temporal displacement with a visit to the target locale for orientation purposes, when that locale still bears sufficient resemblance to its earlier self to make the trip worthwhile. That, self-evidently, is not the case this time. Nowadays, Uruk is only an archaeological mound, and mostly composed of the ruins of later periods—especially the early third millennium, when we believe it was the largest city in the world, with as many as fifty to eighty thousand residents living in a walled area of perhaps six square kilometers. However, it is possible to reconstruct in very general terms what it looked like when it was first founded." He manipulated controls, and part of one of the conference room's walls became a viewscreen, showing a map.

"As you can see, the town is near the southwest bank of what was then the Euphrates River, to which it is connected by canals. At some later point, the river's course changed, which probably contributed to Uruk's decline. You will note that the town is built around two temple complexes, denominated the 'Eanna District' and the 'Anu District.' This reflects the fact that the town was formed, at a time which cannot have preceded our target date by very much, when two smaller settlements of the prior Ubaid culture merged. The Eanna District was sacred to the goddess Inanna. The Anu District was sacred to the god of that name, and was the older of the two. Later it was to become the site of a massive ziggurat. We are certain that it was that district's original temple, built on an earthen terrace, that appears in Father Ernetti's imagery, rather than the Eanna District, which was walled off from the rest of the city. In fact, the Eanna District may not have yet existed in its definitive form in 4004 B.C."

"So," said Jason, "the male Teloi that Father Ernetti filmed there must have been 'Anu.'"

"Presumably. In later mythology, he was Inanna's grandfather. Her father was Enki, the god of—"

"—Eridu!" exclaimed Jason. He turned to Allawi. "Didn't you tell me he was the one his daughter Inanna received the arts of civilization from? And that he was supposed to be some kind of fish-man from the sea?"

"Which sounds like an amphibious being," Mondrago added. "Such as a Nagom."

"But how could he be the son of a Teloi?" was Shartava's reasonable question.

"This is getting more and more puzzling," said Jason.

Reverse-engineered Transhumanist technology made a temporal displacement of almost sixty-four centuries possible, at least for a party of only four people. But even so, a displacement of such magnitude demanded an energy surge comparable to that required by the Authority's old Weintraub-Fujiwara displacer. Such power could only be provided by the annihilation of a significant amount of expensive antimatter. (The council's grumblings still hadn't subsided.) So the old powerplant had to be brought back on line and connected to a displacer to which it seemed grotesquely out of proportion.

At least, Jason consoled himself, the engineering problems gave them more time to grow the beards and long hair which, justifiably or otherwise, they were assuming would be expected of mountain men. He was just as glad that they weren't pretending to be Sumerians, which would have entailed shaven heads as well as faces.

At length, however, all was in readiness. Wearing the rough tunics that, like the hair, they hoped would be considered appropriate, they made their way to the satellite facility housing their displacer, passing the titanic new power connections to the main installation. Here, among the surrounding control panels and consoles, Rutherford waited to administer the traditional predisplacement handshake.

But as soon as they entered the enclosure, Jason heard a familiar voice behind him. "Commander?"

"Julian!" Jason turned and shook hands with the Jesuit. "I wasn't expecting to see you here."

"Well, I wanted to see you off and wish you the best of luck," Father Casinde explained. "And also . . . to express my regret that I'm not going with you."

"I wouldn't mind having you along. But as you know—"

"Yes: this is strictly a job for the Special Operations Section, of which I'm not a member. And I have no specialized knowledge of the period to contribute. Still . . ." All at once, his wistful expression turned to one of earnestness. "Commander, you're going to be traveling back to the very origins of religion—I mean actual human religion, as opposed to the Teloi charade. This must have been the era when humans first began to independently exercise their capacity for genuine spirituality, and fashion their own myths—their first childlike gropings after something higher, however crude and naive those myths may have been, and however much they may have had to accommodate ancestral memories of the Teloi captivity."

"Yes. In fact, we think some of those memories may already have been getting just a little muddled." Briefly, he explained the puzzling Anu-Enki-Inanna relationship.

"Yes," Casinde nodded. "Your perplexity is understandable. But remember, such things can become contradictory and incoherent in later tradition."

"Right. I know from personal experience in Bronze Age Greece how later mythmakers can get things confused. Anyway, hopefully we'll soon find out the answer, in the process of scotching whatever it is the Transhumanists are up to."

"I'm sure you will. And Commander . . . I know this isn't a research expedition, but whatever you may learn about those spiritual origins I mentioned . . . when you return . . ."

"I'll look you up, and you'll be among the first to know."

"Thank you. And God be with you."

"You know, Father," a stubborn honesty forced Jason to say, "I'm not of your faith." Actually, he was far from sure he was of *any* faith.

"Considering what you are going into battle against, I somehow don't think He will let that prevent Him from being with you."

They smiled and shook hands again. Jason turned and strode off toward the displacer stage.

# Chapter Sixteen

Even at daybreak in late October, the leaden heat of the lower Mesopotamian plain was oppressive. The instantaneous transition into that ovenlike stillness took their breath away at first, and drenched them with an unnaturally abrupt outflow of sweat. Combined with the indescribable disorientation of temporal displacement, it almost overcame all of them, especially the inexperienced Allawi. While they waited for him to recover his physical and mental equilibrium, Jason took stock of their surroundings.

One of the innumerable things they hadn't known when planning this mission had been the layout of Uruk's natural and man-made environs. The extent of the town itself could be more or less established archaeologically, but of course they didn't want to arrive there, where people might be up and about just after dawn. It wasn't that there was any danger of their materializing inside the same volume of space already occupied by another solid object. An inherent feedback aspect of the displacement process (which unfortunately did not obtain on retrieval, which was why their displacer stage had to be kept pristinely clear) made that impossible, causing a default to the nearest unoccupied space, while the energy release accompanying the materialization of a displaced object sufficed to shove air molecules out of the way. But to minimize the chance of any turn-of-the-fourth-millennium-B.C. people witnessing four figures popping into existence out of thin air, they needed a place which, without being too far from the town, was vacant of habitation. The obvious solution would have been a spot in the desert to the southwest of Uruk. But their assumed background made it implausible that they would be coming from that direction, where dwelled proto-Semitic tribesmen who (if later historically-attested relationships were any guide) might well be enemies of the proto-Sumerians. So they had decided on a place a little to the northwest, upriver from Uruk and a little inland from where their best guess placed the Euphrates' bank in this era.

Now, as the sun peered over the eastern horizon, Jason saw to his relief that no one was nearby. The river was further away than anticipated, but it was visible in the distance to the northeast, gleaming with the rays of the rising sun which were already touching it, in this perfectly flat land where there were no hills for it to peek from behind. As soon as Allawi was ready, they drank deeply from their goatskins of still-cool water, hitched up their satchels, and set off toward the distant palm-fringed riverbank.

As they walked, the sun rose higher and the blue of the cloudless sky whitened in the shimmering heat. Approaching closer to the river, they entered a region of tiny farm plots, crisscrossed with irrigation canals. Jason recalled from his orientation that this ground had gradually been built up by silt brought down from the north by the Tigris and Euphrates, a process that was not as far advanced in this era as it would later be. He also recalled that humans had had a share in the drying-out process, making the ground firmer by fashioning mats from the reeds that grew from the marshes and using them to cover the slime, and then stamping down the ground. Reeds were also a common building material, used to form the roof of the typical hut, the topmost bundle flaring out into a graceful double curve.

Here, people were about, rising with the sun in the immemorial way of farmers to cultivate the grain from the Zagros foothills that they had domesticated over the long period of the Ubaid culture. That culture was now drawing to a close, with the dawning transition to the urban Uruk culture—not that these stolid peasants showed any awareness that they lived at the dawn of a cultural revolution. They gazed incuriously at the four strangers, then went back to cultivating their wheat and barley as their ancestors had done since time out of mind. And Jason was certain that their ignorance of the past was as profound as their ignorance of the future; they had absolutely no knowledge of the fact that those ancestors had once fled from Teloi enslavement before beginning the cultural climb back upward to being farmers. That had been too long ago for any sort of oral tradition to survive except as the vaguest memories of gods.

As they continued and the sun rose, more and more variety was to be glimpsed, especially to the left along the river. Men could be seen fishing, and tending groves of domesticated date palms in the well-drained soil of the levees. Animals were domesticated as well, for Jason saw several cattle, sheep and goats. And the population seemed to grow steadily denser as they walked toward Uruk.

After a time, they paused by a well where a man was drawing water with a ceramic bucket on a hinged pole. Jason decided it was high time to test their language skills. He asked, with what he hoped was properly respectful attitude, if they could fill their goatskins. After a brief, quizzical look at the odd-looking, odd-sounding strangers, the man grunted assent. It showed Jason two things: they could at least communicate with these people, and foreigners were not objects of automatic hostility—there even seemed to be a certain custom of grumpy hospitality.

They proceeded on, continuing to follow the river, and presently Uruk grew visible ahead. Of course it wasn't as large as it was later to become—Jason estimated about twenty hectares—but it clearly dwarfed its surroundings. Especially impressive in this land without natural hills was the massive mound topped by the temple of Anu, even though that temple was not to be compared with the titanic ziggurat that would one day loom above Uruk. There was a good deal of foot traffic through gates in the low wall, and they entered without drawing any apparent notice.

The archaeologists had never been able to extract a detailed layout of Uruk at this early stage in its development, buried as it was under layers and layers of strata—thousands of years of them. So Jason's optically projected map showed little more than the locations of the Anu District and the Eanna District. But as they walked on, and he looked about him, the map seemed to grow and spread organically as his computer implant used the input of his eyes to fill in the blankness with alleys and canals—a good many canals, for Uruk was well penetrated with them, connecting it with the surrounding agricultural belt and with the Euphrates just to the northeast, where a number of reed canoes and several actual boats were tied up.

"Almost like an extremely low-tech Venice," Mondrago remarked with a smile.

"Minus the tourists," Jason murmured in reply. "Unless you count us."

The more he looked about him, the more he could see evidence of the transition to urban civilization that was the hallmark of the Uruk culture, for the region's agricultural surplus was beginning to permit occupational specialization. And it became clear that the small mud-brick courtyard houses were grouped by the occupants' professions. In front of one house, a potter busily fashioned his wares on a wheel—something whose application to vehicular transportation had yet to be discovered. Through the door Jason could see a closed kiln, enabling the potter to control his temperatures. Further on, in front of another building, a barber used an obsidian-bladed razor to keep a customer in the prevailing shaven-headed style. Still further on, they passed an open-fronted establishment, operated primarily by women, which from the aroma of fermenting barley and a glimpse of certain implements within—a mortar, a kneading tray, a kind of vat, and large pottery jars—Jason identified as a brewery. He recalled that beer was a staple of the Sumerian diet, and he looked forward with no great enthusiasm to sampling the local product, which he had been given to understand probably had the consistency of thin gruel.

The more Jason observed, the more things were added to his map display . . . and then, abruptly, one of the few things that were already there vanished. He blinked, and looked around him. There was only more of the general warren, thinning out toward an open space around what looked like it might be a temple, in some indefinable way old-fashioned-seeming even in these surroundings. The expected limestone-walled enclosure was nowhere to be seen.

"Ahmad," he muttered to Allawi, "this is where the Eanna District is supposed to be."

Allawi also looked around, and nodded. "We knew the enclosed compound was younger than the Anu District. We also knew it was built over a preexisting temple of the Ubaid culture." He indicated the archaic-looking structure. "We just didn't know whether or not it had already been built at this time."

"Well, that's one mystery we've solved. The interesting question is this: does its later construction have any connection with what the Teloi and the Transhumanists are up to here?"

"And what about the Nagommo?" Mondrago put in. "I mean, this strange relationship of Inanna with Enki . . ."

"Let's not theorize in advance of the data," said Jason, unconsciously paraphrasing a certain fictional detective. "Come on. We'll have no trouble finding the Anu District."

Nor did they. Even without the brutal mass of the later ziggurat, the earthen mound and the temple it upheld were clearly visible above the otherwise low structures of Uruk. The temple was a rather featureless rectangular mud-brick structure, but while not to be compared to its successors that would one day rise here it was incomparably the largest building in the city. As they approached it and entered a small open square below its entrance, yet another occupational specialization became apparent: that of soldiers or police, from whom the civilians seemed to be apprehensively keeping their distance. They began to see more and more men carrying short spears with leaf-shaped copper spearheads, and wearing arrogant expressions that might well have been a consequence of their possession of those state-of-the-art weapons. Some of them also had copper-bladed daggers thrust through their cloth belts, and most of them wore a kind of black leather helmet, peaked at the top and extending down almost to the shoulders behind and to the sides. Otherwise, they were dressed like most of the men of Uruk, in white flounced skirts or kilts, with the upper body left bare. (Women's skirts were simpler in cut but more varied in color.) Some of them gave the time travelers frowning glances, but none challenged them; there didn't seem to be any kind of formal guard mounted.

Jason intended to test that. In many cultures, there were traditions of religious centers offering hospitality to indigent travelers. He didn't know if that was the case here and now, but even if all he got for his pains was an answer of "No," it would give an excuse for entering the temple, where his implant should be in range of any Transhumanist bionics. He led the way toward the ramp that ascended the terrace to the temple's entrance.

Here, the guards were more numerous, but they still lounged about in no particular state of alert. Jason wondered if they would be able to simply walk in. But then, near the top, a man stepped forward into their path and planted his spear-butt firmly on the ramp. He was slightly older than the others and wore the first copper helmet they had seen. Jason knew an officer when he saw one.

"What is your business?" The question was not especially truculent, but it was asked in a businesslike way. And, out of the corners of his eyes, Jason saw the guards get up and start to gather around them.

"We are from the mountains to the northeast, and are new to this land. But we know of the great god Anu from afar, and seek to make offerings to him." Jason could only hope that this was the right thing to say, or that if it wasn't it would be chalked up to his foreignness. He had a feeling that actually asking for a handout would have been too crass. But elementary premoney societies generally had traditions of exchanging gifts.

The guard captain (as seemed to be his status) rubbed his none-too-freshly-shaven chin. "I must ask one of the priests. Wait here." He turned, walked up the remainder of the ramp, and vanished into the dimness of the temple's interior.

For an interval that seemed longer than it was, they waited in the sun, and the guards showed no disposition to relax their vigilance. Finally, the guard captain emerged from the entrance above, accompanied by a second man: tall by local standards, and wearing the miter-like headgear Jason had seen in Father Ernetti's recording. In fact, Jason had seen that man, in that same recording, and recognized him for what he was . . .

In a calm corner of his mind, Jason wondered why a little blue light had not begun to flash urgently at the lower left of his field of vision. For now, seeing him in the flesh, he was surer than ever that he was looking at a goon-caste Transhumanist. In fact, beyond the usual subtle indicia that were always there if one knew what to look for, there was a certain individual familiarity about him Jason couldn't quite put his finger on.

He forced himself to remain expressionless. But the priest's eyes widened with sudden realization as he stared at the strangers. Jason didn't know if the Transhumanist, despite the seeming lack of functioning bionics of his own, had the same kind of detection capability he himself had, or if it was just something about the newcomers' general appearance. And at the moment the question wasn't terribly important.

And the goon caste weren't stupid. They were actually fairly intelligent, within their limited scope. And their reactions were very, very fast.

"Seize them!" shouted the priest, in a Sumerian that seemed even more heavily accented than Jason's own. "Alive!" And the guards sprang to obey.

# Chapter Seventeen

Jason's companions hadn't shared his moment of recognition. They were unprepared for the sudden rush of guards from both sides, piling onto them and forcing them down onto the ramp before they could attempt to defend themselves.

Jason, however, had a second's warning of what was coming, and he was standing further ahead than the others, facing the priest. He launched himself forward, simultaneously activating his "walking stick" and bringing it up. With a lunge, he jabbed its business end into the Transhumnist's midriff and pressed the firing stud.

The Takashima was set on "lethal." The fact that its orifice was embedded in its target's belly muffled the usual *crack!* But a puff of steam escaped as the goon doubled over with a choked shriek and collapsed, clutching his fried guts.

But then a guard kicked Jason's legs out from under him from behind. As he fell prone, another guard wrenched the "walking stick" from his hand, and a spear-butt smashed into his kidney with sickening pain. His gasp of agony brought his head up, so he saw a second priest emerge from the temple. Through his haze of agony, he thought to recognize a middling managerial-type Transhumanist, although his sensor remained silent. And, again, there was the elusive sense of familiarity.

"Hold!" the priest commanded the guards. He gazed down at the body of his fellow Transhumanist, lying in fetal position. Then he turned on Jason with a glare of indescribable hate—hate which, if possible, seemed to be redoubled as recognition dawned in his eyes.

"You!" he hissed in Standard International English. Then his voice rose as he addressed the guards in their own language, with an accent as heavy as the goon's had been. "Bring them to the chamber of question!"

*I don't think I like the sound of that,* thought Jason as the guards hoisted him erect and, grasping him by both arms, marched him and the others into the temple.

Coming directly from the glaring sunlight into the temple's dimness, they could barely make out Its interior details. Instead of proceeding directly into the main chamber, they turned to the right, and the prisoners were shoved, stumbling, down a torchlit flight of steps. Evidently the temple complex extended into the artificial mound as well as above it. At least, Jason thought, it was cool down here. Finally they were pushed into a small chamber where the guards inserted torches in rough sconces on the walls, revealing walls with copper rings from which ropes hung. (Chains, Jason decided, hadn't been invented.) The walls were stained with splotches of dried blood. The stench was indescribable.

They were tied crudely but securely to the copper rings, after which the priest turned to the guard captain. "Gather up the walking sticks these people were using—carefully. And place them in the treasury chamber."

The captain blinked, bewildered. "Uh . . . the walking sticks, holy one?"

"You heard me! And leave me alone in here with the prisoners until I call you. Let no one spy on us—not that it would do anyone any good. I will be speaking to them in a strange tongue, for I know from whence they have come."

"To hear is to obey, holy one." The captain hustled his men out and closed the door behind them on its crude, creaking wooden hinges. The priest then turned to Jason, his eyes glittering in the torchlight, and spoke in Standard International English, his voice a tightly controlled snarl.

"You don't remember me, do you?"

Dissimulation was obviously pointless. Jason spoke in the same language. "I know you for what you are. But I don't think I've had the pleasure."

"Oh, yes you have. But then, you wouldn't recognize me, would you? There's been some resequencing of my genetic code since then. But think back to Venice . . . a certain night in 1978 A.D . . . Father Ernetti's cell . . ." And the Transhumanist smiled in an irritating way.

That was what brought recognition crashing home to Jason, for he had last seen that particular smirk—albeit on less full lips, and under a smaller nose—just before its owner had vanished from Mondrago's grip, as he and his companion had been snatched away by temporal retrieval. Now he knew why the faces had seemed tantalizingly familiar underneath the subterfuge of genetically modified features and coloring.

"So it's you!" he gasped. "You're the two who murdered John Paul I."

"Yes . . . the two of us. And now you've killed—!" The Transhumanist halted and took a deep breath, for the snarl had ceased to be controlled. His eyes no longer glittered—they blazed. Jason recalled something they had learned about the Transhumanist underground: male homosexual relationships were common among its personnel, just as they always had been in societies whose women were rendered uninteresting by subjugation. By killing the goon, he, Jason, had tapped into a whole new stratum of hate.

After a moment, the Transhumanist got his breathing under control, and when he spoke his voice held a note—almost a croon— of pleasurable anticipation. "So you see . . . one more grievance, Commander Thanou!"

Jason didn't ask how the Transhumanist knew his name. There were any number of ways—his face was pretty well known among them by now. And besides, the question would only have been a distraction from what must be his main objective: to obtain as much information as he could before escaping. The fact that their captor hadn't killed them at once, while he had the chance, surely meant that he did not know Jason could whisk himself and his followers back to the twenty-fourth century at any time by activating their controllable TRDs. And those followers were Special Ops—he knew he could count on them not to blurt out the truth. So this was a priceless opportunity for gathering intel.

At the same time, he didn't want to goad the Transhumanist by revealing that he knew of the Teloi presence here. The Underground had no reason to know what the Authority had learned from Father Ernetti's recording, and there was no point in spilling those particular beans.

"Well, you've got us," he said, putting as much resignation and despair into his voice as he could without overacting. "But tell me something, since telling me can't possibly do any harm. What are you up to, here and now?"

"Up to?" the Transhumanist queried with a puzzled frown.

"Yes," said Jason patiently. "Why did the Underground send you and your partner back to 4004 B.C. Mesopotamia? What is your mission? To start one of your secret cults, maybe?"

For a moment the Transhumanist stared at him. Then he emitted the bitterest and most humorless laugh Jason had ever heard.

"You just don't understand, do you? There is no 'mission.' We were *exiled!*"

For a stunned instant, Jason could only think, *Well, now I know why my sensor function for active bionics didn't detect them.*

And after another instant, the thought was joined by a second one. *There's no point in concealing my knowledge of his Teloi connection after all. He's not exactly going to be reporting back to his superiors.*

The Transhumanists who had gone back five centuries and across interstellar space to found the secret colony of Drakar in the year which on Earth was counted as 1897 had been fanatics even by their movement's standards; they had volunteered to be temporally displaced without TRDs, marooning themselves in time as well as space to avoid any possibility of Observer Effect complications.

But, as Jason had learned in the course of aborting that colony, it wasn't always voluntary.

It was, in fact, a particularly diabolical form of punishment the Transhumanist leadership held over the heads of its underlings. Their bionics would be deactivated and they would be sent back to some less-than-desirable historical milieu without any equipment or orientation, including the local language. The prospect of having to survive as best they could among the unmodified humans they despised was, Jason had imagined, a more effective deterrent to disloyalty or failure than the threat of death would have been.

The Authority had been appalled when Jason had informed it of the practice. To be sure, the Observer Effect *ought* to protect history from any meddling by the temporal exiles. Anything they did in the past had *always* been part of history, as the standard formulation went and as the council members—the only people privy to the information—kept assuring themselves. But there was always a nagging fear that the assumption might, just possibly, be wrong, or at least conceal unsuspected exceptions or qualifications . . . in which case, the potential consequences did not bear thinking about.

At the same time, there was also the feeling that the victims of this form of discipline must surely burn with resentment against their superiors who had done such a thing to them, and therefore might be turned and used as intelligence sources. But none had ever been encountered.

Until now.

"We *told* Central Control we had succeeded in killing the Pope," the Transhumanist was saying, pouring forth his resentment in a river of querulous self-pity. "But they said it was a sloppy job—doubts and questions about his death would linger forever. As if it was *our* fault that the Catholic Church was stupid enough to bury the silly old bastard hurriedly, with no autopsy. Talk about conspiracy theory fodder! And what could we have done about it anyway? It *had* to work out that way—history said so."

"So the Observer Effect wouldn't have let you do a better job," said Jason with a nod, forcing himself to exude sympathy. "By the way, why were you sent to do it? After all, if it was bound to happen anyway . . .?"

"We weren't told the details. But apparently another expedition of ours had somehow learned that two of our people had done it, so Central Control decided, just to be on the safe side, that —"

"—They had to *make* it happen," Jason nodded.

"And you two were picked to be the fall guys," added Mondrago, evidently understanding the game Jason was playing. "They were looking for scapegoats."

"It wasn't fair! It wasn't our fault!"

"Clearly not," Jason soothed. "By the way, what's your name?"

"Gleb, Category Eighteen, Fifty-Seventh—" The Transhumanist

clamped his jaws shut and resumed in a dull voice. "No. Not anymore. That's in my past. Call me Lugal-tarah. It's the name I've adopted here." His eyes turned inward, and he spoke mostly to himself. "At least our immediate controller decided we deserved a little consideration—after all, the Pope *was* dead like he was supposed to be. So they gave us the local physical type and language—that's more than most exiles get. Of course, the language was mostly speculation. At first it was hard for us to communicate with these Pugs." Jason recognized the Transhumanist acronym—short for products of unregulated genetics—for humans in the natural state.

*Of course,* he thought. *The Transhumanists don't have Father Ernetti's audio recording, so they don't know what this sui generis language really sounded like. So that explains why your Sumerian is even worse than mine.*

"But," he said aloud, "they deactivated all your bionics."

"Yes. They dumped us here, with nothing but the clothes on our backs, among these miserable, filthy, stinking primitives, to grub in the dirt on the same footing as them!" Gleb—no, Jason thought, Lugal—subsided, mumbling to himself.

"How long have you been here?"

"Years," Lugal muttered dully. "I don't know how many. I lost track."

"Well," said Jason, very cautiously, "after the injustice that was done to you, I don't imagine you still harbor much affection for—"

With the sudden wild mood-swing of the insane, and the blinding quickness of his genetic upgrades (they hadn't been able to take that away from him), Lugal slapped Jason across the face with a force that brought the taste of blood to his mouth. Then another slap, and then another, sending him staggering left and right as far as his bonds would permit. The world swam in his eyes and he fought to retain consciousness among the impacts and the pain.

Finally Lugal ceased, breathing heavily and glaring with eyes that were nothing more than blazing points of hatred. "Shut up, Pug! Do you think you can fool me, your evolutionary superior? I know what you're trying to do. But it won't work! I know who is really to blame. It's you! Central Control would have forgiven us for the loose ends concerning the Pope's death—they knew that was inevitable—if it hadn't been for our failure with the chronovisor. That was what they were *really* punishing us for. We were supposed to steal it—or, rather, the specifications for it, so it could be copied—at the same time we were tidying up the business with the Pope. *You* prevented that, you loathsome, contemptible Pug! *IT'S ALL YOUR FAULT!* And now you've killed my—" He stopped abruptly short of saying just exactly what the goon had been to him. Instead, he commenced slapping Jason again, with renewed ferocity and an accompaniment of inarticulate snarls. This time Jason was ready, and was able to roll with the slaps, lessening the impact.

Finally, Lugal paused, gasping for breath. Jason, shaking his head to clear it of the whirling disorientation, spat out blood and ordered himself to concentrate on extracting any possible crumbs of knowledge. "Well," he managed to say, "whoever is to blame for your misfortune, it seems you've done rather well for yourself here."

With another abrupt mood-change, Lugal once again took on his patented infuriating smile. "Yes. You see, I found some . . . useful friends."

"You mean, I suppose, the Teloi."

Jason had the intense satisfaction seeing the smirk depart Lugal's face as his jaw dropped. "How did you know—?"

"Never mind. The point is, we know there are at least two Teloi here, one male and one female, and that they're posing as the Annunaki, or gods, whose priest you are. I assume they're holdouts of the *Oratioi'Zhonglu* Teloi who established themselves as 'gods' on Earth a very long time ago."

"Only the female. The male belongs to the *Tuova'Zhonglu*."

"So you know about them?" Jason tried to keep the surprise out of his voice. He had learned of the interstellar Teloi military subculture (or whatever a *zhonglu* was) in the seventeenth-century Caribbean, where they had been hand in glove with Transhumanist time travelers. But all of those time travelers had, as far as Jason knew, been killed. There was no apparent way the knowledge could have been transmitted to the Underground, unless possibly by a message drop.

Lugal seemed to read his thoughts, at least partially. "I recognized them for Teloi at once. You see, I come from a period well after our expedition to Athens in 490 B.C., when we first made contact with them. In fact, I'm from slightly in the future of your own displacement here. But it wasn't until I established communication with them that I learned the male's origin." All at once, the smile was back. "As they've learned mine."

A horrible suspicion awoke in Jason. "Do you mean—?"

"Yes, Commander Thanou." Lugal's tone became almost one of gloating. "I've told them all about time travel."

# Chapter Eighteen

A couple of heartbeats passed before Jason found his voice.

"You *WHAT*?" he finally blurted, beyond caring that he was in Lugal's power. "Are you crazy? Do you have any idea of the possible consequences?"

"What do I care? The Transhuman Movement has disowned me—spat in my face. And I hate you even more than them! I owe nothing to any of you!"

"But what about the Observer Effect? You and I both know that time travel will be new to the *Tuova'Zhonglu* more than five and a half millennia from now. Haven't you considered—?"

Another tooth-loosening slap cut Jason off. Lugal's eyes were wild, flickering with what Jason now recognized as the flames of madness. "Don't you see? I haven't just transcended both sides. *I've even transcended the Observer Effect!* Nothing stopped me from telling them the secret. That proves that the Effect no longer applies to me! I've moved beyond it! I've beaten it!"

Lugal's voice had risen almost to a shriek. Now he abruptly halted, as though awaiting some kind of acknowledgment of his greatness. But Jason could think of nothing to say in response that would serve any purpose other than to occasion more slaps. Instead, he reflected that he should be grateful for Lugal's insanity. It probably explained why it hadn't occurred to the Transhumanist, who had used controllable TRDs himself in twentieth-century Italy, that Jason might also have them. The recollection of such things had probably been worn away by the passage of years in what must have seemed to him a secular hell.

"So," said Jason after a moment, "what are you going to do with us?"

"For the present, nothing." Lugal was now calm and businesslike. "You will be imprisoned while I consider your fate. I plan to put a great deal of thought into it. I want it to be something truly special . . . something that will last. Of course, I can't wait *too* long. You obviously don't have controllable TRDs, because if you did you would have used them to escape as soon as you were captured. So you're here and now for a fixed time. I just don't know how long that time is—and you'd lie to me if I asked you. But it wouldn't have been cost-effective to send you back for too brief a period. So I have a little time . . . I must think of something special . . ." He trailed off, mumbling to himself.

*All right, so he's not quite as hopelessly mad as I thought,* Jason admitted to himself. *Still, this is the convoluted logic of psychosis.*

There was a hesitant scratching at the door. Furiously, Lugal flung it open, to reveal the cringing guard captain.

"You idiot!" Lugal grated. "I told you I was not to be interrupted."

"Forgive me, holy one, but . . ." The captain drew Lugal aside and muttered to him in an undertone. Lugal stiffened, his anger seemingly forgotten, and departed with the captain, turning and bestowing a last glare on Jason before closing the door behind him. The captives were left in the reeking semidarkness to contemplate the implications of what they had just heard.

"Commander," said Allawi, breaking the silence, "was that true, what you said about the *Tuova'Zhonglu*? I've heard that you were the first to make contact with them."

"That's right. It was in the Caribbean, in 1669 A.D. Transhumanist time travelers were also there. It was a first contact for them as well. Nobody had known of the *Tuova'Zhonglu*'s existence—we thought the Teloi had all been wiped out in their war with the Nagommo. And they had never heard of time travel."

"Right," Mondrago spoke up. "Remember how the Transhumanist leader was able to bamboozle them with lies about it?"

"Yes . . . Romain, Category Three, Eighty-Ninth Degree. I'm not likely to forget him." Jason had always thought himself incapable of actually enjoying killing someone. Romain, with his cannibalistic depravities ordinarily beyond the pale even for Transhumanists, had disabused him of that illusion. "He offered to tell them the times and locations of human extrasolar colonization starting in the twenty-second century, so they could be there in advance and abort the colonies."

"But the Observer Effect—"

"—Wouldn't have permitted it," Jason finished Allawi's sentence. "That's the part Romain didn't bother to tell them. Anyway, they were all killed or stranded on Earth, so the *Tuova'Zhonglu* Teloi we later encountered, in 1897 A.D., still had no notion of time travel."

"Which shouldn't have been the case, if this Lugal had passed the information on to one of them in 4004 B.C.," said Mondrago morosely.

"By the way," Shartava put in, "what's that one doing on Earth? And what's he doing playing the god game along with a female of the *Oratioi'Zhonglu*? It was my understanding that those two groups of Teloi couldn't abide each other."

"That's always been our experience," Jason acknowledged. "There was some contact between them over the millennia, but the *Tuova'Zhonglu* despised the *Oratioi'Zhonglu* as decadent, effete dilettantes, while the *Oratioi'Zhonglu* looked down their noses at the *Tuova'Zhonglu* as boneheaded militaristic boors."

"Both were right," Mondrago interjected.

"So," Jason concluded, "I can't answer your questions. And at any rate, they're not the most urgent questions we're faced with at the moment."

After a brief silence, Allawi spoke hesitantly—but calmly, without a trace of jitters in his voice. "Commander, regardless of what Lugal thinks, you *can* get us out of here at any time, right?"

"Yes, I can. But I'm not going to, at least not yet." Jason turned his head as far as he could and met the eyes of the other three, one at a time. The look he gave them was stern and hard. "Lugal's insane irresponsibility has created a situation whose potentialities are literally imponderable. It's up to us to defuse that situation. Until I'm satisfied that we've done so, I'm not going to activate our TRDs unless we find ourselves in circumstances where there's absolutely no other way to preserve our lives—and I don't mean our *comfortable* lives. Like it or not, the four of us have suddenly become the guardians of inevitability. Is this clearly understood?"

"Understood, Commander." Allawi's young voice held nothing but steadiness. And Jason was already certain he had no worries about the other two.

"All right. What we're going to do is—"

At that moment, the door opened and a figure entered, walking in the crouching position necessitated by his almost eight-foot height.

Jason was by now an old hand with the Teloi, and Mondrago almost equally so. The other two gaped. Despite all the imagery they had studied, seeing one in the flesh was something else.

Twenty-fourth century humans had become fairly accustomed to intelligent nonhuman races, and all but a small minority of incurable xenophobes were able to accept them on their own terms, even though none came even close to being as humanoid as the Teloi. But that, Jason thought, was precisely the problem. Aliens were supposed to *look* alien. The Teloi's eerie not-quite-humanlikeness caused them to seem *wrong* in a way that frankly weird-looking extraterrestrials did not.

What made it even worse was the knowledge that the resemblance was not entirely coincidental.

The *Oratioi'Zhonglu* had chosen Earth, despite certain drawbacks like a somewhat higher gravity than they preferred, precisely because it had held a species, *Homo erectus*, which lent itself to gengineering into a slave race of superficially sub-Teloi appearance. In short, humans looked the way they did because the Teloi looked the way *they* did.

It was a thought calculated to induce disgust in anyone who knew the Teloi like Jason knew them.

At least it was satisfying to see that this Teloi had to continue to bend down in the low-ceilinged room. In a crouching position, it was impossible to really carry off the trademark Teloi arrogance, which reached its zenith in the *Tuova'Zhonglu*.

A second Teloi entered—a female, not having to bend quite as low. Jason was sufficiently familiar with individual Teloi characteristics to recognize the pair from Father Ernetti's recording. He also recognized the indicia of aging in the female. Last came Lugal, in an obvious state of fidgety resentment.

The male Teloi spoke, with his race's subliminal voice-quality that Jason had always found even more disturbing than their appearance. "I am Anu. Our high priest Lugal-tarah tells us that you are time travelers from this world's future like himself." His Sumerian pronunciation was atrocious.

Jason saw no purpose to be served by denials—or by undue obsequiousness. Indeed, provocativeness might elicit more information. "Yes, we are. Did he tell you that we are enemies of the worthless scum he previously served? And that in the end those scum cast him out as unworthy even of them?"

Lugal, eyes blazing and mouth working with inarticulate rage, surged forward. A raised Teloi hand brought him to a comically abrupt halt. It was pretty clear who was in charge of this relationship.

"Lugal did not go into the details, but he has indicated that he is permanently stranded in this time period. He also tells us that you are in your past for a predetermined length of time, almost certainly not a short one, after which you will be returned—alive or dead—to your own temporal point of departure."

"True," said Jason, lying like a trooper. "And now that I've admitted our origin, gratify my curiosity as to yours. I'm surprised to find a lone representative of the *Tuova'Zhonglu* on Earth. And," he added, gesturing with his chin toward the female, "in the company of a member of the *Oratioi'Zhonglu*."

"Yes, Lugal did mention that you're aware of all that. Well, since you know so much else, you undoubtedly know of our war to cleanse the universe of the nauseating interstellar slime known as the Nagommo—and of our eventual complete triumph, of which Lugal has told us."

Jason shot a glance at the exiled Transhumanist, who had broken out in a sweat. Clearly, Lugal had been making a living by telling Anu the lies he wanted to hear, and was terrified that Jason would spill the beans about the war's real outcome.

"At the present time, however, the war still rages. We learned that a Nagommo survey ship had gone to this general interstellar neighborhood. We dispatched a swarm of single-seat scout craft to search for it. I was the pilot of one. My assigned course brought me to this system, where we knew the *Oratioi'Zhonglu* had been established on this planet for a long time. It soon became apparent that they had lost control of their human creations, and that most of them had left this region for areas where the descendants of escaped slaves were even more primitive and therefore easier to overawe."

*Areas to the north and west,* thought Jason. *Where they'll found the empire based on Crete and Santorini, which I discovered in 1628 B.C. And afterward their second generation will give rise to the Indo-European pantheon.*

"However," Anu went on, "one of them, Inanna, had remained." He indicated the female, who he hadn't previously bothered to introduce, with a peremptory jerk of his head in her direction. "On my arrival here, I saw that the automated weapon platforms the *Oratioi'Zhonglu* had placed in orbit around this world to protect their privacy were no longer present. I surmised that the Nagommo ship had destroyed them. After questioning Inanna, I decided there was reason to believe that it had been damaged in the process and subsequently crashed into the gulf to the southeast of here, and that the vermin were still covertly active in this region."

"So you took her on as a junior partner," said Jason, once again seeking to provoke a reaction. He got one, in the form of a glare from Inanna.

"She and I were in a position to be useful to each other," said Anu, continuing to discuss Inanna in the third person as though she hadn't been in the room. "She was well established among her local human worshipers, being the first of the Earth-born among the *Oratioi'Zhonglu.*"

*Well, that explains why she looks older than Anu.* As Jason had learned in the Aegean Bronze Age, the second generation of Teloi on Earth, in addition to being unable to have children (which the Teloi seldom did in any case), had greatly reduced lifespans—extremely long by human standards, to be sure, but nothing like the near-immortal Teloi norm. The last of them were due to die out sometime not too long after 490 B.C. Inanna, he was certain, would not last nearly that long.

"Also, she taught me the local human language," Anu continued. (*Which explains why your Sumerian is so bad,* Jason mentally interpolated. *No direct neural induction, just old-fashioned teaching methods.*) "In return, I was able to provide some impressive displays of 'magic' with my scout craft's equipment."

"No doubt. By the way," Jason added, as though as a casual afterthought, "where is your vessel now?"

"In orbit. I can control it, and summon it."

Jason nodded. He would have expected nothing less than for Anu to be comm-linked with his scout boat's AI via an implanted communicator.

"Well, I'm sure your position as a god has helped you to no end in your search for the surviving Nagommo . . . if any," Jason carefully added. "It seems you've been here for some time"

"A number of the local years. As you may imagine, it took quite a while for the primitive feral humans of this locality to erect this temple to me."

"I gather, then, that you're in no particular hurry to wrap up your mission."

Anu seemed to take no offense at the remark. "Actually, I consider that I have 'wrapped it up,' to the extent that I have satisfied myself that there are indeed Nagommo survivors at work among the feral humans. But I admit that I find something satisfying about the *Oratioi'Zhonglu* pantomime of divinity among lesser beings. In fact, there's something . . . seductive about it."

*Seductive for your race in general and not just the* Oratioi'Zhonglu, *it seems,* thought Jason. Still, none of the *Tuova'Zhonglu* he had encountered before would have admitted to feeling the tug of such a seduction, any more than the Nazis of his own twentieth-century acquaintance would have admitted to a liking for jazz. But those *Tuova'Zhonglu* had been products of the fanatical surviving hard core that had spent millennia after the Nagommo war skulking about the spaceways, stewing in their own embitterment and overcompensation. Anu was just a normal (by Teloi standards) member of a wartime military establishment.

He also recalled that the Teloi, with their lifespans numbered in tens of thousands of years, had a different time scale. Anu probably didn't think he had dawdled here, wallowing in bogus godhood, for an inordinate length of time.

"However," said Anu, suddenly brisk, "I plan to depart soon. I will report the presence of the castaway Nagommo to my superiors, who can send an expedition equipped to deal with them. But in addition, I will have something far more important to report, for which I will be well rewarded: the existence of time travel." The strange Teloi eyes, deep blue on pale blue, suddenly glowed with avidity. "We have always regarded it as impossible—a fundamental philosophical absurdity, in fact. But now, knowing it is possible, we will be able to ferret out the secret . . . especially with Lugal's help. My own craft can accommodate only one, but our expedition to eradicate the Nagommo infestation on this planet can bring him back, to assist our researchers."

Looking at the exiled Transhumanist's face, Jason saw ambivalence. The prospect of spending the rest of his life among aliens who held him in contempt could not be entirely attractive. But at least he would do so amid the high-tech amenities to which he had once been accustomed.

"The four of you," Anu went on, "should also be able to provide useful information on time travel, before you are killed. Lugal will confirm the veracity of your answers. The painfulness of your deaths will be in inverse proportion to your helpfulness." He turned to Lugal. "For now, confine them in the cell with the other prisoner. I have other matters to attend to at the moment, but we must put them to the question soon, as we have no way of knowing how long they are scheduled to remain in this time."

"Yes, lord," Lugal mumbled, giving Jason a sidelong leer of anticipation. He ordered the guards into the room, and they began to untie the prisoners. Anu turned to go, gesturing to Inanna to accompany him.

"You say your vessel can't hold anyone other than the pilot," Jason called out after them, on a sudden impulse. "I assume that includes Inanna."

Anu turned and gave him a look of puzzled annoyance. "Of course," he said shortly. Inanna continued to say nothing. Jason had enough experience reading Teloi faces to recognize careful expressionlessness on hers.

The Teloi pair departed, and Jason and his followers were manhandled through the door and along a short corridor. They were shoved through another low door into an oil-lamp-lit cell barely large enough to hold them and its other occupant.

That occupant was a woman—no, a girl, surely no older than

seventeen or eighteen—wearing a short, dirty tunic. She sat on the earthen floor, curled up in a corner with her bare brown legs drawn up under her. Long, tangled black hair framed a face in which the characteristic Sumerian features assumed an aquiline delicacy. She stared at them with large dark eyes. They stared back—especially, it seemed, Allawi.

"Who are you?" she asked in a husky voice. Her Sumerian held a subtly different accent from that of Uruk.

"That's a long story," said Jason. "Who are you?"

"Zan Zu," she said. "From Eridu."

# Chapter Nineteen

They all sat around in a circle, cross-legged, to hear each others' tales.

"So," Jason concluded, after giving their names and reciting their cover story, "the priests and temple guards set upon us, and we killed one of the priests in self-defense. So they imprisoned us, even though all we had wanted was to pay our respects at this temple. Although strangers from the northern hills, we had heard of the gods Anu and Inanna—"

"The gods of Uruk, to which they and their bloodsucking priests have brought nothing but oppression," Zan Zu cut in disdainfully. "We of Eridu reject their worship."

"Aren't you afraid of their anger?"

"No!" said the girl from Eridu emphatically, giving her head a shake that set her disordered black hair swinging. For all her dishevelment and dirt, her scorn was rich. "These people of Uruk are fools to worship them. They are not true gods at all, but evil beings pretending to be gods. Enki has made this clear to us."

"Enki?" queried Allawi, instantly alert.

"He is the god from the sea—half man and half fish—who has taught us many arts. Or rather, he has taught them to Adapa, who has explained them to us." Zan Zu's eyes grew rapt.

"Adapa?" Allawi's voice and expression held satisfaction at recognizing another familiar name. *But underneath that,* thought

Jason, *is it just my imagination or is there a hint of disgruntlement at the look in Zan Zu's eyes at the sound of that name?*

"Yes. He is the chosen one of Enki—the one to whom so much has been revealed. Useful things, not like the spurious magic of Anu. Things like . . ." She frowned, seeking to frame a difficult concept. "Like the keeping of records on clay tablets using a stylus, using marks to stand for things, not just impressing cylinder seals on the things themselves." Writing, Jason decided, was still so new to the Sumerians, even those of Eridu, that there was as yet no convenient word for it. "Adapa speaks to Enki in his temple of E-Abzu, and acts as the link between the god and King Alulim and his people." Zan Zu's eyes were positively glowing now.

"Zan Zu," said Jason gently, "we are ignorant strangers, and wish to understand. You have called Enki 'half fish and half man.' Can you describe to us what the he looks like?"

Zan Zu frowned again. "Only Adapa sees him regularly. I have only glimpsed him a few times . . . and it is difficult to wrap the mind around such strangeness. He is only a little larger than a man, and has two arms, and stands on two legs like a man—but his feet are webbed, as are his hands, and he has a long, thick tail, with flukes. He is covered with scales like a fish, gray-green except for the belly, where they are light gray. His body is heavy, but his neck and head are long, slender and graceful. His face is nothing like a man's, except for having two eyes—and those eyes are very strange. In addition to air, he can breathe water, through gills in his sides, and even seems to need to do so from time to time. This is why we have built the temple of E-Abzu for him, with water brought in by a canal."

*Uh-huh,* thought Jason, nodding unconsciously at the confirmation of his suspicions. *That's as good a description of a Nagom as I could have asked for. Which means there's one other question to which I need an answer . . .*

"Are there other gods of Enki's kind? Even in our far land we have heard of a god who resembles what you have told me of him, known by the name of Oannes."

"Yes, there are others. But we have only seen them briefly. Enki is the god of Eridu; the others come and go, sometimes back into the sea." (*To salvage more high-tech goodies from their sunken survey cruiser,* Jason mentally interpolated.) "And yes, I have heard of Oannes.

He has also done much for our people. But he has gone away, on some errand known only to the gods, and we have not seen him lately."

Jason tried not to let his relief show. In the Aegean Bronze Age he had met (or was going to meet, depending on how you looked at it) Oannes, aging by then despite the millennial length of his race's lifespans. That Nagom, the last of his kind, would save Jason's life, and die helping strand the first generation of the *Oratioi'Zhonglu* "gods" in their extradimensional pocket universe, his corpse blasted to atoms by the Santorini explosion of 1628 B.C. And—most importantly from Jason's current perspective—he would not, in that year, have any recollection of having met Jason before. Like a cloud blowing away on the wind, Jason now felt the passing of what could have been a major Observer Effect headache.

But that older Oannes would also have no notion that time travel was possible until he met Jason and his fellow time travelers in 1628 B.C. Which meant that neither Enki nor any of the other Nagommo of 4004 B.C. were going to learn the secret—the Observer Effect forbade it. Which, in turn, meant that no situation must be allowed to arise in which they were in danger of learning of it, for whatever it was that would prevent them from learning of it might prove highly unfortunate for Jason and his team.

"But Zan Zu," said Allawi, interrupting Jason's uncomfortable cogitations, "what are you doing here in Uruk? And why are you a prisoner?"

"Enki told Adapa that he needed him to find out certain information about the doings of Anu and Inanna. So Adapa came here with three companions. He chose me as one of them." Zan Zu's eyes gleamed with pride. But then the gleam died and she lowered her head. "Somehow, the temple guards found out about us. I was captured. But Adapa and the others got away. I'm sure they are still here in Uruk. They have a . . . a . . ."

"Safe house," Mondrago supplied, using the literal translation.

Zan Zu nodded. "Yes. And I know Adapa would never leave me behind."

"But he hasn't tried to rescue you," Allawi stated rather than asked—just a bit pointedly, it seemed to Jason.

"How could he?" the Sumerian girl bristled. "They can't attack this temple. Even without the magic of Anu, the guards are too many, and armed with weapons. And the people here would tear them to pieces for seeking to anger Anu." She subsided, and even smiled faintly. "But Adapa will find a way. I'm sure of it."

Allawi had the sense not to pursue the matter, and conversation soon trailed off as Zan Zu, who for the first time since her capture felt able to relax in the company of people who had demonstrated no wish to harm her, drifted off to sleep. Jason and the others huddled in the cell's far corner and, just in case, muttered to each other in Standard International English.

"I gather, Commander, that her description of Enki fits the Nagommo," said Irma Shartava.

"It does," said Jason, who was the only one present—the only living human of his era, come to that—who had actually seen one of the amphibious aliens. "Ahmad, how does what we've heard tally with later Mesopotamian legends?"

"Remarkably well, sir. In the Sumerian king list, Eridu was the home of the first kings, and Alulim was the very first of them. It was during his reign that the culture hero Adapa was supposed to have brought civilization to the city, having learned it from a half human god from the sea—Enki, later called Ea by the Semitic Akkadians. In fact, Adapa eventually got mixed up with him in the usual confused way of mythology, and was identified with U-An, a half-human being from the sea. Even the name of Enki's temple, E-Abzu, is right. It was called that because he was believed to live in an 'aquifer' called Abzu from which all life had emerged. If fact—"

At that moment the door was flung open and a glare of torches almost blinded them, adapted as their eyes had become to the gloom. With a small shriek, Zan Zu awoke from her fitful sleep as guards tramped into the cell, spears at the ready. They were followed by a figure Jason recognized as Lugal-tarah even before he had fully blinked the dazzlement out of his eyes. The guard captain followed.

"Anu has decided that too many of the local rabble saw you kill a priest in the scuffle at the entrance to the temple when we took you," the Transhumanist began, in Standard International English, heedless of the guards' uneasiness at hearing the strange tongue. His eyes were glittering points of hate at the thought of his partner's—and lover's—death, and his face wore an eager leer. "So before questioning you, he's going to reassure them of who's in charge by making a public example of you. Actually, this works out rather well—it will soften you up for the questioning." He switched to Sumerian and addressed the guard captain in hieratic tones. "The god Anu has decreed that these foreigners are to be punished for their impiety in killing one of his priests. We will take them outside, to the top of the ramp, and scourge the skin from their backs! Thus the people will know Anu's power."

"And her, holy one?" asked the captain, gesturing at Zan Zu.

"No, only these four."

Guards grasped them by the arms, hauled them upright, and shoved them out the door. They were marched along the passageway, flanked by four guards and the captain, with Lugal leading the way.

Jason and Mondrago made eye contact. They knew each other too well for words to be necessary.

As they turned a corner to the right, Mondrago seemed to stumble slightly and brush up against the guard to his right. It brought him close enough to grasp the shaft of the guard's spear and, with a swift, smooth motion, pull the spear forward and then shove it backward, jabbing the butt into the guard's midriff. The guard doubled over with a gasp, releasing his grip on the spear, which Mondrago whipped around and thrust the point home at the base of his neck, severing the cervical vertebrae. As he fell, Jason reached past Mondrago with his right hand and snatched the dagger from his belt. Simultaneously, he lunged forward and clamped his left arm around Lugal's neck.

It could never have worked, given the Transhumanist's gene-enhanced quickness, had Jason not taken him totally by surprise from behind. As it was, he wrenched his captive around to face the guards, who were still frozen in shock. He held the dagger's edge to Lugal's throat and spoke in Sumerian. "If anyone moves or cries out, your high priest dies!"

"Do as he says!" Lugal rasped through his constricted throat.

The tableau remained frozen in silence, with Mondrago standing over the dead guard and leveling his spear at the others. Jason breathed a sigh of relief. Had Lugal been a Transhumanist in good standing, he might well have acted with the self-sacrificing fanaticism of his caste. But Jason had gambled—successfully, it turned out—that his exile had burned all that away, leaving only a healthy sense of self-preservation.

"And now," Jason continued, "we're all going to continue up to the entrance as before, very normally, except that I'll be holding this dagger to the high priest's back." After they got out into the open, he thought, it would be a time for very rapid improvisation.

"Commander!" said Allawi. "What about Zan Zu?"

Jason blinked. "What about her?"

"We *can't* leave her behind!"

"We can't?" Mondrago grunted. "Just watch me."

"Ahmad," said Jason with strained patience, "this is *not* the time for heroics."

Allawi took a deep breath and won Jason's respect by standing his ground. "Commander, Adapa is out there somewhere with his friends. He's the only possible source of help we have in Uruk. If he sees her, he may very well come to her aid. But why should he give a damn about us?"

Jason and Mondrago exchanged a look. The young Mithran undeniably had a point, whatever his motivations.

"All right, Ahmad," Jason sighed. "Run back to the cell and get her. And I do mean *run*."

They waited, sweating, with Jason's arm maintaining its unbreakable grip on Lugal's throat and his dagger-point never wavering. After a time that seemed much longer than it was, Allawi returned, leading the bewildered girl from Eridu by the hand.

"Now," said Jason, "let's all proceed, very calmly."

# Chapter Twenty

By now it was late afternoon, but the Mesopotamian sun was still dazzling as they emerged from the temple's dimness onto the top of its great earthen pedestal.

Jason prodded Lugal forward. They proceeded, with the guard captain walking in tight-lipped anger beside Jason and the three surviving guards flanking their five "prisoners." They came to the head of the ramp, where four posts had been inserted in the rammed earth. Those posts featured leather thongs at their tops, and Jason surmised he and his companions were to be bound to them for the purpose of flogging. A leather scourge lay beside them. Below, a crowd had gathered in the square—doubtless the public punishment had been announced—and was being held back by a few other guards on ground level.

"Give yourselves up," Lugal murmured over his shoulder in Standard International English. "I'll invent some excuse to call off the scourging, and afterwards I'll intercede with Anu for you, and—" He gasped as Jason jabbed his back with his dagger.

"Shut up, you lying son of a bitch."

"But you know you can't possibly get away with this!"

Jason put an irritating grin into his voice. "Ah, but remember, Anu has told us that we're as good as dead anyway. So we have nothing to lose." He naturally did not mention that, if absolutely necessary, he could flick himself and his team back to the twenty-fourth century at any time, by mental command. That bit of knowledge was a hole card he intended to keep in the hole. "And now, you are going to step forward—with me and my dagger right behind you, of course—and make the following announcement to the good citizens of Uruk." He whispered a few swift words into Lugal's ear. The disgraced Transhumanist nodded jerkily. They moved to the edge of the ramp, where Lugal licked his dry lips and spoke in a loud voice.

"Anu has decreed that this female spy from Eridu is to be scourged first. Captain, bring her forward and bind her to a post."

"Yes, holy one." The guard captain turned and walked back to where Zan Zu stood beside Allawi. As he did so, Jason looked over his shoulder and met Allawi's stricken eyes. He winked, which he hoped conveyed *play along* in unmistakable terms.

Zan Zu gave Allawi a look of pleading horror as the captain grasped her by the upper arm and jerked her forward. As he dragged her past Jason, her eyes met his, with the same imploring look.

"Don't worry, you'll be all right," he said to her in as loud a whisper as he dared. He only hoped that he wasn't lying, that his horrifying gamble with the life of someone he *couldn't* whisk to safety would work.

The guard captain raised Zan Zu's slender bare arms and tied her wrists to the top of the post. In her numb terror, her legs gave way and she sagged as far as the bonds allowed, almost to her knees. The captain ripped open the back of her tunic, and motioned to one of the guards, evidently the specialist in this sort of thing. In fact, he looked it. He also looked confused by the unexpected turn of events in which they were all caught up. But following the high priest's orders was of course the paramount consideration—and his brain could only handle one consideration at a time. He picked up the scourge (Jason now noticed that it had jagged bits of copper worked into its leather), raised it, and drew back for the first stroke.

Jason was already sweating in the sun, but now his sweat turned cold. *It's not going to work out,* he thought dismally. Out of the corner of his eye, he saw the wild look in Allawi's eyes as the young Mithran bunched his muscles for a desperate lunge . . .

At that instant, a commotion erupted among the crowd below. A tall young man, his head wrapped in a kind of partially concealing burnoose, burst forward and struck a guard a paralyzing blow to the solar plexus, grabbing his spear with his other hand. With a smooth motion, he rotated backwards and hurled the spear, javelin-wise. It transfixed the guard who was still in the process of raising the scourge over Zan Zu.

Jason had no leisure to admire the throw, for pandemonium at once broke loose.

As the javelin thrower bounded up the ramp, Mondrago whipped his spear out from behind his back, where he had been concealing it, and thrust it into the guard beside him. Simultaneously, Shartava brought a knee up into the crotch of the other guard. As he doubled over, she snatched his dagger and brought it sharply upward behind his chin, through his tongue and into his brain.

Lugal, with the quickness of his artificial heritage, dropped to the ground before Jason could react, rolled backwards, sprang to his feet, and ran toward the entrance. As Jason turned to pursue him, the guard captain lunged at him with his spear. Jason dodged it and grabbed the shaft. They both fell, grappling.

Even as he struggled, Jason was aware that Allawi had sprung forward, snatched up the fallen scourge-wielder's dagger, and was cutting Zan Zu loose.

Jason rolled the guard captain over on his stomach and, holding the spear shaft in both hands, got it under his jaw. Jamming a knee into the small of the captain's back, he heaved backwards convulsively on the spear shaft and heard a sickening *snap!* The captain went limp.

It had all taken mere seconds. By the time Jason got to his feet, the young spear-chucker had reached the top of the ramp. No one pursued him, for the guards on ground level were fully occupied dealing with a crowd driven mad by panic. Civil disturbances were evidently uncommon in Uruk.

*"Adapa!"* cried Zan Zu as Allawi finished cutting her bonds. She ran to the young man, flinging herself into his arms. Even at this moment, Jason noted that Allawi wore a somewhat sour look.

Adapa didn't let the embrace last. "Quick! Let's go!"

"Let these other prisoners come with us," urged Zan Zu. She indicated Jason and the other time travelers, her gesture seeming to linger fractionally longer on Allawi. "They've helped me."

"Yes, I saw. And I'm grateful."

Jason decided it was just as well that Adapa—and Zan Zu, for that matter—didn't know he was the one who had told Lugal to order her scourged.

Adapa, whose head cloth had fallen away, met Jason's eyes, and for the first time Jason got a good look at him. He was tall for this milieu, and powerfully built. The characteristic local ethnic features had an exceptionally rugged cast in his case, and he obviously had been a while without being able to partake of the Sumerian custom of shaving the face, for a dense dark stubble was starting to cover his jaws. And he didn't follow the practice of head-shaving at all, for he had a thick head of wavy blue-black hair.

The glimpse only lasted a heartbeat, for Adapa wasted no time. He scooped up the scourge—the nearest weapon available, took Zan Zu by his other hand and spoke urgently. "Come, while the confusion lasts!"

Jason needed no urging. He motioned to his companions and, carrying the weapons they'd appropriated, they followed the pair from Eridu down the ramp and plunged into the chaos below.

The tightly packed, confused mob hampered the guards from doing anything about them as they shoved their way through the crush of bodies. Two young men—Adapa's followers, Jason supposed—managed to break free and join them. But at that moment, one guard managed to work free from the press and plunged his spear into the back of one of the youths. With an anguished cry, Adapa turned and backhanded the guard across the face with the scourge, ripping out an eye and sending a spray of blood flying. As the guard screamed and clutched his butchered face, Allawi stabbed him in the gut and gave his dagger a twist.

For an instant, the crowd drew back, shocked, as the guard fell. Taking advantage of the opportunity, they broke free and left the mob and the struggling guards behind. At full speed, they ran from the open space of the Anu District and entered the labyrinth of alleys and canals that was Uruk. Very few people were about—everyone must have gone to the square to watch the show—and the occasional exception scurried quickly out of the way of the armed and grim-looking group.

They continued on, following a canal, along winding alleys where Jason's map display continued to grow as he observed the surroundings. That display told him Adapa was leading them toward the Euphrates. Presently the small mud-brick courtyard houses began to thin out as they neared the river, and the low wall was pierced with openings for the small canals—one of which openings allowed them a wet egress. There was nothing properly describable as a waterfront, but they entered an area with small huts scattered among spare-foliaged palm trees on a slight rise above the bank. As the sun neared the western horizon, they came to one such hut, back to back with a shed. Outside the door, an elderly man was waiting, looking anxious. His eyes bulged at the sight of the strangers accompanying Adapa, but he gestured them hurriedly inside.

In the oil-lamp-lit dimness of the interior, the old man removed a screen of woven reeds from one wall. It concealed the entrance to the shed, into which he ushered them. There was barely enough space for seven people to squeeze in, and Jason couldn't help feeling a certain skepticism about security. But Adapa evidently felt they were safe, at least for the moment, for he sank to the earthen "floor" and rested his head on his knees as though allowing reaction to catch up with him.

Zan Zu knelt beside him and placed a gentle arm around his shoulders. "I'm so sorry, Adapa."

"Kuda was a good friend," Adapa said tonelessly. But he laid a hand on the girl's, and looked up and met Jason's eyes. "And so are you, for helping Zan Zu." He managed a smile. "Good fighters, too! Who are you?"

Jason again recited their cover story, during which the old man brought in some of the local beer. It lived down to expectations. Jason concluded as he had with Zan Zu by insisting that the temple guards and priests had attacked them for no apparent reason, resulting in their killing of a priest and subsequent imprisonment. "So now we must get out of Uruk—our lives are forfeit here."

"We must also leave. Now that we have Zan Zu back, there's nothing to keep us from returning to Eridu." In a seemingly unconscious gesture, Adapa touched a copper amulet hanging from a leather string around his neck.

"Ah . . . may we accompany you there? Zan Zu has told us much about your great god Enki, and we would pay our respects to him."

"Let them, Adapa," said Zan Zu. Allawi, thought Jason, seemed to brighten slightly.

"Very well. We'll leave shortly, after night falls. It will be safer, traveling by night, as well as cooler. But it won't be easy to find our way out of Uruk in the dark."

"I may be able to help with that," said Jason with a smile. "I have a *very* good sense of direction."

# Chapter Twenty-One

Eridu was about fifty miles southwest of Uruk. In Jason's time, its ruins lay in the midst of desert, south of the Euphrates and a hundred and twenty-five miles northwest of the Persian Gulf. But in the current, almost unthinkably ancient era, coastlines and river courses were different. The Euphrates divided into two channels just northwest of Eridu; the southern branch flowed past Eridu while the other flowed past Ur (now nothing more than a village still slumbering in the Ubaid culture, untroubled as yet by the revolution of the Uruk culture), with both branches emptying into the Gulf only a few miles beyond.

So the most obvious way to get from Uruk to Eridu was to float downriver. Unfortunately, Zan Zu explained, there was nothing available that would safely hold seven passengers. She declared her own people to be experienced sailors whose substantial boats were equipped with sails. But all the landlubbers of Uruk had were canoes and reed boats propelled either by paddles or pole-pushing—not even worth stealing, she sniffed. And anyway, stealing one was out of the question; Adapa's surviving male companion, a wiry youth named Nabi-ilisu, reconnoitered the riverbank and reported that the temple guards were on patrol around the watercraft.

Jason wasn't surprised. Lugal would surely be exerting every effort to redeem himself in Anu's eyes after the time travelers' escape, not to mention the near-riot that had made a fiasco of what was supposed to be a public demonstration of the "god's" power.

So after darkness fell and a quarter moon rose, they slipped out of the shed, carrying bundles of rough food provided by the old man (whose relationship to Adapa Jason was never to learn), unarmed save for whatever daggers they had taken, for spears would be too conspicuous. Cautiously, they began to work their way around the fringes of what Jason ironically thought of as "Greater Uruk," toward the south and the desert. Adapa was unfamiliar with these marginal areas, and Jason even more so. But Jason's computer implant built up his map display steadily, even though he was only seeing by moonlight and starlight and the occasional lamp-lit window. He impressed Adapa with his ability to lead them through the outlying huts, keeping the small structures between them and the occasional patrolling guards.

Eventually they left the last structures behind and relaxed somewhat as they walked on into the agricultural belt. Once in the open, Adapa was quite capable of finding his way by the stars. As for Jason, he marveled at those stars' sheer number, despite the moon's presence, in this crystal-clear air on an Earth without electric lights. And, of course, there were no hills or forest to circumscribe the sky's vastness. Gazing up into that blazing firmament, he began to understand why so many of humanity's great religions had arisen among desert peoples.

They had no desire to continue on into the sandy desert itself. Instead, they skirted the cultivated areas, with their palm groves and tiny plots and networks of irrigation canals. Even out of sight of the moonlit river, Adapa kept them moving southeastward. They trudged on through the night, stopping occasionally to eat sparingly of the old man's dates and tough bread.

Shortly after dawn, Adapa decreed that they should stop and sleep. Jason was inclined to agree that traveling by night was both cooler and safer, in case Lugal had sent his guards to search downriver. They found a fairly isolated palm grove and tried to sleep.

At dusk, they risked resuming their trek, after obtaining water from a local well. Another night of weary hiking passed. As the sun rose, they could see that, as they came nearer to the head of what would someday be called the Persian Gulf, the river was increasingly fringed by areas of thick marshes. Presently, such an area appeared to their left.

"The people here live by fishing, not cultivation," Adapa explained to Jason. He frowned with thought. "Some of the canoes they use could probably carry all of us. And we're far enough from Uruk now that we may be able to risk it."

Jason wasn't certain Adapa's reasoning wasn't that of a man who was trying to convince himself. But he could fully understand that the young Sumerian was tired of walking, as he himself shared the feeling. "Well, maybe we could conceal ourselves among the reeds at the river-margin until tonight and steal a boat."

"Good idea. And besides, we need to get into the open, make ourselves visible. You see, I *know* that Enki himself is going to come and appear to us." And Adapa again fingered the amulet hanging from his neck.

"Yes!" said Zan Zu. "He will come to our aid!"

Jason made what he hoped would be interpreted as a reverent gesture, privately thinking anything that upheld these two's morale should be encouraged.

They turned left and entered the marshes. In contrast to the usual mud brick houses with reed roofs, the huts here were made entirely of reeds, with thick pillars of bundles of the things for support. These were often built on solid earth embankments at water's edge, flanked by what could be called boat slips, and shaded by palms and willows. Reeds covered considerable expanses of the river. By the standards of most of this part of the world, the vegetation was lush.

They saw few people—most of the men and boys were already out on their canoes, and the women were presumably inside—but those few gave them looks that did not overflow with friendliness. Jason surmised that these people, living their immemorial lifestyle in a marginal and partially hidden environment, were even less cosmopolitan than the farmers.

"I'm not sure this is such a good idea," Mondrago muttered to Jason.

Adapa couldn't understand him, but he caught the tone. "Let's get away from the huts," he said, "and find a place to hide."

They turned left and followed the riverbank upstream, feet squelching in the shallows, until the last of the huts was out of sight. Adapa led them to the base of a headland, covered with a clump of palms, which jutted out into the river. "After we get around this, we ought to—"

At that moment three boats, of the largest sort Jason had seen at Uruk, rounded the headland. They were loaded to maximum capacity with temple guards. In the prow of the leading boat was a figure without the leather helmets of the others. Jason instantly recognized Lugal.

*Anu must have assigned him to take personal charge of tracking us down,* thought Jason. *And he naturally assumed we'd head toward Eridu.*

Lugal leaned forward and pointed with one of the "walking sticks" he had seized from Jason's party. *"There they are!"* he shouted. The guards began paddling (no one had yet invented rowing) for all they were worth.

"Run!" And Jason suited the action to the word.

The all turned back the way they had come . . . and stopped dead, for they found themselves facing a semicircle of the local fishermen. They had no purpose-built weapons, but the clubs, staffs and other crude implements they carried could undoubtedly do some damage if wielded with gusto.

Whether they were actually working for Lugal or simply acting out of their fundamental distrust of strangers was immaterial, for either way they were clearly disinclined to let the fugitives pass. And looking back over his shoulder, Jason saw that the boats were rapidly bearing down on the shore.

Those of them who had daggers drew them. Allawi tried to position himself to protect Zan Zu, which wasn't easy inasmuch as they were threatened from both sides. But she looked oddly serene.

"Enki will succor us," she said in a soft voice.

*Right,* thought Jason sourly.

But then he heard a vaguely familiar humming sound.

Everyone else seemed to become aware of it as well. The guards' paddles went slack in their hands, and they and the fishermen looked around anxiously.

A disturbance in the river caught Jason's attention. It was as though a large oblong segment of the water was being pressed down and pushed aside by some invisible force, and flowing away in ripples.

*Grav surface effect,* flashed through Jason's mind. In confirmation, a tiny blue light began to flash at the edge of his field of vision. It was a light he practically never saw on extratemporal expeditions, for it was triggered by a sensor function of his brain implant which detected nearby use of grav repulsion. And then, looking above the water, he recognized a familiar shimmering, or wavering, in the air. A refraction field was powering down, ceasing to confer invisibility by bending visible frequencies of light a hundred and eighty degrees around the space it enclosed.

*Any second now,* thought Jason.

All at once, a sleek, enclosed craft made of an unknown substance that was neither wood nor ceramic nor copper appeared out of nowhere, hovering in midair a few feet above the river.

The fisher-folk went mad with terror. Some fled, screaming incoherently, while others fell to the mud and went into fetal position, moaning and covering their heads. Even the guards, though doubtless not unacquainted with Anu's "magic," had never seen this; the refraction field was, as Jason knew, not part of the Teloi technological inventory. They panicked, capsizing the boats as they frantically tried to reverse direction and get away, ignoring Lugal's bawled commands—which, in any case, were cut off abruptly as he toppled into the water.

Adapa, Nabi and Zan Zu were the only Sumerians unaffected. Their unsurprised expressions reflected nothing more than confirmation of their expectations, and Adapa reverently touched his amulet.

*Homing device,* thought Jason grumpily. *You might have told me.*

*But of course you don't know that. As far as you're concerned, it's just a talisman.*

*And of course Enki couldn't come and snatch you straight out of Uruk. Something that small probably doesn't have much range. And anyway, he needs to stay close to Eridu.*

A dorsal hatch popped open, and an alien head appeared. Jason's companions stared, but he felt memories rushing back as he recalled Oannes. This face held subtle differences—some of which, Jason was sure, reflected a millennial difference in age—but it was unmistakably a Nagommo face.

"Enki!" intoned the trio from Eridu, bowing.

Jason belatedly decided that he and his fellow time travelers had better start displaying the sort of reaction to be expected of a bunch of forty-first century B.C. hillbillies. He genuflected in the mud, gesturing at the others to follow suit.

"Who are these, Adapa?" The indescribable Nagommo voice quality was as Jason remembered, forming a human language with nonhuman vocal apparatus.

"They are friends, lord. They rescued Zan Zu from the dungeons of the temple of Anu, and helped us escape from Uruk. Take them to Eridu along with us."

Jason risked raising his head slightly. He met the Nagom's eyes—large, dark, with nictitating membranes blinking back and forth horizontally. It was always risky, trying to read alien facial expressions, but he could have sworn those eyes held a certain puzzlement. *We probably just don't look like the Sumerians he's used to,* Jason assured himself. *And for this era, I'm tall and Ahmad is very tall.*

"Very well, Adapa," said Enki after a barely perceptible hesitation. "I think there will be room for everyone in my vessel." A side hatch slid open. They all splashed out into the shallow water and began to board.

"That's right, Nagom, take them!" came a shout from the shore, just short of the headland, where Lugal had swum ashore and now crouched, covered in mud. His voice held the quaver of insanity, and it rose to a shriek. "But don't listen to their lies. They are from this world's future! As am I! *As am I!*" And he dissolved into compulsive laughter.

In his entire life, Jason had very seldom wanted anything as much as he now wanted to kill Lugal.

But there was no chance. They were hastily crowding into a passenger compartment too small for seven people. Packed tightly together, they felt the grav raft swing about and head downriver.

Zan Zu and Allawi were squeezed particularly close—*By accident or design?* Jason wondered—and she spoke softly. "Ahmad, what did that high priest mean? It didn't seem to make sense."

"Oh, nothing," Allawi hastily assured her. "He was just raving." She seemed to accept this, for she said no more.

*We can only hope Enki is as easy a sell,* thought Jason. He was still trying to untangle the Observer Effect implications of Lugal's mad outburst, for there was no getting around the fact that in 1628 B.C. Enki's fellow Nagom Oannes would know nothing of time travel.

For now, he thrust it out of his mind, for there was nothing he could do about it. He worked his way through the press of bodies until he could look past the Nagom in his oddly designed control seat and see the forward viewscreen. The outside world showed in blurry shades of gray, as always when viewed from inside a refraction field. But Jason was used to it. And very soon, there appeared up ahead the first city on Earth.

# Chapter Twenty-Two

Eridu wasn't really a "city," of course—nothing really so describable existed yet. But it was an undeniable town, and it was the first of those; Jason's orientation told him it dated back to about 5400 B.C. His practiced eye told him it covered twenty to twenty-five acres, and from what he knew of low-tech urban population densities he guessed it held at least four thousand people. Rising from the midst of the built-up area was what must be the temple called E-Abzu, connected to the river buy a canal, of which Zan Zu had told them.

That was all Jason was able to take in as the grav raft, invisible in its refraction field, passed the northwestern portion of the waterfront and settled gently into the river. Once submerged, it turned up the canal.

Given the race that had built it, Jason was unsurprised that the grav raft had submersible capability. He recalled another planetside vehicle that the stranded Nagommo crew had salvaged from their lost survey ship: Oannes' supercavitating submarine, which had been capable of supersonic underwater speeds. This was nothing like that, but the raft's impellers pushed it slowly through the water until the canal widened into a larger expanse. The raft surfaced, and floated in a pool surrounded by the inner walls of the temple.

"So," breathed Allawi to Jason in Standard International English, "this was the basis of the legend of Abzu, the 'aquifer' beneath the Earth in which Enki lived. Now we know why this temple was called E-Abzu, 'The House of the Aquifer,' or 'The House of the Waters.'"

"Seems surprising that the archaeologists never found this pool."

"Actually, they have noticed—or rather, they *will* notice—a depression that would allow water to accumulate. But remember, the temple will be built over many times. Over the millennia, as the head of the Persian Gulf recedes and the Euphrates changes its course, this site will turn to desert. It will dry up, and fill in."

"So all remains of it will vanish," Jason nodded. "But," he added firmly, "I think we'd better go back to speaking the local language. People always feel suspicious when they don't know what you're talking about." With his chin, he pointed toward Zan Zu, who was looking at them oddly as they conversed in their strange foreign tongue. And out of the corner of his eye, he glimpsed Enki turn his head with his species' unhuman suppleness and give them a sharp glance.

But it only lasted an instant. The Nagom turned his attention back to bringing the raft up against the side of the pool and opening the side hatch.

"Adapa," Enki said, "see to accommodations for your . . . friends. I shall want to speak to them later. And then come back and tell me what you learned at Uruk."

"Yes, God," said Adapa, inclining his head deeply.

Adapa took the time travelers to his family's home. It was typical of the large houses that sheltered extended families: a single-story mud-brick structure, just under fifty feet square, organized around a long central room flanked by rows of smaller chambers. As women and girls prepared food, Adapa departed, having no desire to keep Enki waiting. Zan Zu was left to attend to their needs.

"Zan Zu," said Jason after they'd eaten, "even in our far country, we've heard of Eridu. We'd be grateful if you'd show it to us."

"Yes!" Allawi piped up eagerly.

"Of course," she said, with a glance and a smile for Allawi.

Eridu was, unsurprisingly, much like Uruk in many ways. But there were differences. Located on what was currently the estuary of the Euphrates, only a couple of miles from what would one day be known as the Persian Gulf but which these people called simply *The Sea*, it was a busy port. Zan Zu took them to the busy waterfront, where Jason saw that she had not been bragging about her people's shipping. In addition to the usual reed boats and canoes, there were honest-to-God sailboats. Small, of course, and very crude—almost as broad in the beam as they were long, and with one mast, inserted in a socket and secured by "rigging" that consisted of three ropes extending from near its top and fastened in holes. Just one sail, of course. But this tub was the earliest evolutionary ancestor of all the windjammers that would ever sail Earth's seas. And Jason recalled from his orientation that the archaeologists had found Ubaid culture pots like the ones he now saw being loaded aboard as far away as the Strait of Hormuz.

Another difference from Uruk that Jason noticed was Eridu's—to use a word whose obsessive overuse in the late twentieth and early twenty-first centuries he could personally recall—diversity. Three different lifestyles had come together here and contributed to the building of Eridu. Most important was the irrigated subsistence agriculture with which they were already familiar from upriver, with its canals and its mud-brick buildings. But in addition there were the fishing people they had recently encountered, their reed huts spreading along the riverbank. Finally, there were proto-Semitic pastoralists from the west who had clearly moderated their nomadic habits, for their tents and flocks of sheep and herds of goats were to be seen around the outskirts.

The nascent urban occupational specialization they had already seen at Uruk was just as developed here, including the occupation of soldiers or guards—although they didn't seem to inspire the same kind of nervous apprehension among the citizenry that they did at Uruk. And in fact, there were two occupations here that Uruk had yet to see. As they passed a courtyard, Jason spotted one of these: that of scribes.

Maybe it was a few generations too early to actually call them that. But Jason saw men seated cross-legged on the ground, a couple of them cutting the cylinder seals used to identify items of property, while another working with a stylus on clay, for Enki had taught these people that the symbols of the seals could be used to represent things indirectly . . . and also to represent numbers and sounds. Jason could almost smell Allawi's urge to examine the clay tablets to see if they already held a recognizable ancestor of cuneiform.

The second new specialization was easy to recognize, for they passed a man wearing a kind of hooded cloak covered with a pattern of scales and hanging down almost to the ground behind him, where it divided to resemble flukes. It was pretty obvious what the strange garment was supposed to resemble.

"Is he a priest of Enki?" Jason asked Zan Zu.

"Oh, no. He is a healer. Enki has taught us many things to make the guardians of health enter into the sick, and expel the demons that cause maladies. Those who practice these arts naturally want to look as much like him as possible."

Allawi whispered excitedly into Jason's ear, softly to avoid being overheard but remembering Jason's injunction to speak Sumerian. "It fits! Mesopotamian physicians wore these kinds of getups for thousands of years after this, for symbolic association with Enki. Of course, the costume will later come to look more like fish and less like Nagommo. But that's natural; they'll forget what Enki really looked like, so they'll visualize him more and more as a 'fish-man'. And—" He cut himself off abruptly, for Zan Zu—whose hearing must have been sharper than he had bargained for—stopped abruptly and gave him a quizzical look.

"What was that you were saying, Ahmad? I couldn't quite understand."

"Oh, nothing," said Allawi lamely.

"Yes, nothing," added Jason firmly, with a quelling side-glance for the young Mithran.

The girl's brow remained furrowed. "But I thought I heard you say something about things that are yet to be—"

"He was just marveling at Enki's wisdom," Jason assured her, rather desperately.

"Oh, yes!" Zan Zu's expression cleared, to Jason's relief. "He has taught us so many things, through Adapa. Besides showing us ways to heal the sick, he has told us that we're less likely to get sick in the first place if we keep ourselves and our homes clean." And, Jason now realized, the sights and smells of Eridu seemed somehow more sanitary than those of Uruk.

It all made sense. Technological progress was a cumulative thing, with one development a prerequisite to the next. Contrary to the opinion of some early writers, a primitive society couldn't be converted to a high-tech one overnight; the foundations simply weren't there to be built on. And the technological gap between Mark Twain's Connecticut Yankee and the Britain of King Arthur was trivial compared to the chasm that yawned between the Nagommo and these people, not yet emerged from the Chalcolithic into the Bronze Age. No; all that could be done was to lay the groundwork for future progress by introducing the basic fundamentals. And even that could not have been easy, because for the Nagommo—at least as advanced as Jason's own twenty-fourth century human civilization—those fundamentals lay so far in their race's past that most of them were effectively lost arts. Even if there had been any tin deposits within accessible distance of Eridu, it was a safe bet that not a single member of a spaceship crew knew how to mix it with copper and make bronze. Or how to make papyrus. Or how to build a water wheel.

But concepts could be imparted, such as the idea that human action could improve health, even if it had to be couched in supernatural terms like 'the guardians of health' . . . and the supreme gift of writing, which made all future progress possible by allowing for the accumulation of knowledge. It must have been heartbreakingly difficult to get such an unheard-of notion across. But the thing had been done, here in Eridu, and now the human race's feet were set on the road that would lead to the stars.

Night had fallen when they returned to the house of Adapa's family. Adapa was waiting for them in the central chamber. "I've come from Enki," he began without preamble. "He has certain questions for the four of you. Come with me."

"Yes, of course," said Jason. "But first, can we have a few moments alone? We must . . . perform certain devotions to our own gods."

Adapa obviously considered the request a slightly odd one. To the Sumerians, gods were local, their jurisdiction limited to their own cities. But all were entitled to respect . . . and at any rate, foreigners could only be expected to have different customs. He showed them into a storeroom to the right of the hall, behind a ramp that led to the roof, where there was just enough room for them among the pots and bales.

"All right," said Jason as soon as they were alone, "we're going to be dealing with a being from an advanced, sophisticated culture. And if he's anything like my recollection of Oannes, he's highly intelligent and *very* perceptive. It is essential that we not commit any slip-ups that give him reason to suspect our true origin." He accompanied this with a glare under which Allawi wilted. "We have to be especially careful after Lugal's little outburst."

"Right," Mondrago nodded. "This could be a real Observer Effect nightmare."

"It certainly could. But there's more to it than that." Jason paused, and they all looked at him quizzically—including Mondrago, to whom he'd never told the whole story of his expedition to the Bronze Age Aegean. "If he finds out that we're from the future, he's going to want to know the outcome of the war that his race is now waging among the stars against the Teloi. I don't want to lie to him—and I also don't want to tell him the truth."

"Why, sir?" asked Shartava, puzzled. "Aren't the Nagommo going to win? Of course, I know the hard core of the *Tuova'Zhonglu* will escape, but—"

"You don't understand. Before meeting Oannes, I'd seen the Nagommo home planet. Or what used to be their home planet." Jason drew a deep breath. "It's out beyond my home system of Psi 5 Aurigae—a dim orange star with a liquid-water planet resonance-locked to it. When I was in the Hesperian Colonial Rangers, we were on an anti-smuggling mission beyond the periphery of human settlement. We stopped there and talked to the archaeologists who had been investigating the remains of an ancient civilization that seemed to have wrecked itself around forty-five hundred years before our time by unwise tinkering with its own genotype. We could easily believe it; we saw some of the degraded, gene-twisted monsters that were the only inhabitants, lurking among the ruins. But there were also indications of a great interstellar war, and one of the archaeologists had a theory that in order to win that war the race had gone beyond normal wartime regimentation and gengineered themselves into subspecies, including one of supersoldiers, and that it had gone horribly wrong."

"Like what almost happened to the human race under the Transhuman Dispensation," Allawi nodded. "Except that the Transhumanists didn't have the excuse of having their backs to the wall in an interstellar war."

"One of the supports for that theory was the artwork, which showed what the race had originally looked like. Then, years later, I saw those art works in the flesh, when I met Oannes."

They were all silent, as horror began to dawn on them.

"What clinched the matter was that Oannes told us the marooned crew hadn't been able to have offspring on Earth—even though the Nagommo are fully functional hermaphrodites—because they came from a resonance-locked planet, and their reproductive cycle was rigidly linked to that." Jason grew somber, and spoke as much to himself as the others. "While they were stranded here on Earth, their race was sacrificing itself in an effort—unfortunately not quite successful—to rid the universe of the Teloi. Oannes was the last of the crew members. Which meant he was the last Nagom, period.

"He deduced that we were time travelers, even though his race hadn't thought that was possible. I tried to make him think we didn't have interstellar travel, and therefore had no knowledge of how the war had come out. I failed. So I lied and told him we simply didn't know of his world. He pretended to believe me. But I could tell he knew I was lying . . . and that the lie was rooted in kindness. And that last part told him all he needed to know.

"I don't want to have to go through that again." Jason drew himself up. "Now, let's go."

# Chapter Twenty-Three

Adapa, carrying a torch, led the way to the E-Abzu temple. Once inside the great central court around the pool, he inserted the torch in a sconce, to add its light to the other torches that smoldered around the periphery. He then waited in a silence Jason decided it would be inadvisable to break.

They had not long to wait. A disturbance appeared in the surface of the water, and a Nagommo head appeared. Adapa genuflected, and Jason led his companions in following suit.

Slowly, Enki emerged from the pool. He reclined on a kind of bench that had clearly been designed with him in mind. (Jason automatically thought of the Nagom as *he*, rather than as *it*. He recalled having reacted the same way to Oannes.) "Rise, Adapa. Rise, all of you." They obeyed, and Jason thought to see the same look of puzzled inquiry he had noticed on that alien face when he had first met the Nagom's eyes.

"Introduce your friends, Adapa," Enki commanded. "Your *tall* friends," he added, glancing at Jason and particularly at Allawi.

The young Sumerian gave their names. "They are travelers from the mountains to the north, who were imprisoned in Uruk along with Zan Zu."

"Yes . . . I can see that they are not of this land." Enki addressed Jason. "Why did the priests of Anu imprison you?"

Jason recited the same story he had told Adapa, of an unprovoked attack by the temple guards and the killing of a priest in self-defense. "I don't understand it," he finished in an indignantly self-pitying tone. "When all we wanted to do was—"

"Worship Anu?"

*Nice going, Jason old man!* "Er . . . that is . . . we naturally wish to pay proper respect to *all* the gods of this land." Jason suddenly thought he saw a way to change the subject and also elicit some important information. "Indeed, great Enki, we have heard that there are other gods like you. We even have heard the name of one: Oannes. Zan Zu told us she knew of him, but that he is not here."

The flicking back and forth of Enki's nictitating membranes abruptly halted. Jason suspected it was the equivalent of a human narrowing his eyes and drawing his brows together. "You seem surprisingly well informed, Jason. Yes, there are other gods of my . . . tribe. Including Oannes. And yes, he is now elsewhere, on a journey with my consort Ninhursanga."

*"Consort," eh? Second in command, you mean.* But, Jason thought, it would be a natural way of representing the relationship to the Sumerians, who automatically assumed that the gods had two genders like themselves.

"However," Enki continued, "they will be returning shortly." Jason's heart sank, for he had hoped to avoid coming anywhere near the Nagom who, in 1628 B.C., would never have seen him. There was no telling what might happen to prevent Oannes from getting a glimpse forbidden by the Observer Effect. He would have to be very cautious.

"However," said Enki, hauling the conversation back on track, "while you were prisoners in Uruk, did you encounter Anu's high priest, the one called Lugal-tarah?"

"Yes, great Enki." Jason decided that honesty was the best policy, which has been translated as *hold your lies to the minimum that are necessary.* "I believe he is mad."

"Quite possibly. That would account for what he called out from the shore this morning when I rescued you." The nictitating membranes halted their blinking motion again. "Do you have any idea what he might have meant by it?"

"No, great Enki! None. No idea at all." Jason hoped he wasn't being too emphatic. "He must be even madder than I thought."

"Perhaps. But ever since this Lugal first appeared, I have been curious. There seems something strange about him, as though he does not belong in this place . . . and time. And now . . . do you remember the word he used for me?"

*Nagom*, thought Jason with a sinking feeling. "Ah . . . I've forgotten, lord."

"It was a word he had no business knowing. Of course, I suppose he could have learned it from Anu. Still, it is one more bit of strangeness about him." Enki took on a look Jason had seen in Oannes. He had learned to recognize it as a look of disconcerting perceptiveness. "Come to think of it, there seems something strange about you and your friends as well. As though there is more to you than the simple mountain men you say you are."

*Yes, the Nagommo are altogether too damned perceptive for my taste.* Jason made himself cringe. "We are only humble strangers from a far-off country, lord. Our ways are naturally different from those of this land."

"Naturally. And yet, despite being new to the lower riverlands, you seemed to accept the sight of me very readily. More readily than anyone else has." Enki seemed to reach a decision. "Adapa, I think perhaps we should—"

At that moment, screaming sounds of mass panic came from beyond the walls. There was a sharp *crack!* that should never have been heard in Sumeria, followed by a roar and a crash of collapsing brickwork. Adapa's eyes widened with uncomprehending fear, and Enki surged upright.

Jason saw a tiny blue light flashing at the lower left corner of his field of vision, as his brain implant reported, for the second time in a day, nearby use of grav repulsion. And he knew—and he knew Enki knew—what that cracking sound was: air rushing in to fill a tunnel of vacuum burned through it by a weapon-grade laser.

The door through which they had entered was flung open, and Zan Zu ran into the court, her black hair flying.

"Adapa! Anu is here in his flying boat! And he is spitting lightning bolts! And—"

Another crack—closer and therefore louder—cut her off. A portion of the wall exploded inward with the violence of instantaneous energy transfer, showering them all with debris. The concussion sent them staggering. Zan Zu, who was closest to the blast, fell to her knees. Adapa and Allawi simultaneously rushed to help her. As they did, Uruk temple guards began clambering over the rubble of the wall.

Jason looked overhead. In the light of the fires that had broken out in Eridu, he could make out a craft—small, but with the somewhat arrowhead-shaped configuration typical of vessels equipped with negative mass drive. He could hear the characteristic hum of the grav repulsion on which it was maneuvering at low altitude.

*Anu's scout craft,* shot through Jason's mind. *Lugal must have had some kind of communicator, and sent word of where we were going to Anu, who summoned his boat down from orbit. And Lugal got the guards motivated again and led them here, approaching the town under cover of darkness.*

*All while we were playing tourist.*

A guard rushed at Zan Zu. Adapa, who was closer than Allawi, interposed himself.

Lugal appeared at the top of the rubble. He raised the "walking stick" he must have salvaged from the river. (*Designed to be water-tight,* was Jason's automatic thought.) A sparkling spear of ionized air impaled Adapa, who collapsed with a laser weapon's usual limited knockback effect, dead before he hit the floor.

Zan Zu screamed.

With the kind of sinuous motion of which his species was capable, Enki rose and prepared to dive into the pool.

Lugal brought his weapon around. There was another laser flash, and the water immediately in front of Enki exploded into steam. The Nagom, recognizing a warning shot, instantly went motionless.

While Lugal was thus distracted, Allawi floored the guard with a roundhouse kick, grabbed Zan Zu by the arm, and hauled her to her feet. Together, the two of them ran out the door through which she had entered.

Lugal didn't notice. He held his disguised laser carbine trained on Enki, Jason, and Jason's two remaining companions. "Do not resist," he commanded, as his guards closed in around them.

They didn't.

Allawi and Zan Zu emerged from the temple into a scene of fire-lit pandemonium, with people fleeing hysterically from beneath the "flying boat" that hovered overhead, seeking whatever shelter the town's mud-brick buildings afforded from the god's supernatural lightning bolts. The copper spearpoints of the guards Lugal has stationed in the temple's vicinity to keep the populace away were superfluous.

Zan Zu, Allawi thought, was moving with commendable purposefulness, considering that she had just watched Adapa die. He didn't doubt that the reality of it would catch up with her sooner or later. For now, though, she was keeping up with him.

"This way," he said. "We'll get back to the house of Adapa's family."

"No," she said. "My parents' house is closer." She took him by the hand and led him around a corner . . . where they found themselves face to face with one of Lugal's guards.

The guard was clearly in no mood to merely shoo them away. Recovering from his surprise, he thrust his spear at Allawi's midriff.

Allawi twisted aside barely in time, simultaneously shoving Zan Zu away and batting the spear-shaft aside. He lunged forward and tried to get a wrestling hold. In the awkward grappling, the guard dropped his spear. They fell to the ground, each struggling for a hold. The guard was an exceptionally big man for this era, stocky and strong, and at such close quarters Allawi had limited scope for using the unarmed combat techniques in which he was trained.

With a sudden, convulsive heave, the guard momentarily broke Allawi's clumsy grip and reached for the spear, seeking to grasp it just below the head and use it as a clumsy dagger.

Zan Zu kicked the spear with a sandaled foot, sending it spinning away.

The guard's desperate grab left one of Allawi's arms free. He raised it, and brought the elbow down against the guard's temple. The flexible leather helmet was inadequate protection. The guard went limp.

"Thanks!" Allawi gasped, getting to his feet and taking the girl's hand again. He let her lead the way through the nighttime labyrinth of Eridu, away from the fires and the hovering god-boat.

The house to which they came was a somewhat smaller version of the house of Adapa's extended family. People of both genders and various ages huddled together in the central chamber, moaning with terror and trying to quiet screaming infants. And elderly (by local standards) woman embraced Zan Zu with obvious relief.

"This is my aunt, Amytis," Zan Zu told Allawi after introducing him as the man who had helped her escape from the temple. "My mother died giving birth to me, and my father only survived her by a few years before being carried off by disease despite everything Enki's healers could do," she explained. The mention of Enki obviously brought back the reality of what she had seen in the violated temple, including the death of Adapa—a reality she had been holding at bay. But she was till in a state too closely resembling shock for tears to come. Her face remained expressionless as they found a corner of the crowded room and sat back against the wall. Hesitantly, he put an arm around her shoulders. At first she stiffened, but then nestled against his side and buried her face in his shoulder. Presently he could feel her trembling, and hear a muffled sound of weeping. He tried to comfort her wordlessly, for he did not trust himself to speak, fearing to let something slip that she must not be allowed to know.

*Well, at least Commander Thanou knows where I am,* he told himself. Then came the unwelcome mental qualifier, *assuming he's still alive.*

*I'll just have to trust to his well-known talent for survival.*

Anu's single-seat scout craft was of no use for hauling prisoners, and he departed forthwith for Uruk. But with the population of Eridu either fled or cowering in terror, Lugal had no trouble commandeering boats. The captives, securely bound and (in Enki's case) concealed under a rough tarpaulin, were loaded aboard and the voyage upriver began.

On Lugal's orders, the guards rebuffed any attempt to engage them in conversation. And they were notably nervous around Enki, frequently making certain surreptitious signs. Jason had to grudgingly admire Lugal's achievement in persuading these men to dare to capture a god. At the same time, they also showed a certain defiant swagger. *They probably expect to dine out on this story for the rest of their lives,* Jason surmised.

The trip took somewhat longer than it had to, for Lugal deliberately timed it so as to arrive at Uruk after dark. Clearly, he didn't want Enki to be seen, for he had the guards rig a kind of sling, with which they carried the thoroughly shrouded Nagom as they hustled the prisoners to Anu's temple. They were hastily conveyed to the subterranean cell where Jason and his companions had first been held. There they were immobilized as before.

Enki endured everything with silent stoicism, even though he had been continuously out of water for a longer time than his species preferred, and being tied upright to one of the copper rings was even more uncomfortable for him than for the humans. He said nothing to his companions, and their own conversation was limited by the necessity of concealing their true origin in his hearing. Shartava tried to be in character by bewailing their fate and imploring Enki to use his godlike powers in their behalf. But the Nagom's stony silence was unbroken.

Through it all, Jason had something to occupy his mind: his neural map display, and the red dot that showed the location of Ahmad Allawi's implanted TRD. He was still in Eridu, and therefore had avoided capture.

Jason couldn't let himself dwell on the fact that his own freedom of action had just become curtailed. Allawi was now outside the range within which Jason could activate his TRD. So for the present, at least, he could not flick himself, Mondrago and Shartava back to the twenty-fourth century without leaving the young Mithran stranded.

All of which assumed that the red dot didn't mark the resting place of Allawi's corpse.

# Chapter Twenty-Four

"Enki is dead!" moaned Ibi-ilishu, one of the leading men of Eridu, who were trying to organize things now that King Alulim had been badly wounded by the wrath of Anu and was not expected to live. The rest of the group in the partly ruined court of the aquifer wailed in sad accord.

"No!" Zan Zu's dark eyes flashed fire. Her relationship with Adapa apparently gave her a certain status despite her youth and gender, for these men listened when she spoke. "We never saw Enki die before we escaped."

"That's right," Allawi confirmed.

"And besides," the girl went on, "if he had been struck down by Anu's lightnings, his body would have been here, like . . ." For a moment, she could not go on. When they had returned to the temple, Adapa's laser-burned corpse had been there for her to weep over. But she lifted her head and resumed, pointing theatrically toward the pool. "*There* is where he must be! He has returned to the waters from whence he came, in a rage at the impiety of the men from Uruk who violated this, his temple."

"But that means he's abandoned us!" quavered Ur-engur, one of the eldest of this council of elders. "And we've lost Adapa."

"And now we're caught up in a war of the gods," added Libit-ninub, not as old but even more tremulous. "We're doomed!"

"We're *so* doomed!" echoed the others like a Greek chorus.

*No,* Allawi mentally corrected. *A Sumerian chorus.*

"Wait!" he said. They all turned their attention toward him—including Zan Zu, who had been glaring contemptuously at the Sumerian chorus. He had no status here, but apparently having rescued Zan Zu conferred some creds. And it is a universal constant of the human condition that sheer size makes one harder to ignore. He drew a deep breath. "I know I'm a foreigner among you. But hear my words. My companions were here—Enki was questioning us—when the attack came. And *their* bodies were not found here with Adapa's. So they must have been taken alive, and carried back to Uruk. And if *they* were, then perhaps Enki was as well."

The Sumerian chorus stared at him, openmouthed. Evidently, kidnapping a god was an even more shocking solecism than killing one.

"I have an obligation to try to help my friends," Allawi continued. "So I am going to Uruk. While I'm there, I'll also try to learn what has become of Enki."

Zan Zu met his eyes. (Hazel-green eyes, who had ever had heard of the like?) "So you truly believe Jason and the others still live?"

"I'm certain of it," he replied stoutly.

*Hell no, I'm not certain of it! But they'd better be. If Commander Thanou is dead, then I'm a permanent resident of Chalcolithic Mesopotamia.*

*Which I will be anyway, if I don't get within range of his "control" TRD.*

*The only good news,* he reminded himself anew, *is that, if he is alive, he knows where I am. And as everyone in Special Ops knows, he never, ever abandons a member of a team he leads.*

Zan Zu continued to look up at him and hold his eyes. "And you are willing to go looking for them in Uruk, even though you're known to Lugal and his guards, and easily recognized?"

"Yes, I am. I must."

"They breed *men* in those mountains you come from." Zan Zu nodded with a gravity beyond her years. "Very well. And I'm coming too."

"*What?*" blurted Allawi. "But . . . but the danger! Remember, Lugal knows you too." The Sumerian chorus was speechless.

"Yes, he does. But," she said with a smile, "I don't stand out in a crowd quite as much as you do. And as you say, you're a foreigner. You're going to need help in Uruk."

Which, Allawi reflected, was demonstrably true. Still . . . "No! I can't let you risk yourself."

"I have a right to come," she said, suddenly turning bleak. "I have a score to settle."

"Yes. I suppose you do." Allawi looked into her large dark eyes, which had recently been weeping for Adapa. Now those eyes held nothing but steadiness. He marveled at the high, fine courage contained, quivering, within her slight frame.

*If I do end up stranded here,* he found himself thinking, *there might be compensations.*

"All right," he heard himself say. "Let's go."

Periodically consulting his map display, Jason saw to his relief that Allawi still lived, for his TRD had departed Eridu and was moving steadily toward Uruk. He also frequently called up his neurally displayed digital clock. In the subterranean cell, there was no way to tell day from night, and time stretched like an eternity of miserable discomfort.

But Jason's computer implant told him that less time passed than seemed to before the door creaked open and, in a flare of torchlight, Anu entered with Lugal following deferentially behind.

At first Anu paid no attention to the three humans. Instead, he brought his face within a couple of feet of Enki's and smiled a gloating smile that failed to disguise the disgust and hate that underlay it.

"I was already fairly certain there were Nagommo at work here," he began, in the Sumerian they had in common. "The stories I heard of Eridu's god Enki and his kin resembled your nauseating species too closely for coincidence. But now I have confirmation. And so I believe I will change my plans. Instead of departing immediately to make my report and arrange for an expedition to come here and root you out, I will first remain a while longer and eradicate as many of you as possible myself."

"Thus making yourself look better in the eyes of your superiors," said Enki tonelessly.

*And allowing yourself to spend a little more time here playing god,* Jason mentally added.

"Precisely. But first there is one matter to attend to." The gloating was now in full force. "Tomorrow you will be displayed in front of this temple, for the inhabitants of Uruk to see. There you will be slowly and carefully flayed alive, before being sliced open and gutted. Thus the humans will see who their *true* gods are. It will solidify our authority, and rob you Nagommo of your support—which, in turn, will make it easier for me to hunt you down."

"One question, out of curiosity," said Enki, with more equanimity than a human could have managed under the circumstances. "Why did you go to the trouble of capturing these humans and bringing them back here? At first I thought it was because they were escaped prisoners of yours. But that didn't seem a good enough explanation. And now they seem strangely unsurprised by what you've been saying. From the first, I've been unable to rid myself of the feeling that they are somehow more than they seem."

"Oh, indeed they are!" Anu seemed hugely amused. "Didn't they tell you? They, like my servitor Lugal-tarah, come from this world's future. He and they are on opposite sides of some kind of time war."

Alien though Enki was, his stunned amazement was unmistakable. And a black tide of despair rose in Jason . . . until he recalled that Enki was scheduled to take his knowledge of time travel with him into death in the morning.

His relief at that thought was instantly followed by a spasm of self-disgust for having felt it.

"We never thought time travel was possible either," Anu allowed. "But now, thanks to Lugal, we know it is—and with his help we're going to experiment until we learn the secret. It's subject to limitations I don't fully understand, but still it should have military uses in our war to exterminate you Nagommo filth. A war, incidentally, which Lugal assures me that we are going to win. These others will also assist us before we kill them—which will be soon, since unlike Lugal they are to return to their own time at some not very distant date. Unfortunately, one of them escaped capture, but he can do no harm. In fact, I believe that as part of tomorrow's ceremony we'll soften them up a bit, just to make them more amenable to questioning." And on that note the Teloi departed.

Lugal started to follow him, then paused. He thrust his face close to Jason's and hissed in Standard International English. "Something I forgot to tell you earlier, Pug—something else to think about tonight. Before I was exiled they told me that they were going to send a second party back to 1978 Venice to correct our failure to steal the specifications for the chronovisor. They should arrive at that funny little monk's cell shortly after you left it; to him, it will seem like we've returned after an hour or so! So now you can die knowing you failed!" Without warning, he spat in Jason's face. Then he was gone, closing the door behind him.

There was a very long silence. Enki finally broke it.

"So what Lugal said, there by the river, was true. You are time travelers."

Jason felt neither the energy nor the inclination to lie. "Yes. I know it sounds impossible, given the paradoxes it would seem to allow for. Take my word that the 'limitations' Anu mentioned—we call them the *Observer Effect*—make those paradoxes impossible."

"Yes, I can see how it would have to be that way." Enki reflected a moment. "Anu indicated that you are scheduled to return to your point of origin at a fixed time. A pity you cannot do so at your own discretion." A flash of grim humor. "If so, perhaps you could take me with you!"

"No. I'm sorry. It doesn't work that way." *True as far as it goes,* Jason told himself. Admitting to what Enki already knew was one thing; volunteering additional information about time travel was quite another, however limited the Nagom's life expectancy might be.

After another pause, Enki spoke in a very different tone. "Where— or, I should say, *when*—do you come from?"

"Almost sixty-four hundred local years in the future."

"Anu said Lugal told him the Teloi are going to succeed in exterminating my race. You must know whether or not he is telling the truth." The Nagom's voice held a mixture of eagerness and apprehension.

By twisting as far to the left against his bonds as possible, Jason was able to meet Enki's eyes. He did so now, and spoke the same lie he had told—or was going to tell—Oannes in 1628 B.C. "No. In my era, we have no knowledge of your race. And we've never encountered the Teloi in our own time, only when traveling into the past. Lugal is just lying to please Anu." The last two sentences, at least, were true. And the rest was a kindness.

"I see." Jason couldn't be sure Enki believed him. But the Nagom said no more. (*Leaving well enough alone,* Jason surmised.) Silence descended again.

Time crawled. To take his mind off what was going to happen in the morning, he concentrated on keeping track of Allawi's TRD. The young Mithran was now nearing the outskirts of Uruk. But he was still well outside the extremely limited range of Jason's "control" TRD. And, he admitted to himself, Anu was right. What could Allawi do?

The clock built into Jason's brain told him it was nearing sunset when the door creaked open and once again their eyes were dazzled by torchlight. *Back to gloat some more?* thought Jason. But then their eyes adjusted. The figure holding the torch was crouching, as the Teloi had to do in the confines of the cell—but not crouching as low as Anu had.

It was Inanna.

For a moment the "goddess" simply looked them over, her strange Teloi eyes glowing in the torchlight. Then she abruptly addressed Enki.

"Nagom, are you aware of what is to happen to you in the morning?"

"Your partner Anu made it clear enough."

Inanna's thin lips curled in a remarkably humanlike sneer at the word *partner.* "How would you like to avoid being butchered?"

"I would not be averse to it."

"Then perhaps you would be interested in a proposal. I know there are other members of your ship's crew active in this part of the planet. So far, they have always kept a low profile, not wishing to call attention to their presence. But surely they want to rescue you. I can help, from the inside."

At first, Jason could hardly believe what he was hearing, for it flew in the face of everything he knew of the insensate hostility these two races nourished toward each other. Come to think of it, Inanna's whole aspect seemed to lack the sheer, concentrated loathing Anu had displayed in Enki's presence. But then he recalled the fragmented nature of Teloi culture, with its mutually unsympathetic subcultures. Inanna belonged to the *Oratioi'Zhonglu,* poles apart from Anu's

*Tuova'Zhonglu,* the race's fanatical vanguard against the Nagommo. Jason recalled something a turn-of-the-twenty-first-century North American acquaintance had said: "America is not at war; the Marine Corps is at war, America is at the mall." This might be a more extreme case of the same thing.

Enki seemed to take it in stride, for his reply was matter-of-fact. "Why would you wish to help me? What do you want in return?"

"I want your help in restoring me to my rightful place as supreme deity of the local humans, and ridding me of that insufferable *Tuova* martinet!" All at once, Inanna's long-pent-up resentment gushed forth. "I've been able to endure his pompous arrogance—barely— because it was only temporary. I kept telling myself he'd have to report back to his base. But he stayed on and on and on, brazenly usurping the *Oratioi'Zhonglu's* right to be worshipped by this slave race that we created! And now he's come up with a rationalization for lingering still longer. I don't think he *ever* intends to leave. I'll never be quit of him!"

"And if we reestablish you in Uruk, will you leave us unmolested in Eridu?"

"Yes, I suppose so," said Inanna with no particularly good grace.

"In that case, we may indeed be in a position to help each other. You have correctly surmised that there are others of us in this region. In fact, two of them are returning here even now. And although I am unable to communicate with them, they will be aware that I am in Uruk, and will deduce that I am a prisoner."

*An implanted tracking device,* thought Jason. *Like the ones incorporated in our TRDs. And, like them, purely passive. So he doesn't have any active bionics for my implant to detect.*

*And now I know why he's been so stoical. He's had hopes for a rescue mission all along.*

"The problem is this," Enki went on. "While we were able to salvage a certain number of auxiliary vehicles from our survey cruiser, none of them are specialized combat craft. We have nothing that is even close to being a match for Anu's scout vessel. Where is it, by the way? Has Anu sent it back into orbit?"

"No. He wants immediate access to it, so he can use it as part of tomorrow's ceremony. It's parked in the desert just outside Uruk. I'm no mechanic." Inanna's unspoken, supercilious *of course* might just as well have been audible. "But I believe I can disable its weaponry. I'll try to do the same to its controls."

"Good. I suggest you do so tonight. I have no way of knowing when my colleagues are going to make their attempt. But if they do not do so by morning, the question becomes academic."

"Very well." Inanna started to leave.

"Wait a moment!" said Jason. "We can help too."

For the first time, Inanna deigned to notice Enki's fellow prisoners. She gave Jason the kind of inspection she might have given something unpleasant in a plate of food. "What possible assistance can imprisoned feral humans offer?"

"You forget that one of my 'feral humans' is still at large out there. In fact, I have means of knowing his location. He's near the outskirts of Uruk, by the river to the southeast. I can't communicate with him, but I can tell you exactly where to find him. If you tell him what to expect, he can stand by to create a diversion or something."

"And what do you expect from me in return?"

"Our lives, for one thing. And your promise to always keep silent about time travel. But what we really want is the chance to contribute whatever we can to the killing of Anu . . . and Lugal."

"Ah, yes: Anu's slimy little sycophant." This seemed to make Jason more sympathetic in Inanna's eyes. "Very well. Agreed. Tell me where this friend of yours is."

Jason described the location in as much detail as his map display allowed. Inanna again turned to go. "Hey!" Mondrago called out, his voice ragged with hours of wretchedness. "Aren't you going to cut us loose?"

Inanna had clearly not thought of this. But she had a ceremonial obsidian dagger—perhaps an appurtenance of goddesshood—in her girdle. With great effort she cut the rope holding Enki's wrists to the copper ring. He collapsed to the floor, rubbing feeling back into his hands.

Inanna offhandedly tossed the dagger down on the floor beside him. "You may free them if you see fit." Then she was gone.

"Nice lady," Shartava commented drily.

"Still and all," said Mondrago, "for the first time ever, I feel an urge to kiss a Teloi."

Jason said nothing. As Enki started sawing at his rope, he met the

Nagom's eyes. It occurred to him that, if there really was a chance of them getting out of this, it also meant there was a chance that Enki— and his knowledge of time travel—might survive.

*Well,* he philosophized, *you've got to take the bad with the good.*

Once again, he wasn't especially proud of himself for the thought.

# Chapter Twenty-Five

Ahmad Allawi squinted into the setting sun as he peered across the expanse of cultivated flatlands at Uruk.

He and Zan Zu lay prone on a low ridge (the only kind of ridge that existed in this region) just downriver from the town, concealing themselves in a palm grove with the Euphrates just to their right. The ridge marked a break in the checkerboard of tiny, irrigated farm plots, so they had chosen it to pause and take shelter from the late-afternoon heat. Now the farmers were departing their fields, and soon they would risk their final approach to Uruk.

Zan Zu pointed ahead and slightly to the right, where Uruk thinned out toward the riverside, outside the low wall. "After dark, we can sneak in along the river and seek shelter at Utu's hut."

"Utu? Would that be the old man who hid us before?"

"Yes. He's been a boatman on the river for years, sometimes going as far as Eridu. Once he was sick, and Adapa was able to help him with some of the wisdom he'd learned from Enki. So ever since he's considered himself in the debt of Adapa and Adapa's friends." She paused, and her expression grew pensive in the twilight. This was the first time she had mentioned Adapa since they had departed from Eridu, and Allawi had carefully avoided the subject.

Now he found he could no longer do so.

"You loved Adapa, didn't you?"

He had anticipated any of several possible reactions to his question. None of them came. Instead, there was a long pause before she replied.

"Like everyone else, I respected him greatly as the chosen one of Enki. People always looked up to him even before Enki picked him as his messenger, to bring new arts to Eridu."

Which, Allawi thought, was a somewhat oblique answer. "But did you love him?"

"I felt great affection for him," she insisted, a little defensively, not meeting Allawi's eyes. But then she subsided and spoke as much to herself as to Allawi. "Whenever I thought of the two of us, I imagined him on a pedestal. It's not easy to get very close to someone on a pedestal. He could never for a moment forget the great mission that Enki had entrusted to him. It made him different from all other men . . . different and somehow strange." She turned her head to face Allawi and smiled. "There's a strangeness about you too. A different kind of strangeness. But it's there."

"Well . . . er, I'm a foreigner, so naturally—"

"No, there's more to it than that. Somehow, you seem a foreigner not just to this land but to everything I know and understand. I still can't put Lugal-tarah's strange words out of my mind."

A chill stabbed Allawi's heart, and he tried to keep his voice casual. "Oh, he's mad. Pay no attention to his nonsense."

"Still . . ." She turned very serious. "You're not like Adapa, who was the instrument of a god. But it's as though you're serving something larger than yourself—something larger than I can imagine." There was still enough light to see that her eyes held a question, and a plea for candor.

*She must* not *be allowed to know,* Allawi told himself sternly. *I must not lay the doom of the Observer Effect on her.*

*So change the subject fast, dummy!*

"Er . . . I only want to rescue my friends—and, of course, serve Enki, who was kind to us. Do you think Enki's kin will aid us?"

"I'm sure of it." Zan Zu's voice held sublime certainty.

"I hope you're right. But how will they know where we are?"

"Oh, they'll know." The girl's eyes suddenly twinkled mischievously. She reached inside her tunic and pulled out something hanging from a string around her neck.

In the twilight, it took a moment for Allawi to recognize Adapa's amulet.

"I took it while no one was looking, before they carried his body away," she said matter-of-factly. "Enki gave it to Adapa to mark him as the chosen one. So I know I have no right to it, and I'll have to ask Enki's forgiveness. But Enki also told Adapa that he would always be able to find him as long as he was wearing it, and thereby be able to come to his aid. Surely Enki's kindred gods have the same magical powers, and can find whoever wears it."

"Yes," said Allawi slowly. "I think they very well might."

*Enki doesn't have a bionic implant that can detect this tracking device,* he thought. *Commander Thanou would have detected it. So he must do it by means of instrumentation in that submersible grav raft of his—which, as far as I know, is still in the aquifer. Therefore, the other Nagommo currently in this area ought to be able to use it.*

*So I'd better hope they* are *currently in this area.*

"Then perhaps we really can hope for assistance from the gods," he continued, in what he hoped was the right tone of reverence. "But we shouldn't rely on it. We should proceed as though all depended on us. My people have a saying, 'The gods help those who help themselves.'"

"Very wise, Ahmad. Sometime, you must tell me about the land you come from. I'm sure it would all seem very strange to me."

"You have *no* idea," he said with feeling.

"I want to know about it. I want to know about its people. There are so many things I want to know."

He became aware that, without apparent intention, they had worked their way closer together each other, and were now lying on their sides, facing each other. Their faces were now very close indeed.

Moving as though by its own volition, and in defiance of all his good resolutions, his hand reached out and brushed her hair away from her face. Her eyes closed, and she smiled.

The sun vanished below the western horizon and the stars began to abruptly appear in their multitudes. The moonlight was sufficient to see—but, Allawi hoped, not sufficient to be seen—by. It should be dark enough in a few minutes. "Ahem! I suppose we'll need to get moving soon."

"Yes," Zan Zu said softly. Her eyes remained closed. "Soon."

Their lips touched tentatively.

"Soon," she repeated. "But not just yet."

He took her in his arms. Their kiss lasted and lasted.

Then, to their right, a sound of disturbed water came from the river.

With a small cry, Zan Zu broke free of Allawi's arms and scrambled to her knees. Her dark eyes grew huge in the moonlight as the surface water flowed away in all directions and a large oblong hole appeared in the river.

*They've got their refraction field on,* thought Allawi as rivulets of water ran down the sides of the invisible grav raft, defining its shape as it rose to the surface.

A rectangle of light appeared in midair over the river as the side hatch slid aside, leaving an opening in the field. A Nagom emerged through the hatch, seemingly from thin air, and stepped into the shallows, clad only in a kind of harness from which hung various items of equipment, including what Allawi thought had the look of a laser pistol. A second Nagom appeared, silhouetted against the craft's interior light.

It was too much for Zan Zu. With a soft moan, she genuflected, hiding her face between her arms. Allawi decided he'd better do the same.

The first Nagom halted, as though puzzled. "I am Ninhursanga, consort of Enki. Where is Adapa?"

"He is dead, great Ninhursanga," said Zan Zu, raising her head just enough to look up. "Anu's high priest Lugal-tarah, wielding Anu's lightnings, killed him when he and his guards stormed Enki's temple, with Anu himself hurling greater lightnings from his flying boat above."

Ninhursanga stepped ashore, followed by her companion. (Allawi decided to think of this particular Nagom as female, in keeping with the assumed role of "consort.") She stood over Zan Zu. "But who are you?"

"I am only Zan Zu. I know I have no right to be wearing the amulet Enki bestowed on Adapa, and I beg your forgiveness. But it was through its magic that Enki was always able to find Adapa in times of need. And I was not able to ask Enki's permission, because no one knows what became of him after the attack."

"Then why are you here?"

Zan Zu indicated Allawi. "Ahmad, a traveler from the mountains to the north, seeks to rescue companions of his who he believes were taken from the E-Abzu temple and brought here to Uruk. He thinks Enki may also be here, imprisoned by Anu."

Ninhursanga turned her gaze on Allawi. *Commander Thanou could probably interpret Nagommo facial expressions, from his experience with Oannes,* thought Allawi as he looked up and met those alien eyes. *I can't. But I could swear she's giving me a very shrewd once-over. Is it possible that the Nagommo have been on Earth long enough to be able to recognize ethnic differences among humans?*

"Ahmad is right," the Ninhursanga stated abruptly. "Enki is indeed in Anu's temple."

"By means of certain powers, we can divine each other's location." Zan Zu inclined her head respectfully at the mention of the supernatural. "That is why I have come here with my nephew Oannes."

*Junior officer,* Allawi mentally translated "nephew," as he stared at the second Nagom. He didn't know the indicia of age among the Nagommo, but Oannes had to be young, for he would still be alive almost twenty-four centuries from this night, the last of the shipwrecked crew of his long-lived race left on Earth—and probably the last member of that race in the universe. And he would meet Jason Thanou . . . for the first time.

*Well, he won't be meeting* me *in 1628 B.C.,* Allawi assured himself. *Therefore, so far so good with the Observer Effect.*

Zan Zu's eyes were alight with joy. "Then, great Ninhursanga, you can use your magic lightnings to rescue your consort Enki!"

"We can try. But I must tell you that our lightnings are not as powerful as those Anu can wield from his great flying boat."

*Uh-huh,* thought Allawi dourly. *This utility grav raft may have various bells and whistles like submersible capability and a refraction field, but its airborne performance is a joke and it's unarmed. Anu's scout craft would eat it alive. All they're got are hand-held weapons.*

He decided to risk speaking up. "Great Ninhursanga, you may not be able to attack Anu directly. But if—as I believe—my friends are also held captive in Anu's temple, perhaps we can help. If you could use your magical invisibility to enable me and Zan Zu to . . ." He found himself at a loss for a Sumerian word for *infiltrate.*

But Ninhursanga seemed to grasp the point without it. "Yes. Perhaps we can help each other."

"Perhaps we *all* can," came a new voice.

Ninhursanga and Oannes whirled in the direction of the sound with the seemingly boneless sinuousness of their species, simultaneously drawing their laser pistols. Allawi leaped to his feet, his hand going instinctively to the hilt of the copper dagger he had brought from Eridu, and stared in the same direction.

He had viewed recorder-implant imagery from Commander Thanou's expedition to the Aegean Bronze Age. So he had seen the kind of grav platforms used as flying chariots by the Teloi "gods" among the Achaeans (although of course no one would think of them that way in this era, which lacked chariots or any other sort of wheeled vehicles). They were graceful but somehow overelaborate in accordance with the vaguely Art Deco-like aesthetic precepts of the *Oratioi'Zhonglu*. Now he saw one at first hand, floating a yard or so above the ground with a practically inaudible hum. And seated on it was a Teloi he recognized as Inanna.

*She must have come from the town with the lights off and the grav repulsion powered down, so no one noticed her,* raced through Alawi's mind. *But how did she know to come to this particular place?*

Zan Zu choked off a muffled scream.

Inanna addressed the two Nagommo, her empty hands raised in the light from the moon and the open hatch. "I am unarmed. Put away your weapons. I come from Enki. And also," she added, turning to Allawi with what seemed an oddly amused look, "from your friends, who are imprisoned with him. Their leader told me you were here."

*So that's how she knew where to find me,* thought Allawi, commanding himself not to go weak at the knees with relief that the Commander still lived.

Out of the corner of his eye, he saw Zan Zu stiffen. Even at this moment, he decided, she must be wondering just exactly how his compatriots could possibly know where he was.

"How did you know *we* would be here?" demanded Ninhursanga. Neither she nor Oannes had lowered their laser pistols.

"I didn't. It was pure chance. *She* must be the key." Inanna pointed at Zan Zu. "You must have known her location, as I knew his. The fact that they are in each other's company brought us all together. Very fortuitous. You see, Enki and I have reached an understanding."

"An understanding?" The obviousness of Ninhursanga's skepticism transcended species and cultures.

"Make no mistake: I have no more affection for you than you do for me. But we can agree on this: Anu has overstepped his bounds, first by usurping my place in Uruk and now by assaulting a fellow god. In exchange for his guarantee that I will be supreme in Uruk, I promised to help you rescue him."

"And leave him as supreme god of Eridu?" Ninhursanga slowly lowered her laser pistol.

"Yes. That is the pact."

*They're both phrasing it this way for the benefit of the natives,* Allawi thought. But then Inanna flashed him a smirk of cynical irony. And a chill ran through him as recollection came. *She knows. Lugal told her and Anu about us.*

But, he told himself, Inanna was keeping up the pretense in the hearing of Zan Zu, who lay, wide-eyed and open-mouthed, listening to this conclave of gods. Which, of necessity, meant she also had to keep it up within the hearing of Ninhursanga and Oannes. *So with any luck she'll continue doing so, and not let anything slip about time travel. And if Commander Thanou told her where I am, he must be in on this little anti-Anu conspiracy.*

"I have agreed," Inanna was telling Ninhursanga, "to . . . work a spell cancelling the lightnings on Anu's great flying boat." (Another amused side-glance at Allawi.) "So you, with your trick of invisibility, should be able to get into Uruk and use your lesser lightnings to attack the temple."

"Good. How long will it take you to . . . work your spell?"

"I don't know. To be safe, you should wait as long as possible. Time your raid for just before dawn."

"Very well. Let us . . . contemplate it."

"Good idea." Inanna stepped off her grav platform. She and the Nagom huddled, synchronizing their respective timepieces. It occurred to Allawi that the interspecies cooperation he was witnessing was historically unique, with the possible exception of the Oannes/Zeus link-up engineered by Commander Thanou in 1628 B.C.

"Great Inanna," he spoke up, "I beg you: take me into Uruk on your wondrous . . . flying sledge, and help us enter the temple. I'll alert Enki and my friends to your plan." He recalled reading that while the Teloi grav platforms were single-seat they had a certain amount of additional carrying capacity.

Zan Zu swallowed hard, got to her feet, and stood beside him. "Take me also," she said with a steadiness that amazed Allawi, considering that she faced the prospect of riding a flying vehicle. The fact that it belonged to one she regarded as an evil false god must, he thought, make the prospect even more alarming. But she did not tremble.

*Having her in there with us could make things awkward,* he thought. *We'll have to watch what we say around her.*

*But . . . do I really want to leave her out here, in danger without me?*

"Yes, take the girl too," he heard himself say. And he felt her hand clasp his.

Inanna considered. "Your leader Jason spoke of leaving you to act from outside. But now Ninhursanga and Oannes are going to be doing that . . . and I believe I can carry the two of you. Very well." She seated herself. "Get on the floor."

They arranged themselves beside Inanna's feet. As the platform rose—a little sluggishly, Allawi thought—Zan Zu's eyes grew huge, and she clutched his hand more tightly. A gasp escaped her as they swooped away toward Uruk.

# Chapter Twenty-Six

In an age without artificial light, practically no one in Uruk was up and about at night. Even without benefit of a refraction field, Inanna's nearly silent "sledge" slid unobserved through Uruk, flying slowly and cautiously by moonlight, to the square at the foot of Anu's temple.

Two drowsy guards sat at the top of the ramp, backs propped against the base of the temple. As the supernatural vehicle rose before them and shone its clearly supernatural running lights in their faces, they scrambled upright and immediately went to their knees, foreheads almost touching the ground.

"You are no longer required here tonight," Inanna intoned in her eerie alien voice. "Go. And tell no one of my command, on pain of death."

One guard dared to raise his head. "But great goddess, the high priest said—"

"I said go!"

The guards needed no further urging. They scuttled away. Allawi and Zan Zu got up from concealment behind the grav platform's curving façade. Inanna again switched off the running lights. "I go now to deal with Anu's flying boat. Your companions are in the same cell as before, and Enki is with them. It is unlocked. Tell them when to expect Ninhursanga and Oannes to act. And in the meantime, act with caution in there. We don't know when or how often the guard is changed, but sooner or later others will arrive, and they probably inspect the lower levels." With its almost inaudible hum, the platform swung away and glided off into the night.

Very cautiously, the two entered the temple. No one was about, at least in the immediate vicinity of the entrance. Anu and Lugal must, Allawi decided, be elsewhere. They turned right and descended the flight of steps into the dungeon level. The corridor was empty of guards—apparently, no need for them was felt. It was also illuminated by only a single torch in a sconce. Allawi took it and they proceeded to the remembered door. As promised, it was unsecured.

Jason had been following the red dot of Allawi's TRD as it zoomed into Uruk at a speed that could only be accounted for by a Teloi grav platform, and fretting over why Inanna was bringing the young Mithran back into the belly of the beast. Even at the highest magnification of his map display, that red dot eventually came almost into contact with the two representing Mondrago and Shartava. So he was prepared when the door swung open and the cell's dimness was illuminated by torchlight.

What he was not prepared for was the diminutive form of Zan Zu at Allawi's side.

*A complicating factor,* he thought sourly. Enki's knowledge of the truth about the time travelers had at least had the virtue of simplifying things. Now they would have to go back to being circumspect. He only hoped the Nagom would understand what was going on, and play along, without having it explained to him.

"Sir, are you all right?"

"We're fine, Ahmad—thanks to the goddess Inanna." Jason added the last part heavily, as a hint to keep up the subterfuge.

"Yes, she told us you were here, with the great god Enki." Allawi solemnly inclined his head toward the Nagom.

Jason gave Enki—whose expression he could not read—a side glance, and indicated Zan Zu with a jerk of his chin. His meaning apparently came across, for Enki held his peace.

Zan Zu went to her knees. "Great Enki, your people in Eridu are in the depths of despair at your absence. But help is at hand. Your consort Ninhursanga and her nephew Oannes are outside Uruk in your invisible boat. They plan to loose their lightnings on Anu just before dawn. We will free you from your captivity and defeat this false god!"

*All right, that explains why Inanna brought Ahmad back,* thought Jason. *We don't need him on the outside—we've got help from that direction. And now, thanks to him, we know when we can expect the Nagommo to attack, so we can coordinate.*

*It's still too bad she had to bring Zan Zu back as well.*

But then he looked at the girl's face—full of respect as it gazed at the being her people worshipped as a god, but without fear, even though she had just offered to plunge into what was, by her lights, a war of the gods.

*There is a Power in her,* he thought. *I can feel it. I don't understand it. But it frightens me, because I know I can't control it and we're now at the crux of events that could potentially affect the structure of reality itself. Bad enough that Enki knows what he now knows.*

Zan Zu's brow furrowed as she turned to practicalities. "Lord Enki, it will be difficult for us to know exactly when to be ready, here beneath the ground."

Jason spoke up before Enki could, once again, shooting the Nagom what he hoped would be recognized as a warning look. "We will know when that time arrives. Enki has bestowed upon me an ability to know the time without seeing the sun and moon and stars." Zan Zu looked awestruck that he should have been so favored by a god. Jason had a sudden inspiration. "In fact, this means we can get some rest while we can; I'll give the alert. Zan Zu, you must be fatigued after your journey from Eridu."

She blinked, as though remembering her exhaustion after all the extraordinary experiences she had undergone in the last hour. "Well, yes, I *am* a little tired . . ."

"Lie down in the corner here and get some sleep," Jason urged. "I'll wake you."

Allawi added his voice. "Go ahead, Zan Zu. You'll be all right, I'll keep watch." Their eyes met, and they shared a smile that was difficult to misinterpret.

*Hmm . . . we just may have a problem here,* Jason thought morosely.

"All right." Zan Zu curled up in the indicated corner.

"Alexandre . . . Irma," said Jason, "keep your ears to the door in case any guards come around." He motioned Allawi and Enki to sit with him against the wall opposite Zan Zu as though composing themselves for rest. They waited until the girl's breathing grew regular, then huddled together.

"All right," Jason murmured. "I think she's asleep." He decided there were more immediate concerns than lecturing Allawi about the Service's strict and eminently sensible policy against its personnel forming emotional attachments with people of the past. "First of all, Ahmad, Enki here knows the truth about our being time travelers. Anu revealed it to him."

Allawi swallowed hard but merely nodded. He gave Enki a look that Jason hoped the Nagom would not interpret correctly. *Ahmad understands the potentially ugly Observer Effect implications as well as I do. And he also understands the inadvisability of talking about them in Enki's presence.*

"Now, about Ninhursanga and Oannes. You didn't—?"

"No, sir! As far as they're concerned, I'm nothing more than what our cover story says I am. I didn't reveal anything about time travel to them."

"Or to Zan Zu?" queried Jason with a slight smile.

"Of *course* not, sir!"

Enki spoke up with a diffidence that Jason knew full well was deceptive. "I must own to a certain curiosity about why you are so concerned with concealing the fact that you are time travelers from my colleagues—especially inasmuch as I myself am now aware of it. Could it have anything to do with that *Observer Effect* you mentioned earlier but never really explained?"

*Why do the Nagommo always have to be so goddamned sharp?* Jason moaned inwardly.

He decided that, when dealing with this being, he'd better not lie outright. Half-truths, on the other hand . . . "I told you that the *Observer Effect* precludes any of the paradoxes time travel would seem to permit. And we believe that to be true. But we prefer not to take anything for granted. That's why we're very cautious and circumspect. The fewer who know that we're from the future, the—"

"So it *is* true!"

The new voice seemed to congeal the very air of the cell. Slowly, Jason turned to face Zan Zu, who had half-raised herself from the floor and was staring at them. Her face was frozen.

*I guess she wasn't quite asleep after all,* Jason thought, seeking momentary refuge in banality. And he belatedly realized that, partly because it was the only language they had in common with Enki and partly out of sheer habit, they had been speaking in Sumerian.

In less than a heartbeat, a recollection flashed through his mind— a story Mondrago had told him when they had been in the Athenian camp in the days leading up to the battle of Marathon. Mondrago had made a friend, Myron son of Epilycos, among his fellow *ekdromoi* or light-armed troops. Somehow, Myron must have overheard the two of them talking, and interpreted what he had heard as meaning that his friend Alexander could foretell the future. He had also understood just enough about the Observer Effect to believe himself under a curse for having heard forbidden things. And he had proven to be right, for the following day, just as he was confronting Mondrago with his knowledge, he had been killed in a skirmish with Persian foragers. Yes, truly the doom of the Observer Effect had been on him. As always, reality had protected itself, showing no pity.

*I wonder how reality is going to protect itself this time,* thought Jason miserably, looking into those dark young eyes that now held knowledge which could not be permitted.

He grew aware that Mondrago and Shartava had turned from the door and were regarding Zan Zu. Mondrago turned and met Jason's eyes. His look was somber. The Corsican, as Jason knew, could make it painless. And Mondrago knew that he knew.

Allawi looked from Jason to Mondrago and back, his eyes full of desperation.

*I have one certainty that I can—and must—cling to,* Jason told himself firmly. *The Special Operations Section of the Temporal Service is not an assassins' guild. And it never will be one as long as I'm in charge of it.*

He broke the silence, because someone had to. "Yes, Zan Zu. We're from your future—far in your future. I won't try to explain how. I'll only tell you that we're not gods."

The girl looked at Enki, trembling. Her voice was haunted. "Are you also from the future . . . and no god?"

"No. I am of this time. I and my fellows come from the stars. And while we have powers your people do not yet possess, and live a very long time, we are mortal. The same is true of the Teloi—those you know as the Annunaki. I have told you they are not true gods, and that is the truth. They did create the human race, as they claim. But they created it only to serve and worship them."

From somewhere, a quotation came into Jason's mind. "Our people have a story in which a god, urged to create a hero, laments, 'I can only make slaves. A free man must create himself.' But Enki's people—the Nagommo—are trying to enable you of Eridu create yourselves as a great people, and help set your feet on the path that will someday lead to freedom from the Teloi."

"That is right," Enki affirmed. "We have no wish to play god. We have so presented ourselves to your people, simply because that was the only way you would be able to understand and accept our powers, and learn from us."

Zan Zu had ceased to tremble. She addressed Enki with a gravity beyond her years. "You and the Annunaki—the Teloi—must be enemies."

"We are. And Anu belongs to another, more powerful group among them. He plans to return to his kind and send more of them here, to wipe out us Nagommo and bring great grief to this world. That is why we have agreed to help Inanna. Anu must be destroyed."

"Yes, he must." Zan Zu rose to her feet and surveyed them all, one by one. And for all her youth and tininess, she seemed to dominate the scene. Again, she spoke to Enki. "You say you are not really a god. But if all the things you have taught us do not make you a god, I do not know what a god is. The Teloi are demons, not gods. Let us stand together against them." She looked around and met, and held, each of their eyes in turn.

*Yes,* thought Jason, suddenly aware that his mouth was hanging open. *I was right. There is a Power in her.*

But then her eyes met Allawi's, and she smiled and was, for an instant, girlish again.

# Chapter Twenty-Seven

The night crawled.

Watching the minutes and hours tick away on his neutrally projected digital clock, Jason stewed over his inability to know, except approximately, what time dawn would break. Not knowing just exactly how long before that Ninhursanga and Oannes would make their move added another dimension of uncertainty.

While they waited, they spent their time making contingency plans and taking turns pressing their ears to the door.

Jason was telling himself that it must be nearly dawn when Shartava, currently on guard duty at the door, gave a warning gesture.

They immediately fell into their prearranged places. Jason, Mondrago, Shartava and Enki stood up against the rear wall and held up their arms as though their wrists were still tied to the copper rings. Enki, whose wrists were as flexible as the rest of him, held Inanna's ceremonial dagger concealed. Allawi and Zan Zu, who weren't supposed to be there, flattened their backs against the wall to the right and left sides of the door respectively.

There was a stamping of feet and a clatter of accoutrements, and the door swung open. Two spear-carrying guards entered from the passageway, blinking as their eyes adjusted to the greater dimness within. They stepped forward, not thinking to look behind them.

With a quick, economical movement, Allawi clamped an arm

around the neck of the right-hand guard from behind, forcing his head back, and with his other arm slashed his throat across with the copper knife he had brought from Eridu.

At the same instant, Zan Zu sprang forward onto the other guard's back and clung, wrapping her arms around his neck and her legs around his waist. He threw himself backwards, slamming her into the wall. She gasped but hung on. Before he could fling her off, Enki lunged forward in his almost otterlike way. He must, thought Jason, have learned something of human anatomy; he plunged the obsidian dagger into the guard's midriff below the rib cage, and then up.

Jason and Mondrago scooped up the spears dropped by the guards. Allawi helped Zan Zu extricate herself from beneath the gutted guard. Despite having had the wind knocked out of her, she steadied quickly in his arms. "All right," Jason snapped. "Let's go."

They exited into the corridor, turned to the left . . . and stopped dead, for between them and the steps leading upward were several guards, led by Lugal.

The guards looked somewhat apprehensive at facing a god who was free and armed—but not quite as apprehensive as Jason would have expected. He immediately saw why: they had supernatural powers on their side. Lugal raised the "walking stick" that spat forth the lightnings of the gods, and aimed it at Jason. His face wore a leer of insane glee.

Suddenly, noise erupted from above: panic-stricken shouts and other less easily identifiable sounds. Startled, Lugal instinctively looked upward. The motion exposed his throat.

In the course of his career, Jason had become proficient with a variety of low-tech weapons—including javelins. The short spear he was carrying wasn't really intended as one. But it would do. He grasped it underhand, leaned back, and with a single fluid motion hurled it. It transfixed Lugal's throat. The exiled Transhumanist's scream instantly turned into a gurgle, and blood flew from his mouth. The "walking stick" clattered to the floor. With a perfect sense of timing, Enki surged forward.

It was too much for the guards. Screaming, they turned and fled, some of them dropping their spears.

"After them!" yelled Jason, running forward and retrieving the disguised laser carbine.

The guards were crowding into the short stairwell when they caught up with them. One of them, less incapacitated by panic than the rest, turned and thrust his spear (which he, at least, hadn't dropped) at Jason, who couldn't bring his laser weapon to bear in the press. Jason twisted aside, barely avoiding the copper spearpoint. The guard drew back and began to thrust again. As he did, Zan Zu sprang up from below, plunging a spear she had grabbed into his gut. He barely had time to scream before Shartava, who had also armed herself with a dropped spear, finished him with a hard stab from behind to the base of the neck.

By this time the remaining guards had ascended the steps, rushed through the entrance chamber, and were emerging onto the terrace atop the temple mound. Leading the rush after them, Jason heard the *crack!* of a weapon-grade laser in atmosphere. It repeated several times, and one by one the guards fell.

*It's the Nagommo!* thought Jason. "Enki, you'd better go in front. They won't shoot at you."

As they came through the temple door with Enki in the lead, Jason swiftly took in the scene, illuminated by the first rays of dawn to the east. Uruk seemed deserted although a low sound of moaning or wailing rose from the mud-brick town whose inhabitants must be cowering indoors. The Nagommo grav raft, not bothering with invisibility, rested on the terrace amid a litter of bodies. A Nagom stood before it, holding what looked like a laser pistol.

"Ninhursanga!" Enki called out. He gestured at the humans following him and said a few words in his own language which Jason assumed boiled down to *Don't shoot, these are friends!* He could only hope that Enki wasn't revealing anything about the origin of those friends.

The Nagom replied in the same language. He pointed at the grav raft and uttered one word Jason recognized. "Oannes."

*Oannes,* thought Jason bleakly. *He must be inside at the controls, ready for departure.* He'd had other things on his mind, but that name reminded him of the Observer Effect tangle in which he was already enmeshed. *He mustn't be allowed to see me . . .*

Then all such considerations were abruptly driven from his mind as the little light that indicated nearby use of grav repulsion began to blink at the fringe of his field of vision.

From behind the temple, a great metallic shape like a thick, blunt arrowhead rose with a humming sound. Anu's scout craft was quite small as interstellar spacecraft went, but at this extremely low altitude it sufficed to block out a good portion of the sky.

Zan Zu sank to her knees. For the first time in Jason's experience her face wore a look of something like despair.

And on the roof of the temple stood Anu, decked out in what must be his space-service kit, silhouetted against the backdrop of the killing machine he had summoned.

*Summoned it with his implant communicator, linked to the ship's AI,* Jason thought. It was the sort of thing that was well within the technological capacity of twenty-fourth century humanity, but forbidden by the Human Integrity Act. He had never succeeded in persuading the mossbacks of the Authority to seek a special exemption for it, however useful the ability to communicate with fellow members of extratemporal expeditions at long range would often have been.

And as he watched, the vessel dropped even lower and moved directly over them, and its ventral weapon turret began to swivel toward them.

*Another wrinkle,* Jason thought, oddly calm because there wasn't a damned thing he could do about it with his pathetic little laser carbine. There wasn't even any point in running. *He can also control the weapons the same way. The boat's brain must be able to remotely project a neural HUD through the communicator; he is, in effect, seeing through the weapon's sights, and communicating commands to it.*

The turret finished swiveling. The snout of the laser pointed directly at the unarmed Nagommo grav raft . . .

And nothing happened.

"Inanna did it!" Mondrago whooped. "Goddamned if she didn't do it!" Zan Zu's look was uncomprehending, but exultation began to dawn in her eyes.

Jason looked up at the roof. He couldn't make out Anu's facial expression, but the Teloi was visibly agitated.

"And now, you miserable son of a bitch . . ." he said quietly, and started to bring his "walking stick" into line . . . only to lower it quickly, remembering that Ninhursanga mustn't see that he knew how to use such things, or even that he possessed them.

He was still thinking about it when Anu suddenly rose aloft and began to drift slowly through the air toward the scout craft. Zan Zu gasped.

*Tractor beam,* thought Jason, instantly recognizing that remotely focused application of artificial gravity. Anu must have communicated a command to the AI to pick him up and bring him aboard. In confirmation, a hatch began to slide open in the craft's side.

Ninhursanga uttered what sounded to Jason like a Nagommo curse and fired her laser pistol at Anu, now coming overhead. At this range, a weapon that struck at lightspeed couldn't miss. But the crackling beam of ionized air stopped and dissipated just short of its target. The light-duty vac suit Anu was wearing must, Jason thought, incorporate a small generator for a magnetic field, and include an extremely thin layer of thermal-superconducting material, like many twenty-fourth century human models. In addition to their primary purpose of deflecting charged particle radiation, these countermeasures also had a certain ability to neutralize coherent energy. The suit wouldn't have done any good if struck by a weapon-grade laser of any power. But against Ninhursanga's popgun, it sufficed. *It probably would have sufficed against my "walking stick" too,* Jason realized.

Enki, standing at Jason's side, spoke as though to himself—but in Sumerian, in accordance with years of habit. "He must *not* escape!" Before Jason realized what he was up to, he squatted on his webbed feet, bunching his legs under him. And as Anu floated directly overhead, he jumped.

Jason had always noted that Nagommo legs looked very muscular—hardly surprising, given the requirements of underwater locomotion. But he had never known the species was capable of spectacular standing high jumps. Or, he reflected, perhaps it was a case of desperate determination calling forth an extraordinary effort on Enki's part. But however he managed it, the Nagom caught Anu by the legs and grappled with him.

With a nonverbal roar of rage, Anu fought back. The two aliens thrashed furiously in midair, struggling against each other and the invisible, nonmaterial force that held them in its rubbery but unbreakable grip. As they did so, the scout boat's AI, with no orders to the contrary, continued to reel Anu in.

The wrestling figures vanished into the hatch, which slid shut. For a moment, nothing occurred to suggest to the watchers below what was transpiring inside.

Then the scout craft began to wobble and lunge about. *Did Inanna succeed in sabotaging the avionics?* Jason wondered. *Or is it the fight for control going on within?* As he watched, the craft skidded sideways, its prow colliding with the upper parts of the temple with a crash and a rain of rubble. Then it swung away, turned on its longitudinal axis, and swept away over the flat fields that the rising sun was beginning to illuminate.

Looking out over the reed- thatched roofs of Uruk, they watched as the craft flew on its side, perpendicular to the ground. Then one of the twin nacelles of its drive made contact with the surface, plowing a monstrous furrow in the field before being ripped off in a shower of flame. The scout craft cartwheeled several times before crashing and exploding with a roar that shook Uruk to its foundations.

For a long moment they all stared at the flames that, Jason knew, were consuming the bodies of two beings whom the Observer Effect had not permitted to live, because of the knowledge they had possessed. Ninhursanga lowered her head in a surprisingly human gesture of grief. Then Jason noticed Inanna, who had emerged from the temple where she had been hiding. She was looking out at that funeral pyre with a small, tight, satisfied smile.

*There's still her,* Jason reminded himself. *Her, and Zan Zu.*

The hatch of the grav raft opened. A Nagommo head emerged.

Jason slipped behind Allawi and spoke in an undertone, in Standard International English. "Ahmad, I've got to get inside. Oannes mustn't see me. I know you won't spill the truth about us to him or Ninhursanga. Make sure Zan Zu doesn't either."

And he made his inconspicuous way back into the temple.

# Chapter Twenty-Eight

They gazed somberly at the wreckage, which lay in the mud of a ravaged barley field and tilted crazily into an irrigation canal. The fire had been intense, for much of the metal portions were carbonized and all the plastic and composites were melted into unrecognizability. Of course there was no trace of the two beings who had spent their final moments in ferocious, insensate combat aboard the out-of-control craft, reflecting in microcosm the hate-fueled, mutually suicidal interstellar death-struggle in which their respective races were even now consuming each other. Bits and pieces of junk were scattered about the farm plots, where they had been hurled by the explosion. No one else was in evidence; the nearby farmers were still too terrified to approach the scene of that blast.

Even after the elements had worn away all trace of the wreck, Ahmad Allawi suspected it would be a very long time before this ceased to be a place of ill-omen.

"Well, that seems to be that," Jason said with an air of finality, and turned toward Uruk. Mondrago and Shartava followed suit. "Coming, Ahmad?"

"We'll be along in a little while, sir," said Allawi, putting his arm around Zan Zu's shoulders.

For a moment, Jason gave him an appraising look. Then, with a small shrug, he led the other two away.

When they were alone, by common unspoken consent, they walked arm in arm toward the nearby bank, where the river showed beyond the date palms. Zan Zu finally broke the pensive silence.

"Will you and your friends be returning to your own time, Ahmad?" she asked in a small voice. Her eyes did not meet his.

"Yes. Soon. We must."

"But must *you*?" Now she turned and looked up into his face.

"Yes. When our leader Jason gives the command—which he can do by thinking it—we all will return together. And at any rate, it is my duty."

Zan Zu reflected. "I know I can never hope to understand how you travel in time. But *why* do you do it? What is this duty of yours that drives you? As I once told you, I've always felt that you were on some great mission, serving something larger than yourself."

"You see, there are others who travel in time—Lugal was one. *Transhumanists*, they are called. They are more evil than you can imagine, and seek to litter the past with certain kinds of traps, to ensnare the people of the future. It is our duty to root them out and destroy them, wherever—and *whenever*—we find them."

"So I have known a warrior who fights a war across time itself." She smiled. "No one will ever believe me."

Allawi drew a breath. This could no longer be put off. "Zan Zu, remember I asked you to say nothing to Ninhursanga or Oannes about us?"

"Yes. I didn't understand why. But I kept your secret."

"Good. Now I want you to promise me you'll never tell *anyone*. Ever."

"But why, Ahmad?"

*How do I explain the Observer Effect to her when I don't understand it myself? When* nobody *understands it?* "You've only just learned that time travel is possible, so you haven't had time to think about some of its implications. But . . . well, there's a paradox my people have been posing for a long time. What if I were to go back in time and kill one of my own ancestors?"

For a moment she looked blank. Then a crease of perplexity appeared between her eyebrows. "Then you couldn't have been born. But if you weren't, then—"

"—Who was it who killed the ancestor?" he finished for her. "We've learned that such things can't happen. Something will prevent it. Everything we do in the past has *always* been part of the past." This was even harder to express in Sumerian than in Standard International English, but she seemed to be following, albeit with difficulty. "We call this the *Observer Effect*."

"Yes, I remember hearing Jason using those words to Enki, just after I woke up."

"And because of it, observed history is fixed. The *Transhumanists* always have to work around that in their schemes. Well, history says that that nobody in your era had any idea of traveling in time. That means you're not going to spread the story—for one reason or another." Impulsively, he took her by the shoulders and tuned her to face him squarely. "Please make sure that the reason is because you *chose* not to. Otherwise, as I say, something else will happen to prevent you—maybe something that will hurt you."

She thought for a moment. "As I told you, I don't think anyone would ever believe a tale so strange. And if they don't, then what harm could it do for me to tell it?"

"It's possible that you're right. But it would be better to take no chances. Remember what I said: you could get hurt. Such things have happened. And . . . I can't endure the thought of you being hurt."

Zan Zu smiled and closed her eyes. "In that case, Ahmad, I promise I'll never tell anyone. Of course I don't want to get hurt . . . but the idea that my getting hurt would cause you pain makes me want it even less." Her eyes opened, and she looked up at him.

He had to bend down to kiss her.

This time no aliens interrupted.

Afterwards, he mentioned that thought to her, and she giggled. "There was something else they interrupted, that time. I'd told you I wanted to know more about the land you came from. Now I *really* want to know." She nestled into his arms. "Please tell me!"

*How do you describe a whole world, across a gulf of six and a half thousand years?* he wondered desperately. *Where do you begin?*

He tried his best. She couldn't get enough of his tales of wonder. They lost track of time, as the sun moved across the sky to the west.

Finally, they began walking back toward Uruk. Their route led them through the riverside area. There, among the huts and sheds, they saw a priest—one of the late Lugal's subordinates—addressing a small crowd of perplexed-looking listeners.

"—And so, oh people, Anu has not departed from us—at least not forever. He has returned for now to dwell for a time among his fellow gods. But Inanna remains, to watch over us—"

Zan Zu made a face. "I suppose I'll also have to pretend to believe *that.*"

"Yes—especially because I'm sure Ninhursanga will be spreading some similar story about Enki in Eridu."

"And my people *must* believe that, if everything Enki did is not to go to waste." She sighed, and nodded.

They walked a little further. Before they reached the town wall, Zan Zu halted and took Allawi by the hand. "If I'm only to be allowed a few hours or days with my warrior out of time, I don't want to waste any of them." She gestured over her shoulder toward the river, in the direction of a certain hut that he remembered.

"I'm sure old Utu would allow us the use of the shed behind his hut for the night, Ahmad," she said demurely.

He needed no urging.

Allawi awoke with the dawn. By the pale light that streamed through a window of the hut, he saw Zan Zu's naked, still-sleeping form. As he hitched himself up on one elbow and gazed on her, a feeling he had never yet known in his young life suffused his soul. It included, but was not limited to, a desire to protect her from anything that might threaten her, for the idea of harm coming to her was intolerable to him, so infinitely precious was she.

*How small she is . . . like an exquisitely perfect miniature . . .*

Then, all at once, like an explosion in the brain, it came to him: the perfect solution to everything.

*Why didn't I think of it before?*

He started to awaken Zan Zu and share it with her. But just before his hand touched her shoulder, he stopped himself.

*No. I mustn't tell her until I've had a chance to broach the idea to the Commander. I'll bring it up with him as soon as a good opportunity presents itself.*

He settled back down onto his back to await her awakening.

# Chapter Twenty-Nine

Inanna had a stool to sit on, so she didn't have to crouch in the human-scaled chamber within the temple. But that evidently didn't make up for the distasteful necessity of dealing with Jason and the other three feral humans from the future. She fairly oozed disdain.

"Now, then," Jason was saying, "we've kept our side of the agreement. You do remember yours—specifically, the part pertaining to the secret of time travel?"

"Yes, yes," Inanna snapped impatiently. "I won't reveal it to any fellow members of my race. I'll keep my word . . . as long as Ninhursanga and Oannes keep theirs."

The two Nagommo had already departed for Eridu. Before leaving, they had reaffirmed their agreement to leave Inanna alone in Uruk.

"In the meantime," Inanna continued, "I'll confirm what the priests have been saying, and maintain the fiction that Anu is still a god—we can't administer too sharp a jolt to the rabble's faith—but has withdrawn from direct involvement in earthly affairs. And to cement my status, I'll have a new temple—and residence—built for myself on the site of that wretched old temple, which is so unworthy of me." She seemed to have an afterthought. "And I'll have it surrounded with an enclosure."

Jason and Allawi exchanged a look. They both realized that the Teloi was describing the Eanna District, as the archaeologists would one day call it, and devise various theories as to why it was walled off. One such theory would even get it right: the purpose was to provide the goddess with privacy, since temples were regarded as the literal dwelling places of deities on Earth. But of course the archaeologists wouldn't dream that it really *was* the goddess's dwelling place.

Allawi spoke up. "I can tell you, on the basis of our own era's knowledge of this world's history, that you'll succeed. You will be remembered as the tutelary deity of Uruk." This was true, as Jason knew from conversations he'd had with Allawi.

"Naturally," Inanna sniffed. "So there's no more to be discussed." Without waiting for a reply from lower life-forms, she rose to leave. To Jason's delight, her loftiness couldn't quite survive the need to bend down while exiting the door.

It occurred to him that, even though she knew them to be from Earth's distant future, she had never once asked him how the *Oratioi'Zhonglu* would be remembered—or *if* they would be remembered—in his time. Perhaps she was too haughty to reveal any interest. Or perhaps she didn't want to hear the answer.

"Do you think she can really be trusted to keep her word, Commander?" wondered Shartava after the Teloi was gone. Mondrago's skepticism didn't need to be verbalized.

"Actually, I do. After all, the rest of the *Oratioi'Zhonglu* have moved elsewhere. And anyway, I don't think she has any desire to share secrets with them. I got to know the Teloi of that subculture when I was in the Bronze Age Aegean, and I can tell you they're a bunch of loners— and she must be worse than most in that respect, considering that she's stayed behind in this part of the world while the others have moved on. They're also compulsive intriguers against each other." Jason recalled what a snake pit the community of Greek "gods" had been—a fact of which he had taken advantage. "And finally, I don't think she's going to be around all that much longer, at least by Teloi standards. Remember, the Earth-born among them have reduced lifespans—and she was the first of those."

Allawi nodded. "I think you're right, Commander. What we know of later Mesopotamian religious beliefs tends to confirm it. Eventually, she sort of fades away in the myths, merging with other female deities into Ishtar. Of course, all the legends will get thoroughly confused. Anu will be superseded in the third millennium by Enlil, lord of the air. And Inanna will somehow become the daughter of Enki, from whom she steals the skills of civilization."

"I'm not sure which of them would hate that more," said Mondrago drily.

Shartava and Allawi chuckled. But Jason only mused, "Yes . . . Enki." He wished he'd gotten to know the Nagom better.

"Did you hear what Ninhursanga and Oannes were saying for human consumption?" asked Mondrago. "Enki isn't really dead, he's merely withdrawn to his aquifer and no longer appears in the flesh to his human worshippers. In short, the same kind of crap that Inanna is going to shovel out in Uruk to explain Anu's absence."

"That's neither here nor there," said Jason firmly. "The point is that Enki really has died, as has Anu, and that their knowledge of time travel has died with them. Ninhursanga and Oannes have no knowledge of it. And we've confirmed by direct inspection that Anu's vessel was reduced by fire to meaningless wreckage, which will rust away to nothing. And I've managed to stay out of Oannes' sight, so the slightly younger me will be new to him in 1628 B.C."

"That," said Shartava quietly, "leaves Zan Zu."

An uncomfortable silence descended.

Allawi spoke hesitantly. "She's promised me that she'll never tell anyone the truth about us. And besides . . . doesn't the fact that nobody in subsequent Mesopotamian history is recorded as having mentioned the concept of time travel show that she's going to keep her word? Or that if she doesn't, she won't be believed, but just written off as a teller of tall tales?"

"Yes," said Jason patiently. "That's how we *think* the Observer Effect works. In fact, everything we know seems to point to it. So I grant you that this doesn't seem to be a serious problem. But as you know, loose ends that seem to allow for *possible* anomalies always make us nervous. We operate on the premise that reality helps those who help themselves."

Allawi met Jason's eyes and spoke unflinchingly. "Sir, you've admitted it isn't a serious concern. But if you have any concerns whatsoever, I have a solution to offer."

"What solution is that, Ahmad?"

"I could take her back to the twenty-fourth century with me."

Not even the usually irrepressible Mondrago broke the thunderstruck silence.

Before anyone could speak, Allawi hurried on. "Commander, like everybody else in the Service, I've heard the story of how you got Dr. Chantal Frey back to our time even though the Transhumanists had chopped her TRD out of her." (He didn't notice Mondrago's wince.) "You took advantage of the all-you-can-conveniently-carry rule."

It was a fundamental fact of temporal displacement, imperfectly understood but beyond doubt because it was the reason why time travelers didn't arrive nude and empty-handed. In some manner the temporal energy potential of an object, living or otherwise, encompassed anything—clothing, accessories, carried objects up to a certain size—that was in contact with it. And the principle applied equally when temporal energy potential was restored for retrieval. Thus it was that time travelers were able to bring back lost works of art and literature, specimens of technology at early stages of development, and other assorted items such as the souvenirs that filled the display case behind Kyle Rutherford's desk. Some time travelers got greedy and returned heavily laden indeed.

"You proved that it applies to a living organism, by picking up and carrying a small woman when you were retrieved." Allawi smiled. "I can't believe Dr. Frey was much if any smaller than Zan Zu. And, with all respect, sir, I'm larger and quite possibly stronger than you."

"But," Shartava expostulated, "Dr. Frey was native to our time! Zan Zu isn't."

"What difference should that make?" argued Allawi. "Dr. Rutherford's prize displays aren't native to our time either."

"I wasn't talking about the temporal physics of the thing. I was talking about the culture shock, which you seem not to have considered. You'd be snatching her from the Chalcolithic era directly into the twenty-fourth century. The experience of temporal displacement itself is disorienting even to those of us who are prepared for it and can fit it into a rationalistic mental universe. But beyond that . . . five minutes in one of our cities, without a single familiar thing for her to get a mental handhold on, and she'd go mad! Just think of all the small things that we take for granted because they aren't even new technology to us anymore. The first time she was in a room and somebody turned on the electric lights, she'd panic—she'd think she was in a furnace, complete with psychosomatic heat." Shartava paused, seemingly as surprised by her own out-of-character vehemence as Jason was. "No. The gap between her world and ours is just too great."

"She'd have me to help her bridge that gap. She'd always have me." Allawi turned from Shartava to Jason with a beseeching look.

Jason regarded the young man somberly. He knew how much time Allawi had been spending with Zan Zu since their breakout, in old Utu's hut—time that must seem all too brief to him. "Ahmad, as you know I'm not given to high-flown speechmaking. But the very reason we're fighting the Transhumanists is that unlike them we believe in human dignity and self-determination. It's not our place to play God with Zan Zu; the fact that we belong to a more technologically sophisticated civilization than hers doesn't give us that right. Does *she* want this?"

Allawi's eyes fell. "I don't know, sir."

"Well, until you find out we can't even reach the question of whether *we* think it would be a good idea." Jason's aspect grew a shade less stern. "Talk to her. I can delay our retrieval a little longer. Some stewing won't hurt Rutherford."

Allawi and Zan Zu lay by the riverbank, beneath a stand of willow trees, sipping a kind of wine her people made from pomegranates and watching the sun set, as he told her more of his world. The first stars began to appear in the ultramarine sky to the east of the zenith.

Zan Zu, in the crook of Allawi's arm, snuggled closer and looked up at those stars. Despite the warmth, she shivered slightly. "And you say your people can sail to those stars in boats?"

"Not exactly boats. But yes, we can travel to them. You see, the stars are other suns."

"But how can that be? They're so tiny!"

"You know how something looks smaller the farther away it is? Well, the stars are very, *very* far away. If the sun were as far away as they are, it would also look like a little point of light. Except that many of the stars are much bigger and brighter than the sun, and much more distant. So distant that we're seeing them as they were many years ago, for it takes that long for the light from them to reach our eyes." He didn't even try to quantify the magnitudes involved. It would have been impossible to express them, for the Sumerian language had no need of such numbers.

Zan Zu sat up so she could meet his eyes. Hers looked dazed. "But if they are so far away, how can you travel to them?"

"We can travel faster than light." Again, he contented himself with a gross oversimplification, not attempting to explain how the negative-mass drive cheated Einstein.

Zan Zu wore a look of painfully intense thought. "If the stars are suns like ours . . . do they shine on other worlds like ours?"

"Many of them do. And many of those have become new homes to men. In fact, I was born on a world of another sun, even though my ancestors came from this one. In fact, my father's family came from this very land."

Zan Zu's eyes grew very wide indeed, and looked upward. "Which of the stars was your birth sun?"

"I can't find it." He had tried to locate Zeta Tucanae, his home sun, but the "fixed" stars had changed position in Earth's skies considerably in six and a half thousand years. "Anyway, many other worlds hold races of their own. Not gods, but mortal races different from man."

"But . . . but . . . how can there be worlds other than *the* world?" She looked around her at the familiar, solid landscape as though in search of reassurance.

"The worlds are balls, and go round and around their suns—just as this world goes round and around its sun. And at the same time, it revolves. That's why the sun seems to move across the sky."

"You mean the world is *moving*? Whirling round and around? And spinning?" Zan Zu seemed to try to plant herself more securely on the ground, almost clutching at it. "Why don't we fall off?"

"Uh . . . you'll just have to take my word for it."

"I know you would never speak other than the truth, Ahmad. But . . ." Her face was a battleground in which all her life's assumptions struggled against unfathomable new concepts.

*It's possible,* Allawi thought, *that hers is the very first human face ever to wear such a look.*

"And," she continued, "there are all the other things you've told me of. The things the Teloi and the Nagommo can do, and which your people can also do—or *will be* able to do. Things I'll never know."

The moment he had been leading up to had finally come. He took a deep breath. "Zan Zu, remember I told you that I and my companions must soon return to our own time?"

"Yes, I remember, although I've tried not to think about it," she said in a very small voice. "I know I'm going to lose you."

"But we don't have to lose each other. You could come with me."

"I could?" Her voice had grown even smaller.

"Yes! I could carry you back with me. And you would know all the wonders of which I've told you."

She hugged her knees tightly and looked around her—at the trees and the river and the cultivated fields, and up at the mysterious stars, now coming out in their multitudes. For a long time she said nothing, and Allawi restrained himself from pressing her. When she finally spoke, it was in a soft voice, and her eyes avoided his.

"We have always thought the Teloi and the Nagommo to be gods because of the things they could do. Now we—or at least *I*—know they are not gods. For humans can do these things too, and *will* do them—all they need is the time to learn them. In fact, by learning to travel in time, they will possess powers beyond those of any gods we have imagined." Now her eyes met Allawi's, and it was not yet too dark for him to see the sadness in them. "I and my people come before that. You come of people who have turned themselves into what seems to us like gods, and more than gods. I now know that Enki and the other Nagommo have tried to start us on the road to learning these things. But I have not yet learned them, and I don't think I could live in your world—or worlds. But perhaps I can help keep my people's feet on that road. And that, I think, is why I must remain in Eridu."

Allawi said nothing. He could only marvel at her and, looking at her, know for the first time the real reason he loved her, and could not have her.

And thanks to her he also knew for the first time in his life the reason humanity would not just survive but prevail.

Then she took his hands in hers and smiled, and was just a girl again. "And you'll be leaving me something of yourself, Ahmad. You see . . . I think I am with child." Her smile widened at his expression—and at a thought that suddenly occurred to her. "So perhaps you are, at many, many removes, your own descendant!"

He could only stare.

"So you have given me a great gift, Ahmad. And now I ask for one more gift. Allow me to be present when you depart."

Jason decided no further harm could be done by acceding to Zan

Zu's request. Thus it was that she stood facing them in a torchlit temple chamber. She and Allawi saw nothing but each other.

"All right," said Jason. "Ready?"

Allawi and Zan Zu simultaneously reached out to each other, without stepping any closer. Their fingers touched, and caressed.

"Let her go, Ahmad," said Jason gently.

Allawi slowly withdrew his hands. When an inch separated his fingertips from hers, Jason gave the mental command, and Zan Zu and the rest of her world dissolved into the chaos of temporal transition.

# Chapter Thirty

Kyle Rutherford's eyes kept going to the Acropolis in the virtual window of his Athens office. Perhaps, Jason thought, he was reflecting on the fact, of which he had now been forcibly reminded anew, that there were even deeper strata of ancientness. Far deeper.

"Well, Jason, It appears that you dealt rather decisively with the problems involving Anu and Enki. A good thing, too; the possibility that Anu might actually have summoned a *Tuova'Zhonglu* expedition to forty-first century B.C. Earth was particularly worrisome. However, you seem to have left a loose end."

"I've explained my reasons for believing that Inanna would keep her knowledge to herself. Those reasons were based on my reading of the *Oratioi'Zhonglu* character—of which, as you may recall, I have more first-hand experience than anyone else. You can be sure they were *not* based on blind trust in her word."

"I have no doubt of that. And I wasn't really thinking of Inanna. Rather, I was thinking of the local female . . . Zan Zu, was that her name?"

Jason settled a little more deeply into his chair and steepled his fingers. "Well, Kyle, there comes a time when we just have to trust to the Observer Effect. There is nothing in recorded history to suggest that Zan Zu ever spilled anything that had any measurable effect. As Ahmad Allawi observed, even if she did break her promise to him, what she said would probably be dismissed as a whopper, and soon forgotten."

"Ah, yes . . . Constable Allawi. I gather he acquitted himself very well on this, his first extratemporal expedition, despite his youth and inexperience. But, reading between the lines of your report, I can't avoid the impression that he might not be entirely objective on the subject of this Zan Zu."

"I'm certain there's no problem there," said Jason reassuringly. He wasn't inclined to blame Allawi for his lapse in the matter of emotional involvement—especially inasmuch as he was sure the lesson had been learned and there would be no repetition. So he had downplayed the hardness with which the young Mithran had fallen for a remarkable girl, when he had composed his report to Rutherford. The old fart wouldn't have understood.

"However," he said in a subject-changing tone, hitching himself up in the chair, "as you will recall from my report, there is one extremely serious loose end with which we have to deal." He reminded Rutherford of it, and as he spoke the older man's expression grew more and more alarmed, and as he often did when in search of strength, he glanced at his display case—and, in particular, at a certain saber that had once been used to draw a certain line in the sand.

"This probably doesn't fall within the scope of my discretion as operations director," Rutherford temporized.

"You're probably right. So," Jason concluded with a despairing sigh, "I'm afraid we're going to have to involve the governing council."

The elegant—or pompous, depending on how one chose to view it—conference room was almost fully occupied, for a quorum of the council was present. Helene de Tredville, who currently held the rotating chairmanship, sat at the head of the long table. Jason and Rutherford were at the other end.

"By now you've all perused my report," said Jason, registering more confidence than he felt. "So you know Lugal let slip that at the time they exiled him—or, strictly speaking, the time when they are *going* to exile him—the Transhumanist underground was, or will be, planning to send a second team to 1978 Venice to finish the job he and his partner had botched."

"Ah yes, I recall," de Tredville nodded. Jason often wondered how she was able to nod, so tight was the bun into which her white hair was pulled back. "Their plan was to send a second party to Father Ernetti's cell—for which they had precise coordinates—that same night."

"Right—an hour or so later, Lugal said. Now, he didn't know that we spent some time with Father Ernetti after his own retrieval, learning about the chronovisor and viewing the recording from 4004 B.C. However, this second team demonstrably didn't—or doesn't, or won't; let's just use the past tense—arrive while we were still there. So they must have arrived very shortly after that. And in this case we can't simply sit back and trust to the Observer Effect to prevent it. There's nothing in recorded history to prove the Transhumanists *didn't* steal the data on the chronovisor in 1978."

"But Father Ernetti isn't recorded as having subsequently said anything about such a theft," protested Alastair Kung. Jason knew it was a fallacy to expect deep voices from the obese, but he had never ceased to find something incongruous in the squeak produced by Kung's tonnage of blubber.

"That doesn't necessarily mean it didn't happen, Councilor. Remember, he swore to me that he'd keep everything connected with time travel secret."

Serena Razmani wore a bewildered look, as she so often did. "But . . . but we have no evidence to suggest that the Transhumanists possess the chronovisor now!"

Jason hoped he wasn't letting his exasperation show. "As you will undoubtedly recall from the report, Ms. Razmani, Lugal & Co. came— or, I should say, will come—from slightly in our own future. Which means the second Transhumanist team also will. Who's to say, at this point in time, that the underground isn't *going* to be building a chronovisor shortly?"

Rutherford wore a haunted look. "It is a disquieting fact that it was only by sheer chance that Commander Thanou obtained this bit of intelligence from Lugal. And I agree with him: this is an instance in which we must take action ourselves." A rumble of agreement, at various levels of reluctance, ran around the table. "But, Jason, we don't know exactly when to expect the second Transhumanist party to appear in Father Ernetti's cell."

"No, we don't. But from what Lugal said, I think it can't be very long after we were retrieved. So I propose that I take a small Special Ops team back to just after that retrieval time—which can be pinpointed from my brain implant's record. We'll use 'controllable' TRDs so we can stay as long as is necessary." Jason smiled. "I need to go back there anyway, to keep my promise to Father Ernetti and return the tape he lent me."

"Very well," said de Tredville, "provided that you don't arrive until at least a minute after the moment when you departed."

"Yes!" exclaimed Alcide Martilleto with a flutter of wrists. "We simply *must* have some safety margin!" This time the noises of agreement were emphatic. Coming even close to the potentiality of a time traveler encountering himself—even though, as in this case, the Observer Effect almost always seemed to forbid it—never failed to give these people an attack of the vapors.

"Now, then, Jason," said Rutherford, "who do you want to take?"

"The same two as before: Mondrago and Julian Casinde."

"But Father Casinde isn't—"

"—Special Ops. I know. But he's shown he can hold up when the action gets gritty. And in matters touching on Father Ernetti, I think he ought to be involved, just in case."

"All right. The three of you have already received the orientation for that milieu, which simplifies things. You'll be able to depart without delay."

"I'll tell them, then. And with your permission, I'd like to let Julian in on the report, and my recorder implant imagery." Jason grinned. "He'll never admit it, but I think that, in his heart of hearts, he'll be just a tiny bit relieved at the confirmation that the Sumerian gods weren't real."

# Chapter Thirty-One

For a long moment, Father Pellegrino Ernetti stared at the space where the three time travelers had stood, and from which they had vanished with a faint *pop* just after he had made the sign of the cross. His mind was so numbed with the unfathomable strangeness of what he had seen and heard that staring was all he could do.

Finally, he shook himself. There was no point in trying to make sense of it all, in his present mental and spiritual state. He must try to get a little sleep, in the few hours of night remaining. He turned and stumbled toward his bed.

He had just reached it, and was preparing to lower himself gratefully into it, when he felt against the back of his neck a breeze that had no business in the enclosed space of the cell.

Guts clenched with terror, he swung around. Two men stood in the cell. They wore the same kind of nondescript clothes as the two earlier Transhumanists. They began to slowly advance on him, their faces expressionless.

*How can they be back so soon?* flashed through his fear-gripped mind. But then he saw they were not the same men.

*If, indeed, they may be called "men,"* he thought, recognizing certain subtle signs of similarity that had at first glance caused him to assume that the first two had somehow returned, and remembering what Jason had told him of the Transhumanists. *Do they have souls? Dare I assume that they do not? And yet . . . surely no human, however godless, would be capable of such transcendently monstrous evil as theirs—the distortion and perversion of God's noblest creation, Man—without the direct intervention of the Adversary. They must be possessed.*

And with that thought, he knew what he had to do. And his fear lost its hold on him, for, at the risk of the sin of pride, he knew himself to be one of the most accomplished exorcists of the present generation.

The problem was, he had no time to do the thing properly. No time for the Litany of the Saints, the canticles and the doxologies. And most certainly no time for him, as priest, to go to confession and then vest himself in surplice and purple stole. Nor was there anyone to deliver the responsive readings, nor any holy water to sprinkle at the correct moments. No: in his present desperate pass, all he could do was hastily offer up one of the prayers of exorcism—or part of one, for surely these intruders would not give him nearly enough time to complete it— trusting that his omissions would be forgiven under the circumstances. But which prayer?

He knew without even having to consider the matter. St. Michael the Archangel, who had cast Lucifer and his fellow rebel angels into the Pit, was the great defender of both saints and men against evil, and appeared in the Litany just below the name of the blessed Virgin herself. He, Pellegrino Ernetti, had now become engaged on the front lines of the war Jason and his people waged across time itself against the Transhumanists for the soul of mankind. He, however unworthy, had somehow been appointed to bear St. Michael's arms. So it was appropriate that he should appeal to the most militant of the archangels.

He grasped the crucifix he wore around his neck and held it up before him, causing the Transhumanists to come to a surprised and somewhat bewildered-looking halt. He drew a deep breath, and commanded himself to steadiness. When he spoke, his voice was unshaken. Indeed, his voice crashed out like thunder, startling in so slight a man, as he began an abbreviated version of the Exorcism Prayer of St. Michael.

*"Most glorious Prince of the Celestial Host, Saint Michael the Archangel, defend us in the conflict which we have to sustain against principalities and powers, against the rulers of the world of this darkness . . . Come to the rescue of men whom God has created in His image and*

*likeness . . . Seize the dragon, the old serpent, which is the devil and Satan, bind him and cast him into the bottomless pit, that he may no more seduce the nations . . ."*

The two Transhumanists, now clearly at a loss, remained motionless and uncertain.

*"We drive you from us, whoever you may be, unclean spirits, Satanic powers, infernal invaders . . . Cease by your audacity, cunning serpent, to deceive the human race . . . This is the command made to you by the Most High God, with whom in your haughty insolence you still pretend to be equal . . . Thus, cursed dragon, and you, wicked legions, we adjure you by the living God, by the true God, by the holy God . . . O Prince of the Heavenly Host, by the Divine Power of God, cast into hell Satan and all the evil spirits who wander throughout the world seeking the ruin of souls. AMEN."*

And at that instant, three figures appeared from nowhere in the now-crowded confines of the cell. At once, Father Ernetti recognized them, for they had departed a mere minute ago.

For an instant, all five of the intrusive figures stood disoriented—the Transhumanists from sheer startled surprise, and Jason and his companions perhaps by some effect on the transition across the span of centuries. But then the Transhumanists seemed to recover, and with a sickeningly unhuman abruptness turned on the newer arrivals.

Jason, groggy though he seemed, managed to jab a walking cane he was carrying into the midriff of the Transhumanist who was mere inches from grasping him in some kind of wrestling hold. There was a sharp *crack!* and a line of sparkling light very briefly emerged from the Transhumanist's back, accompanied by a puff of steam. One of Jason's men, the one named Mondrago, also had a cane, and he also used it in the ridiculously close quarters of the cell, with the same results. The closely confined air was filled with a stench of burned cloth and flesh, and the other concomitants of death.

It was all over in a heartbeat. Father Ernetti found he had collapsed to the floor. Father Casinde's arm was around his shoulder.

Still trying to shake dizziness of temporal displacement from his head, Jason knelt beside Father Ernetti. "Are you all right?"

"Yes . . . yes. Thank you, my son. But . . . how did you return so quickly?"

Jason smiled. "It didn't seem quick to us. Quite a while has passed, in terms of our stream of consciousness—and we've done quite a lot. I'll tell you about it shortly. Anyway, I'm just glad we arrived here in time."

"Of course you did," said Father Ernetti serenely. "God works in mysterious ways."

"What do you mean?"

"When those men appeared, something came to me that I should have realized before. Such evil as the Transhumanists' can only be a result of demonic possession. So I attempted to perform an exorcism, as best I could in the little time available. Perhaps it succeeded, and God will have mercy on the souls of these two."

("I hope not," Mondrago muttered. Casinde shushed him.)

"And then," Father Ernetti continued, "You arrived. I shouldn't be surprised. After all, I had prayed to St. Michael . How else would that particular saint have answered my prayer?"

Jason wasn't sure what he meant by that. "Well, Father, I'll express no opinion on that, one way or another."

"Either way," said Mondrago, "right now we need to get rid of these bodies."

"Right. Fortunately, the Transhumanists aren't noted for flexibility in their methodology. I'm sure these two have 'controllable' TRDs like the last two. So with the leader dead, those TRDs will never be activated. I'm also fairly sure that when they don't return the Underground's leadership will get discouraged and decide trying to steal the chronovisor is more trouble than it's worth." Jason turned to Father Ernetti. "Can you find some rope and a couple of heavy weights?"

In the darkness, they lugged the two bodies to the pier in front of the church of San Giorgio Maggiore, and dumped them into the Canale di San Marco, at the bottom of which the two TRDs would lie, forever dormant, as the bodies decomposed around them. To Mondrago's ill-concealed annoyance, Father Ernetti made the sign of the cross as they sank into the dark water.

"Now, Father," said Jason, "I don't wish to imply that you might forget your promise to keep silent about the things you've seen and learned. I only wish to remind you that it covers the events of tonight."

"Yes . . . yes, of course." The Benedictine looked back at the water and shivered.

"Good. And speaking of promises . . . before we depart, I want to return this." Jason reached into a satchel he was wearing on his belt and withdrew the Father Ernetti's tape.

"Thank you. Of course, it seems to me that I only just now lent it to you. But you say time has passed in your life since then."

"Yes. I said I was going to tell you about that. You see, we went back to 4004 B.C. and investigated the things you saw, and recorded on this tape." Even in the darkness, Jason could sense Father Ernetti's stiffening. And he hesitated to go on. He had a pretty good idea what the knowledge of humanity's true origins would do to this man.

Casinde came to his rescue. "Father, there are things we are not permitted to tell you. But this you may know: we established beyond a shadow of a doubt that the pagan idols of the Sumerians were *not* gods. I swear to that by all that is holy."

The Benedictine seemed to deflate with relief at Casinde's half-truth. *No, not really a half-truth,* Jason decided. *Entirely true, as far as it goes. And an act of kindness.*

"Thank you," said Father Ernetti in a barely audible whisper. "But I will not tempt fate again. After I know for certain that the Holy Father is dead—which you say I will learn in the morning—I will consider myself free of my promise to him, and destroy the machine. And I will devote the rest of my life to making certain that no one takes seriously the possibility of building another one."

*Just as well,* thought Jason. "And now, Father, we must return to our proper time. As I've told you, I don't think the Transhumanists will trouble you again."

"I'm certain of it. I believe my prayer has been answered, and in the most appropriate of all possible ways. Remember, I told you I prayed to St. Michael—the patron of soldiers and police officers. God be with you!"

As Jason gave the mental command and reality wavered, the last thing he saw, dimly in the darkness, was the Benedictine making the sign of the cross.

# Author's Note

First of all, let me acknowledge my debt to—or, as would be truer to say, confess my theft from—the late, never-to-be-sufficiently-lamented Jack Vance. The idea of appropriating Zan Zu, the girl from Eridu, simply tempted me beyond my character.

I would never presume to apologize to Vance's shade in an afterlife in which I know he did not believe. So I address this to his shade wherever it may reside in my own memories of the innumerable hours of reading pleasure he has given (and continues to give) me, with infinite but nonetheless inadequate thanks, and with my assurance that I have understood the poem he wrote for the mad poet Navarth in *The Palace of Love*. In fact, one might say that I have endeavored in this novel to create a kind of backstory to that poem. Vance is on record as having regarded *Palace* as one of his two best works, the other being *The Face*, another "Demon Princes" novel. I was delighted beyond words to read that he did, because I wholeheartedly agree. I can do no better service to his memory than urge everyone to read the "Demon Princes" series. Those who do not do so are depriving themselves of one of the true treasures of twentieth century science fiction.

Father Pellegrino Ernetti actually lived, and the biographical facts about him are as Julian Casinde sets them forth in Chapter Three. As Father Casinde points out, everything connected with the chronovisor (including the deathbed confession a distant relative of his supposedly claimed to have heard) is urban legend. I am 99.9 percent certain that that is all it is. I am almost but not quite equally convinced that there is nothing to the various conspiracy theories surrounding the death of Pope John Paul I.

Aside from the obviously science-fictional elements involving the Teloi and their Nagommo enemies, everything herein about Mesopotamia at the beginning of the fourth millennium B.C., when the Ubaid culture was giving way to the Uruk culture, is consistent with modern archaeological findings. That the people of these early cultures were already Sumerian-speakers is not universally agreed upon, but the smart money says they were. Of course, the remains of such very ancient sites as Eridu and Uruk, under the accumulation of numerous strata of subsequent levels, are of necessity incomplete and subject to interpretation. The names of the various deities are also factual, although our knowledge of their worshipers' ideas about them is based on writings of much later times. As Ahmad Allawi somewhere mentions, their functions and relationships changed over the millennia, which is why I have felt justified in allowing myself a certain latitude.

Father Ernetti's quick-and-dirty exorcism in Chapter Twenty-Nine is patched together from bits and pieces of the actual Exorcism Prayer of St. Michael the Archangel. But of course it bears no relationship to the full Roman Catholic rites of exorcism. These rites, by the way, are publicly available. But don't try this at home.